PELOTON OF TWO

Andrew Bowie was born in Scotland, grew up in Australia, and now lives in Oxfordshire in the UK. *Peloton of Two* is his first novel.

For more information, visit: www.andrewbowie.net

PELOTON OF TWO

Andrew Bowie

AUGMONT BOOKS

First published in 2016
by Augmont Books

ISBN 978-0-9956490-0-2

There ain't no surer way to find out whether you like
people or hate them than to travel with them.
    – Mark Twain, *Tom Sawyer Abroad*

Le grand départ

Catherine Pringle sat alone in her car on the crest of the last hill before Base Camp. She was watching the sun set over the Wiltshire Downs and stubbornly pretending there was all the time in the world before she would have to arrive.

In London a few hours earlier, she had thought she was ready for the summer to begin. But now, after a prolonged battle with eve-of-departure nerves, she was wavering. The doubts were back, swirling through her head again, and she was going nowhere until an inner calm had somehow been restored. With the driver's window down, she let her eyes drift across the downland, following its contours into the shadows cast by the setting sun. She focused on her breathing – inhaling deeply, slowly exhaling – and willed herself to relax.

It was just beginning to work when she noticed a break in the hedgerow a little ahead of the car. Leaning forward, she saw that it gave her a clear view across the neighbouring field and, beyond that, all the way into Base Camp. On the lawn in front of the cottage, two men were wrestling with the outer shell of a tent. It flapped between them in the breeze until they managed to bring it under control and spread it on the grass.

Even from a distance Catherine recognised both of them. Brendan Stillwater, broad-shouldered, tall, his wild rust-red hair stirring in the breeze, was impossible to mistake, especially on the threshold of his own home. His companion, a fraction shorter, dark-haired and lean, was a little harder to be sure of. But when he dropped to his knees on top of the flattened tent and began to crawl across it, feeling slowly along the seams for defects, she could tell that it was Nick.

Watching him covertly like this sparked a flurry of guilt. Catherine rummaged inside her bag for her smartphone and dialled his number. 'Nick,' she said quickly, when he answered, 'it's me.'

'Catherine, where on earth are you? You should have been here ages ago.'

'I'm almost there. Close enough that we could practically reach out and touch.'

She glanced at the newspaper lying beside her on the passenger seat. She had to know if he'd seen it. And if he had, she wanted the inevitable overreaction out of the way before they were face to face. 'Did you happen to read our favourite tabloid today?'

'That's about the last thing I had time for. You do know how much there was to do here, don't you?'

'There's an article about us. I couldn't stop them putting some serious spin on it. They're saying it's entirely down to me that we're going.'

He laughed, harder than she'd heard from him in months. 'I find it highly unlikely that anyone will believe that.'

She decided not to take offence and tried instead to find a way of reaching out to him. She knew she should be down there with him, should have been there all day. But she couldn't bring herself to admit this openly. Finally, she managed to say, 'I want you to know how much I'm looking forward to this trip.'

'Me too,' he replied after a pause. 'Look, I still have things to do before the light fades. Let's talk when you get here.'

Catherine hung up, wondering what she'd got herself into and whether there was still a way out. Picking up the newspaper, she opened it at the first page of its Lifestyle section. Above the fold and stretching across three columns was a picture of her sitting on a tandem bicycle. She'd studied it half a dozen times already that day but couldn't resist another look.

The shot was well posed. She was on the tandem's rear seat, looking back over her shoulder at the camera. Her hair, dirty-blonde, and cut in a shaggy bob, was partly hidden under a mushroom-shaped cycling helmet. Her eyes, pale blue, slightly down-turned, were staring directly into the lens. Egged on by the photographer, she had arched an eyebrow and creased her lips into a conspiratorial *I won't take any of this too seriously as long as you don't* grin.

The rider in front of her was facing forward and deliberately out of focus. It should have been Nick, would have been if she'd been able to coax him out of his Wiltshire lair for long enough to attend the photo shoot.

Inevitably she found herself rereading the text below the picture:

Catherine Pringle's Tour de France

This weekend, our lifestyle reporter Catherine Pringle begins a 2,500-mile circuit of France on a bicycle built for two. She'll be sharing the ride with her partner, the adventurer Nicholas Farne.

Catherine has never done anything active in her life before, not unless you count running to catch the occasional bus. She's more at home in a coffee shop than on the stoker's seat of a purpose-built expedition tandem. So we couldn't resist the chance to pair her up with her explorer boyfriend for a summer-long cycling and camping Tour de France.

Will she make it across the Channel, let alone around France? Can she convince a man who always travels alone that two means twice the adventure and twice as much fun? Will three months on a tandem bind them together, or drive them completely apart?

We told Catherine not to come back without the answers to all of these questions. You can follow her quest for cycle touring enlightenment in her new column in Saturday's Travel Section, and in her daily blog on our website ...

The full text, all five hundred words of it, had seemed funny when she drafted it twenty-four hours earlier. Now it was taunting her. She knew she wasn't ready, physically or emotionally, to go anywhere. And certainly not on a tandem with Nick.

Reading it again had given her an idea, and she let it form while the final act of the performance outside Base Camp unfolded. Brendan had disappeared into the house, leaving Nick alone with the tent. Catherine watched as he threaded a pair of aluminium poles into the outer shell and, in a single well-practised gesture, tensioned it into a low-ceilinged dome. Then he picked up the empty tent bag, a nylon stuff sack with a drawstring at one end, and slipped it over his head. In a moment of pure slapstick he fumbled blindly around, collapsing and re-erecting the tent a few metres across the lawn.

This was enough to convince her that her instinct was right. She picked up her phone and scrolled through her work contacts. It was a long shot – calls to her editor almost always went straight to voicemail – but in what she took as an exceptionally positive omen, she somehow got an answer.

'Liz,' she said, talking over the greeting, 'it's Kate.'

'Shouldn't you be halfway to Plymouth by now?'

'You're a day early. But I'm impressed that you've taken the trouble to memorise the route.'

'I do read a surprising amount of what goes into this paper, you know. Especially the pages I'm responsible for.'

The last few words had been delivered over the frenzied rattle of fingers on a keyboard. Realising that she had only seconds to get her message across, Catherine said, 'Please don't hang up on me. I really need a favour.'

'A reporter to her editor kind of favour? Or is it one of those *Liz, I wouldn't ask if you weren't my best friend in the world* situations?'

'Both, actually. I'm having a massive attack of cold feet about this tandem thing. And you're the only one who can help.'

The silence on the other end was so long that Catherine thought the connection had been lost. But the appeal to her friend's ego was perfectly placed. As the keyboard began to rattle again Liz cautiously asked, 'What do you want me to do?'

'Find me a last-minute job that means I have to be in London tomorrow.'

'I hope you're not trying to bail out on us. I went out on a limb to get you this column.'

'For God's sake, Liz! He's out on the lawn right now with a blindfold on, practising low-visibility erections. Of the tent, I mean.'

Liz burst out laughing, and Catherine couldn't help joining her. They both knew that she could expect plenty more of this from Nick during the summer in France.

'All right,' Liz said, when she could speak again, 'you've got me hooked. But if I do this, and I'm not saying there is anything, it's only because I have enormous sympathy for you. I wouldn't get on that thing at all, and definitely not with the oddball you're doing it with.'

Ignoring the jibe at Nick, Catherine replied, 'I really owe you for this.'

'And you'll do anything?'

It was a dangerous concession, but Catherine knew she had no choice. 'Yes. But only if you call me back on Brendan Stillwater's landline. This has to look like it's all your idea, not mine.'

With just the hint of an escape route opening in front of her, Catherine started the car and continued down the lane to the row of chestnuts that marked the beginning of Base Camp's front garden. She turned into the driveway and sounded her horn in what she hoped was a suitably breezy start-of-holiday flourish. But the front lawn was deserted now, devoid of tents and adventure travel experts, and she had to continue along the side of the cottage towards the dilapidated barn that served as a workshop and garage.

She tucked her Mini neatly between Base Camp's two ancient Land Rovers and had just enough time to hide the newspaper under the seat before Brendan arrived to envelop her in a hug.

'Kate,' he said, standing back to inspect her. 'I was beginning to wonder if you were actually coming.'

'How could you even think a thing like that, Bren.' She kissed him lightly on the cheek just above the rusty thatch of his beard. 'I'm completely ready. Very nearly, anyway. How much trouble am I in for being late?'

He shrugged. 'In a couple of days you'll both look back at this and laugh. But until then, if I were you, I'd plan on keeping a very low profile.'

'That's going to be a little hard, don't you think, on a tandem tour.'

'I didn't say it would be easy. Only that it's your best bet for avoiding some serious fireworks. He's pretty upset that you left him to do everything down here on his own this week.'

She turned to shut the door of her car. If she could find the right way to explain it, there was a good chance Brendan would help argue the case for a slight delay.

When she turned back the moment had gone. Nick had come out of the house and was walking towards them. He was wearing a set of coordinated cycling clothes, shorts and a matching jersey, both with the manufacturers' labels still dangling from them. Even on his toned frame, the skin-tight fit and mottled basil-green livery were comical, making him look like a partly used tube of pesto. She began to laugh, but it died in her throat when she realised she was about to spend the entire summer squeezed into something similar.

He was walking oddly too, hobbling across the gravel like a poorly shod pony. When she looked down she found the reason – two very different models of hard-soled cycling shoe, one black and the other tan, that he had slipped on but not bothered to lace.

'Which is best do you think?' he asked, staring at his feet. 'I'm leaning towards the tan.'

When he looked up again, she was afraid he might see a hint of what she'd set in motion with Liz. But he was already deep in the altered state he retreated to on the eve of any departure, and his eyes, pools of the deepest brown that could still melt her when he wanted them to, had a cool detachment. Catherine knew immediately that she would have to tread carefully around him for the rest of the evening.

She said, 'If I have to wear a pair too then my vote goes with the tan.'

She'd meant it as a joke, but the tone sounded a little too reluctant. Coldly, he replied, 'I was asking Bren, actually. Between us we've pretty much done all the deciding already. We picked out your gear too. Had to. Couldn't risk waiting for you to get round to it on your own.'

'I've still got tonight, haven't I? I'll be ready.'

'Catherine, I'd be shocked if you were ready a month from now.'

This got completely under her skin, largely because he was dead right. She opened her mouth to retaliate but Brendan, who was still at her side, squeezed her elbow.

'Let me help you with your bag, Kate,' he said, pointedly. 'There's still plenty for all of us to do inside.'

Base Camp was a rambling half-timbered cottage that had been considerably remodelled and extended in the twenty-five years Brendan had called it home. His most substantial addition was the Map Room, a single-storey, oak-clad barn that he used as the repository for his four-decade history of global travels. Equipment and paraphernalia from his early expeditions, including the sled he'd used in Hudson Bay and a dugout canoe he'd brought back from Africa, hung from the walls. Coils of rope, each a separate strand of history from his climbing period, hung from cleats driven into the oak beams. The walls were plastered with faded but well-annotated maps that described the detail of his major expeditions.

It was a museum devoted to one man's travels but it still had a working heart. A refectory-style oak table ran for more than four yards down the spine of the room. Half of it, Catherine saw when she followed Brendan and Nick inside, was covered in Michelin maps detailing the tandem's planned route from Brittany down to the Loire. The other end of the table was littered with equipment, most of it unidentifiable to her. In what she hoped was a show of interest, she began to rummage through this, classifying it as far as her expertise allowed into either cycling or camping, or not really sure.

When the phone rang a half-hour later she was still at the table, struggling to understand the technical instructions for a heart rate monitor that Nick was insisting she wear on the tandem. Brendan took the call in the hallway and, after a short conversation, signalled that it was for her.

'Liz Madison,' he said, waving the phone at Catherine.

She did her best to look completely astonished, an act that was lost on Brendan, who handed her the phone before disappearing back into the Map Room.

'Liz,' Catherine said, with exaggerated surprise, 'I didn't expect to hear your voice again for at least a couple of months.'

'Kate, I'm impressed. You've almost convinced me this call was my idea.'

'Don't,' Catherine replied, lowering her voice to a whisper. 'I feel unbelievably guilty about this.'

'But not enough to hang up on me?'

'All I know is, if I don't have another day to get myself mentally ready, I won't make it as far as Plymouth.'

'Just make sure this all goes into your blog. And remember what the contract states: it only has to be true if you can't think of anything better.'

Catherine's idea of confessional journalism differed radically from that of her editor. She had no illusions about which would eventually prevail, but hoped to delay the inevitable for as long as possible. 'Have you found me a job for tomorrow?'

'Oh yes. And it's right up your alley. We're going to shoehorn you into one of the more extreme creations from Christian Baltieri's autumn collection. Then we're going to send you out into the real world for the rest of the day. Christian swears the whole collection is perfect for the working woman. Tomorrow, you're going to write eight hundred laugh-out-loud words that prove him wrong.'

'Not the stuff from his Milan show. There must be something

– anything – else.'

'It's what you're good at. And it will practically write itself. The conscious part of your mind can get busy psyching itself up for three months in the company of your alleged soulmate.'

When Catherine returned to the Map Room Nick and Brendan were arguing vigorously over the relative merits of two solar battery chargers. It looked serious but she saw in their eyes that it was nothing more than extreme banter, the constant struggle by Nick to step out of his mentor's shadow, and Brendan's determination not to let this happen. She stopped in the doorway and leaned against the post, hoping that the mock heat would go out of their argument before the time came to announce her own news.

Nick noticed her eventually and tried to draw her into the discussion. 'If you really want a vote on something you can decide which of us is right.'

'No way am I stepping into that minefield.' She took a breath and added, 'Something's come up at work. I have to be in London tomorrow.'

'Well, you'll have to call them back and turn it down. We're collecting the tandem first thing.'

'I can't say no. I'm not giving Liz or anyone else the slightest excuse to spike the new column.'

'Christ, Catherine. The ferry is booked. The accommodation is locked in as far as the Loire.'

'All I'm asking for is one more day.'

He threw up his hands. 'If it wasn't for the help I've been getting from Bren we wouldn't be going anywhere at all.'

'If that's the way you feel why don't you just take him instead of me. Then we'll all be happy.'

The passion in her voice stopped the conversation dead. The wall clock, an old railway timepiece that Brendan had somehow liberated from a Swiss station, ticked out a half-dozen crisp seconds before she felt able to open her mouth again. 'Nick, I'm sorry. I didn't mean that. But I can't start tomorrow. I just can't. I'll be ready on Friday. I promise.'

'Maybe it's not such a bad idea, Nick,' Brendan broke in. 'You and me on the tandem.'

Nick turned to him as if he were mad but Brendan just chuckled, and added, 'Let Kate go up to London if she wants. You and I can collect the tandem from Taunton. We can put it through a better shakedown ride than you would with her on board. And cover a greater distance too. She can drive down in the evening and switch with me for Friday's leg down to Plymouth.'

Catherine loved the idea and she could tell that Nick did too. But they all had to wait while he made a show of thinking it through. He unfolded an Ordnance Survey map and ran his finger along the route he'd already selected from Taunton down to Plymouth.

While he did this Brendan joined him at the map table. 'This way, everyone is a winner. You get to stay on schedule. Kate does her day's work. And I get the chance to be part of the trip even if it's only for a day. What do you say?'

Nick lifted both hands and ran them through his hair. His body was shaking slightly and for a moment Catherine was afraid her antics had driven him to tears. But when he turned she could see that he was laughing. 'All right, Catherine Pringle. I know when I'm beaten. But once we're in France things will have to change. We have a tight schedule and the only way we can make it all the way round is to stick to the plan.'

Catherine crossed to the table and put her hand on his shoulder. It was a truce signal, one that he was happy to accept. He put his arms around her and kissed her and, for now at least, the tension was gone.

As they parted, she said, 'I'd better get started with my packing. It looks like I have some serious catching up to do.'

2

It was almost dark when Catherine arrived at the West Devon rendezvous. She was late, delayed by traffic, and wasn't surprised that Nick and Brendan were no longer waiting for her in the car park opposite the village pub.

She squeezed her car into one of the few remaining spaces and checked her phone for messages. There was nothing from either of them. More worrying still, when she tried calling, was the discovery that they both had turned off their phones.

She wondered for a moment if Nick might have changed his mind about taking her to France. It wasn't beyond him, if the day with Brendan had gone particularly well, to consider cutting her loose from the tour. She imagined him another dozen miles down the road, congratulating himself on a narrow escape. Twenty-four hours earlier she might have looked on this as a happy outcome. But the extra day made all the difference. Heading back to London on her own now would feel like a personal and professional disaster.

It occurred to her that the missing tandem was something she should tweet about. Liz had ambushed her on the way out of the office and extracted a fresh commitment to share every waking thought on social media. With this in mind Catherine opened the Twitter app on her phone and wrote:

> *Lost. Two adventure travel experts on a heavily laden tandem. Last seen in car park of west country pub. #whereismytandem?*

The obvious answer came to her as she finished typing. In a new tweet, she added:

> *Doh! Will check inside.*

Scanning the crowded interior she spotted Brendan at the bar, deep in conversation with a cluster of locals. She watched him for a moment: the wild red hair flecked with grey; the right hand, which was missing its three middle fingers, gesturing to embellish some point in his tale; the wide, travel-crazy eyes that drew his audience into the spell of the story. From the way his hands clawed at the air she could tell it was something to do with mountaineering, probably a retelling of his favourite yarn, the near-death experience in the avalanche on Mount McKinley. She had heard it so often that she knew every detail, but still enjoyed watching it unfold on the faces of a fresh audience.

When the tale ended Brendan looked up and saw her standing just inside the door. He waved, then drained his glass and came over to meet her.

'I somehow thought I'd find you here,' she said, as she prised herself free from his bear hug greeting.

He chuckled. 'It didn't make sense to stand around outside a pub when I could be enjoying its charms with the locals.'

'Nick isn't with you?'

'Not likely. He decided he couldn't risk leaving the tandem all alone in an empty campsite. Perfectly sensible too. Every touring party should have someone like him along for the ride. One is probably the optimum number, though.'

He stepped back and made a show of inspecting her clothes. 'Well, well. You really look the part.'

At a motorway service station she had made a last-minute decision to change into cycling clothes, a gesture intended to signal her total commitment. But in a pub teeming with a country-set crowd, the skin-tight red polka-dot jersey and matching lycra shorts felt completely out of place. Self-conscious, she tucked a strand of hair behind her ear, and replied, 'He's going to fall down laughing when he sees me like this.'

'You're wrong. I think he'll be touched.' Gesturing towards the door, he added, 'Come on. We'd better get moving.'

They stopped at the Mini to collect her overnight bag and a cardboard box with the overspill of her new travel clothes. Catherine locked the car and made a show of presenting him with the keys. 'It's better I don't have these any more. I might still bolt for it when I get my first look at the tandem.'

She was inviting him to comment on her performance twenty-four hours earlier at Base Camp, maybe even to gently chastise her. Coming from him the truth was something she could just about stand to hear. But he let the opportunity pass, smiling enigmatically as he took the box from her, and she was left feeling almost disappointed.

They crossed the road and started along a lane that cut between two crumbling stone-walled cottages. It soon narrowed into a rutted path that was flanked and overhung by beech trees. In the dark Catherine stumbled on a ridge of exposed roots. As she recovered her balance she couldn't help asking, 'Will it be like this every night?'

'God no. Camping in France is much more civilised. Mostly you won't notice a difference from being in your own home.'

'Oh, I think I'll notice. Home is completely sealed from the elements, with four encouragingly thick walls and a sturdy roof. And there's a city right outside the front door catering to my every possible cultural and culinary need.'

Brendan stopped to transfer the box from one arm to the other. 'If you don't think you can stick with this right to the end then it's better that you tell him tonight. Waiting until you're in France will cause no end of trouble.'

She stared directly at him, wondering how best to respond. In the shallow moonlight his face and hair were drained of colour. He looked like an ancient soothsayer who had stolen a glimpse into the future and was bearing a warning he knew would be ignored. Her first instinct was to laugh it off, to tell him he had completely misread the runes. Then she realised that he might be trying to offer her a way out.

'I want to do this,' she replied, conscious that her voice still carried a stubborn trace of doubt. 'It's what we need. Three months together, just the two of us. If that doesn't put everything right, then I don't see what will.' She wanted to say more, to tell him about her fear of trespassing so profoundly into Nick's world. But she held back. Brendan had come to think of Nick as the son he'd never had and, try as he might, he was never going to be completely impartial.

'Kate, this will be no holiday. Living together, even part-time like you do, is one thing. But travelling with him – I'm not sure even I could cope with that any more. After the Amazon trip he won't let go of the tiniest detail. Right now, for instance, he's adjusting the tension in the spokes on the rear wheel. It's been put together by a master wheel-builder, for Christ's sake.'

Catherine smiled. 'I may have had a major wobble yesterday but I'm over it now. I know that every day for the next three months will be like a military operation. Setting up camp in exactly the same way every night. Eating only during prescribed times. Covering fifty miles on the back of a tandem every day, five days a week for ten weeks. I'm going to do it, and I'm going to enjoy it.'

He reached across and squeezed her arm. 'You're beginning to sound like you actually mean that.'

'I do. But I'm not sure I can display this level of bravado for more than a few minutes at a time. At the office they're running a sweepstake on how soon I'll give up. If you're interested in a flutter you can still get pretty good odds on me being back at work in under a week.'

'I've never thought of you as a quitter. Put me down for you going the whole distance.' He smiled and added, 'Remember, my job is to support you both. If you need me I'm just a phone call away.'

'Thanks Bren. Just one thing, though. I won't be able to get through if you keep forgetting to turn it on.'

A few minutes later they passed through a kissing gate and found themselves in a gloomily lit camping area. Just inside its fence line were three ancient caravans, deserted and in disrepair, their shells daubed with streaks of lurid green mould. Beyond them the path wound past a stone-walled toilet block. As she rounded the corner of this Catherine saw two lights at the far end of the field. The first was set low to the ground. Its diffuse glow told her that this was their new gas micro-lantern. The other, an intense, narrow-focused blue-white beam, jigged and bobbed in the air like a drunken, high-voltage glow-worm.

From the shape of the light-cone she knew this was Nick, wearing a head-torch exactly like the one he had given her at Base Camp. He turned as she approached and blinded her with a blast of high-intensity light. When her eyes had recovered she saw that he had picked up the gas lantern and was holding it in front of the tandem.

'Well,' he said, grinning ferociously, 'what do you think?'

The tandem's lustrous yellow frame glowed in the gas light, inviting her to reach out and run a finger along its enamelled steel top tube. It was cold from the night air and damp with condensation but this only added to its sense of strength. The frame rested on a pair of gleaming alloy wheels, each with a plate-sized disc brake set into the hub. The front handlebars, those ahead of Nick's seat, were traditional touring drops, curling like ram's horns above the front wheel. Set behind his seat post were the more upright butterfly bars that she would use.

It looked just right, the ultimate touring machine and a perfect vehicle to carry her hopes for the summer. 'It's fabulous, Nick. I can't wait to get started.'

This was exactly what he wanted to hear. Beaming, he put his free arm around her waist. 'It was a perfect first day. We were late getting away from the framebuilder's shop but we still covered a hundred miles. It practically pedals itself.'

She doubted this very much and was searching for a positive response when he surprised her by changing the subject. 'How about you? How was your day?'

'A bit of a trial actually. Does the name Christian Baltieri mean anything to you?'

When he shook his head, she continued, 'The fashion designer. He was on TV recently, one of those trace-your-ancestor shows. The big reveal was that he's directly descended from a Milanese armour-maker to the Medicis. He's so obsessed with the idea that it featured in the finale of his latest collection.

'I spent the whole day wearing a dress he made out of tailored chain mail and wafer-thin armour plate. I had to be bolted into it. Couldn't take it off even to go to the loo. It was like a cross between a suit of armour and a ball gown. More battledress than little black dress.'

There was more, eight hundred words more. The struggle to stand up and sit down. The surprising number of magnetic fields she'd encountered on the Tube journey back to work. The exhausting weight of it. And all the time knowing that it was a self-inflicted burden, the result of a moment's panic outside Base Camp. 'You can read the rest in Tuesday's Lifestyle section if you're interested.'

She knew this wouldn't happen. Nick was already on his way back to the tandem. Over his shoulder he said, 'I just have a couple of things to finish here before we eat.'

She watched him squat beside the rear wheel and realised it was a perfect picture for her blog. Close up and in profile, with a misty rain soaking into his thick dark hair, she could see that he was in his element. It reminded her of their first meeting almost two years earlier, when she had been sent by Liz to interview him. He'd been promoting his first book, an account of his journey by bicycle along Central Asia's Silk Road. He was brimful of the experience, alive with endless tales from the road. She had fallen for him instantly.

Smiling at the thought, she reached across and touched his shoulder. He grinned back and it felt as if they were connecting for the first time in weeks. Then they both seemed to remember the unaccountable gap that now lay between them. They turned away at the same moment, Nick settling back over the rear wheel, and Catherine catching eyes with Brendan who had been watching with interest.

He was still carrying the cardboard box with her excess clothes. Setting it down in front of her, he said, 'Let me help you get your gear sorted. Then I should be going.'

'You're going back to Base Camp tonight?'

He nodded. Leaning a little closer, he whispered, 'You can't take all of this with you. Have you any idea how much room there is inside a pannier?'

'I do, actually. Forty litres total on the rear rack, twenty-five on the front. Divide that by two, and my share is about thirty-two litres. Plenty of room.'

He laughed. 'Google is a wonderful friend. But it wouldn't

have told you that the panniers will be mostly full of cycling gear, camping equipment and food. If you want me to spell it out in terms you can understand, you can take three tops, two pairs of shorts, one fleece, a rain jacket ...'

'Enough. I just have to make a few last-minute decisions, that's all.'

'You'd be surprised how little you need. Just a credit card and a change of underwear, and you're good to go.'

'The wisdom of a man who's walked from Cape Town to Cairo.'

'Exactly. You'll always have support back at Base Camp if there's anything you need. All you have to do is sit on the back of that thing and pedal. And, as you said, enjoy it too.'

'That's just what I intend to do.'

My Tandem Tour de France
By Catherine Pringle

Saturday 18 June, 4 a.m.
Mid-Channel, aboard the overnight ferry MV Armorique

By the time you read this post Catherine Pringle will be in France and well into the first day of her epic 2,500-mile cycle ride.

Denial experts among you will have noted the deliberate (perhaps you're also thinking desperate) use of the third person in that opening. When my resilience is low – and there are no prizes for guessing we're deep in that murky little place right now – I find it enormously comforting to imagine that Catherine Pringle is someone else entirely. How else can I reconcile the fact that she'll soon be in France doing something she'd never in a million years imagine herself doing?

A long-distance journey by tandem is a proposition that would never have entered my head without someone standing on the other side of it pushing and shoving pretty hard. That someone is the man who will be sitting in front of me all the way around France – my boyfriend, the explorer Nicholas Farne.

We've been together for almost two years, but for most of that time he's been out of the country on one of his many solo adventures. The longest we've actually spent continuously in each other's company, having what you might think of as a normal everyday relationship, is something like a fortnight.

So when his promise of a summer at home together was threatened by another lengthy expedition, I just had to put my foot down. Ultimatum time. His choice. Me or another trip.

I fired everything I had at him: that we hardly spent any time together, had few shared experiences, weren't really a couple. Which turned out to be a major tactical blunder. I'd backed myself so far into a corner that there was no reasonable way out when he suddenly said: 'Then come with me to France!'

Since then — and this is pretty typical of anything organised by him — the whole thing has assumed epic proportions. In my mind *Come to France* is in a whole different category from *Ride with me on a tandem around France. Oh, and we're going to camp as well because my employer is an outdoor equipment retailer and they insist on us testing their entire catalogue while we're away.*

One slightly hesitant *yes* somehow led to another and, before I knew it, we were discussing routes, equipment, everything right down to choice of tyres. (Schwalbe Marathons, if you have to ask, a decision thankfully that only required me to nod in agreement.)

I've done a lot of nodding over the last few months. That and praying the whole thing might never get off the ground. Hardly my finest hour. But don't worry. Yesterday, the first day on the tandem, I paid for that attitude in spades.

It was hell. Over and over again the rolling Devon countryside exposed me as a breathless, weak-limbed dead-weight. A total humiliation. Nick insists he went easy on me but from where I was sitting I can only describe it as brutal.

Deliberate or not, it almost broke me. I can't tell you how relieved I was to freewheel downhill into Plymouth. I even felt a surreal sense of accomplishment when we rolled onto the ferry's car deck.

Somehow, against the odds, Catherine Pringle survived her first 50 miles on a tandem. Which leaves another 2,450 to go. I know what the philosopher Laozi would say about that — you know, a journey of a thousand miles begins with a single … etc., etc. But I'm pretty certain he didn't magic that up on the back seat of a tandem with an unrelenting partner sitting up front setting a savage pace.

I think Catherine Pringle can make this work, but only time will tell, and I've got a nagging worry that something in all of this will eventually have to give. I just hope it isn't me.

No place for a passenger

3

Deep in the down-filled cocoon of her sleeping bag, Catherine clung for as long as she could to the last comforting remnants of a fitful sleep. But with daylight growing and the steady patter of rain on the roof of the tent, her senses reluctantly tuned in to a new day. Slowly she became aware that she was in a campsite, and that it was now her second day in France with another ninety still to go.

She opened her eyes and saw that she was pressed tight into the curve of Nick's back. She loved moments like this, when they were as close as it was possible to be, when her breathing matched his and their bodies were almost one. It was infinitely preferable to having him awake. Awake, he would be up and herding her towards the next leg of the journey.

After two exhausting days on the tandem she knew that a third was really going to hurt. Fifty miles in Devon and the same again along the rain-swept coast of Brittany had been a shock. Everything ached, especially her legs. She had breached a contract with them, a lifelong agreement that standing and walking, sometimes in not very sensible shoes, was all they would ever have to do. They needed time to recover, time that she knew they weren't going to have.

To prolong the peace she peeled herself carefully away from him and rolled onto her other side. Before the first day's ride her plan had been to spend an hour at the end of every day writing a blog entry. For two days in a row this had failed completely. She had been too tired to do much more than eat, crawl into bed and send a few half-hearted tweets.

Today, she realised, it was time for Plan B, a radical reimagining of herself as a morning person. She began by pulling together her first impressions of cycle touring in France. Already there was plenty to write about – from the physical effort of cycling all day through to the trials of sharing the snug tent with a man who had lately become painfully distant. She searched for a theme that would weave these strands together.

Glancing at her sleeping partner, she remembered the 'discussion' he'd insisted they have the night before. They had just arrived at the campsite and she had been lying on the ground with her thighs tucked soothingly into her chest. The sight of her, totally inert and seemingly unwilling – she completely denied this – to play her part in unpacking the panniers and setting up the tent, had been too much for him. He'd been spoiling for another fight since Base Camp and two days of less than stellar performance from her had given him all the ammunition he needed.

Most of what followed – exactly the kind of colour Liz had sent her to France to write about – was still too raw for publication. But one particularly barbed line had lodged deep in her head and she couldn't resist using it as an opening sentence.

Picking up her smartphone, she wrote:

There is absolutely no room on a tandem tour for a passenger. It's a team effort, a relationship, two people pulling together to make something better than the sum of their parts.

It takes commitment and compromise. And it hurts. Boy, does it hurt! There are parts of me I didn't know were capable of feeling this bad.

But here's the shock. I'm beginning to think it might be worth it. Travelling by bicycle, moving through the landscape at your own pace and under your own steam, somehow lifts the spirits like nothing I've ever experienced. Yesterday's struggle through a heavy rain squall around the Baie de Morlaix was proof of this. Yes, there was the pain. But with the suffering there was also an exhilaration, a pleasure that sometimes had me laughing through the tears.

By now you must be wondering if Catherine Pringle has taken leave of her senses. You might well be right. An unaccustomed mix of physical effort and exposure to the elements has, at the very least, left me in an emotionally unpredictable state.

But there's another, more alarming possibility, the consequences of which are profound. There's just a chance that a tiny little bit of Catherine Pringle might come to enjoy this. Just a tiny little bit.

She was still editing this half an hour later when Nick began to stir.

'Rain,' he said, coming instantly alert. 'You'd better check the forecast.'

As she waited for the Météo-France site to load, he added, 'The nearest *code postal* is 29690.'

She stared at him, wondering if he'd already memorised the postcodes for all of their overnight stops. He looked knowingly back at her and she decided it was better to leave the question unasked.

Her French wasn't good enough for the full text of the forecast, but the simple graphics in the *Aujourd'hui Matin* segment of the screen needed no interpretation: heavy grey clouds were sending thick sheets of solid grey lines towards the bottom of the screen.

'Brilliant sunshine on the Côte d'Azur,' she said, handing him the phone. 'Shame we aren't there.'

'Rain always sounds much worse from the inside of a tent. The sooner you're out in it, the better.' He disappeared through the front flap, taking his rain jacket with him. Tossing the phone back to her, he added, 'It says this will clear by lunchtime. Sunny and warm after that.'

She watched him cross to the toilet block through a soaking rain that swirled across the campsite. Discouraged, and aware that another full day in the saddle would only provide more evidence of her incompetence as a cyclist, she zipped the fly down and pulled the sleeping bag over her head. A part of her, a very substantial part, hoped he might lose himself in the mist at least until noon.

He was back long before she was ready, squatting in front of the tent to light the micro-stove. Her instinct was still to stay dry and warm but his dogged persistence outside shamed her into action. She pulled on her rain jacket and waterproof leggings and crawled reluctantly into the world.

'God, it's worse than I thought,' she said, as rain beat against the hood of the jacket. 'Maybe we should wait this out and go on in the afternoon.'

'Maybe we could take tomorrow off too. Better still, why don't we stay here in Brittany for the rest of the summer? Nice try, Kate. But you're a professional traveller now and that means being completely weather-blind. Come on, a cup of tea will brighten everything up.'

She gave up and hobbled over to the toilet, happy enough that today, at least, she was Kate again after several days of mostly being Catherine.

A steaming mug of tea was waiting for her when she returned. As Nick handed it to her, she smiled at him through slightly gritted teeth. They stood in the rain, sipping at their tea, trying not to catch each other's eye. Inevitably, when they did, they both burst out laughing.

'How about this,' he said, his voice softening. 'Huelgoat is only three kilometres away. Why don't we get everything packed away, ride up there and find a warm dry bar to have breakfast in. In a few hours this should have cleared and we can still complete a full day's ride.'

'Thanks Nick.' Aware that he was doing it solely for her she put her arms around him, pushed the hood of her jacket back, and planted a rain-soaked kiss on his lips.

She felt him respond and for a moment it seemed that they might edge back inside the tent after all. Reluctantly he broke away and, still smiling at her, said, 'We should get going before this rain gets heavier. But tonight let's go out for dinner – a kind of celebration of making a start. I hope you managed to sneak some off-cycle clothes into that pannier of yours when I wasn't looking.'

'There's a distinct possibility that I did,' she replied, surprised and pleased by the sudden turn in events.

On a dry, sunny day the short uphill ride around the edge of the forest to Huelgoat would have been a pleasure. But with mist swirling across the road and rain driving into their faces, Catherine was content to tuck herself close to Nick's back. She kept her eyes down, half-focused on the bitumen below, and watched the steady rise and fall of her feet as they slowly turned the cranks. Even with the rain, perhaps because of it, she felt absurdly positive. The compromise they had just made over the day's ride seemed proof that they might conceivably put their troubles behind them.

She was dragged out of this reverie by the arrival of a tractor which swept through the rain onto their tail. For a hundred metres it sat just behind Catherine, its engine howling as the driver held it in low gear ready to pass. He tried on the first stretch of straight, clear road, swinging out and coming level with the tandem. But a string of cars loomed out of the mist, forcing him to brake and tuck close behind her again.

He tried again just before the blind, right-hand sweep at the top of the incline. This time the high, studded rear tyres drew level and inched ahead, spewing a cocktail of mud and spray into their faces. Catherine began to turn her head away but froze when a flash of white further up the road caught her eye. Another vehicle, a van, was on the apex of the corner and gathering speed towards them.

Swerving out of the van's way, the tractor cut sharply into the tandem's path. Seeing this, Nick flicked the handlebars sideways and hauled the cycle onto the verge. On the thick wet grass the wheels slid uncontrollably and the whole machine toppled into the steep-walled roadside ditch.

Catherine glanced off the embankment and rolled into the ditch where she sat winded in a few inches of murky water. Adrenalin drove her up after a few seconds and she climbed onto the road, shouting after the tractor as it disappeared around the corner. Deprived of this outlet for her anger, she turned and saw that Nick was still lying beside the tandem. He was on his side with his head raised a little and his left leg bent at a worrying angle.

'Be careful!' he said, when she dropped into the mud beside him.

Already there was an ugly swelling around his left knee. Fearing the worst, she asked, 'Do you think it's broken?'

Cradling the joint in his hands, he eased it up and found that it would bend. 'I don't think so.'

'Then we should get you out of the mud.'

'Don't touch me. Just let me sit here for a while.'

She was about to argue when a movement on the edge of the mist further down the incline caught her eye. A walker, clad in a charcoal rain jacket and waterproof leggings, was striding steadily up the hill towards them.

Catherine hurried down the road, rehearsing a few lines of her meagre French as she went. Explaining what had happened was beyond her – she couldn't think of the word for leg, let alone knee. But she was determined to secure the newcomer's help.

When they were only a few metres apart she saw that the face huddled inside the charcoal hood of the rain jacket was male and, encouragingly, set in a cheerful grin.

'*Excusez-moi, monsieur,*' she started. Then, defaulting to the easiest option, she added, '*Parlez-vous anglais?*'

The grin widened. 'Last time I checked I was pretty much fluent. But it has been a couple of weeks.'

'You're Australian. Thank God.'

He laughed. 'It's not often I get that kind of reaction. What can I do for you?'

'It's Nick. My boyfriend. We've had an accident and I need your help to move him.'

Realising there was someone in the ditch, he hurried across and stepped down into the mud. Squatting, he said, 'Nick, I'm Steve. It looks like you've found yourself a little bit of trouble.'

'It's nothing that a stiff drink and a couple of painkillers won't fix.'

'That sounds like a bloody good idea. I'll pass on the painkillers but I wouldn't mind joining you for a drink. But first we should get you to somewhere a little more comfortable.'

Catherine watched as he pulled back his hood for a better look at Nick's leg. He was, she guessed, in his mid-thirties, with longish fair hair that was completely wet through from the rain. His face was broad, with wide-set blue eyes and a large slightly crooked nose. His cheeks and chin were rosy from exposure to the rain. There was something in his manner, a combination of ease and directness, that managed to cut through Nick's usual reticence about accepting help. It drew Catherine closer too and she stepped down beside him, wanting to take part.

Indicating the low stone wall on the far side of the road, he said, 'Nick, the first thing we're going to do is carry you over there. I want you to relax and let us do all the heavy lifting. No arguments. Okay?'

To Catherine's amazement Nick simply nodded and let them ease him into a sitting position on the grass verge between the ditch and the road. From there, after a short struggle, they lifted him and shuffled across the road to the wall.

'So far so good,' Steve said. He turned as a car came around the corner from the direction of Huelgoat. When it was about two hundred metres away he pointed to it and said, 'Rule number one in an emergency: never be shy about asking a local for help.'

He stepped into the middle of the road and held up his arms. The car, an old Renault Clio, slowed to a crawl and its occupants, an elderly couple who peered warily through the windscreen, exchanged a few words before deciding to stop. Steve disarmed them with another smile, then leaned into the driver's window and began a halting conversation in pidgin French.

'Languages aren't exactly my strong point,' he said, when the short interaction had come to an end, 'but I think they're offering to drive you down to the nearest Accident and Emergency. They're going to Morlaix now, so if you want to take a chance, then you should hop in.'

They helped Nick across the road and into the back seat of the car. Catherine passed him his bar bag with his documents and wallet. Then she turned back to Steve. 'I can't let him go on his own like this. I know it's a really big ask, but would you be willing to wheel the tandem back down to the campsite for us?'

'Sure. I'm only too happy to help.'

'No,' Nick cut in. 'I can cope alone. I'll feel better knowing that you're looking after our gear.'

She stared at him, exasperated. She was certain he'd need her but he seemed more concerned about the tandem. And, quite possibly, happier on his own. 'All right. But put your phone on and let me know what's happening.'

'Of course,' he replied. He leaned out and touched her arm. 'Don't worry. I'll see you later.'

Catherine watched the car until it had disappeared around the bend at the bottom of the hill. Then the nervous energy that had carried her through the accident and its aftermath deserted her. Steve, who saw her knees begin to buckle, was at her side in time to stop her fall.

'Are you okay?'

'I think so,' she managed, letting him take her weight. She eased the sleeve of her coat up and saw the beginning of bruising where her forearm had struck the wall of the ditch. Her right hip and shoulder were both throbbing now but she didn't want to look at them until she was alone. 'I'm just a little shaky, that's all.'

'There's no hurry to go anywhere. Let's sit down for a while.' He took her arm and guided her back to the wall. They sat side by side and he eased his arm around her for support. She let her head fall against his shoulder, her mind empty except for the blurry realisation that the accident could have been a lot more serious.

After a while he passed his water bottle to her and she took a steady drink. When she handed it back, he said, 'In all the rush I don't think I caught your name.'

'It's Catherine. My friends call me Kate, unless they feel like being formal, or I've just done something they find particularly irritating.'

'Well, I'm not formal at all. And so far I haven't found you even the tiniest bit annoying. Play your cards right and it will always be Kate with me.'

She smiled, aware that he was trying to put her at ease. Nodding towards the ditch on the other side of the road, she said, 'Nick might not agree but I'm beginning to realise just how lucky we were. Look where we ended up. It's incredible.' There were tears now, rolling down her cheeks. 'God, I hope he's all right. I can't believe someone could be so irresponsible. On a blind corner. They didn't even stop.'

She wiped her eyes and forced herself to stand. 'I don't suppose the tandem's going to get itself out of that ditch by itself. Do you feel like having a go at rescuing it?'

Halfway across the road she turned suddenly and gripped his arm. 'Thanks, Steve. I don't know what we would have done without you.'

Embarrassed, she hurried ahead and dropped into the ditch to unload the panniers. She passed them up to him, being careful to avoid eye contact. Then he jumped down and helped her lift the cycle onto the road. It had survived the accident almost entirely unscathed. A few scratches on the paintwork, a slightly misaligned front mudguard and a bent bottle cage gave it a gravity that it had lacked before.

They wheeled it slowly down the hill and were back at the campsite in less than twenty minutes. Near the riverbank they leaned the tandem against a picnic table. Catherine turned and smiled at Steve. 'Thanks again.'

This was more gratitude than he seemed able to handle. 'Well,' he said, 'I might be on my way. I've got a pretty full day's walking ahead of me.'

She wanted him to stay but didn't feel it was right to ask. Instead, she just nodded.

'I won't be back till late,' he added. 'If you're still here, I'll see you then. If not, good luck with the trip. I hope everything works out for you.'

She watched him walk out of the campsite. As he turned along the road towards Huelgoat, she wished that she'd found the words to make him stay.

4

When Nick was travelling, which he did for more than nine months of every year, weeks would often pass without Catherine hearing a word from him. On one occasion, when he had been journeying by dhow along the spice routes of the northern Indian Ocean, they had lost touch for well over a month. It was early in their relationship, the first real separation after they had met, and the weeks of worry had taught her a lasting lesson: Nick only ever got in touch when he had something useful to say.

Calling to tell her that the boat was slowly sinking never entered his head. Hearing on his return that he had almost drowned triggered their first fight. In his shoes she would have moved heaven and earth to deliver a final message, and she couldn't understand why he didn't feel the same. No amount of arguing bridged this gap and she had gradually resigned herself during their frequent periods of separation to just not knowing if he was dead or alive.

But the tandem accident felt like something entirely different. She had actually been right there on the spot with him and this had convinced her he'd follow through on the half-promise to call from the hospital. When it didn't happen she made excuses for him, accepting that there might be practical or technical reasons for the delay. But as the morning dragged into afternoon she slowly realised she was fooling herself. She was still worried, but the concern was tempered with a growing irritation.

For a while she distracted herself by unpacking their wet gear and spreading it out to dry in the sun. Then she assembled the stove and made herself an instant coffee. It wasn't the *grand crème* she'd imagined when they started uphill towards Huelgoat, but it was still refreshing and it gave her the extra satisfaction of feeling self-sufficient.

With a second cup in front of her she cast around for someone to discuss the accident with. Liz started at the bottom of the list. A close interrogation followed by demands to publish on social media wasn't exactly the gentle debrief Catherine had in mind. On reflection she shied away from her other close friends too. They all knew each other, most of them worked in the media, and the story would get around, quite possibly to Liz, before there was a chance to tell it herself.

By a process of elimination she settled on her mother. Just that morning Eleanor Pringle had surprised her daughter with one of her infrequent text messages. Catherine opened it again and scanned it:

> *Good luck in France, Darling. Hope you're not setting yourself up for a very public humiliation. I expect you'll cope.*

It was typical, Catherine thought, a perfect combination of love, double meaning and ego demolition. But she still wanted to hear her mother's voice, and she texted a short plea for a voice call.

Her phone buzzed a few minutes later and a short, pointless exchange of texts followed:

Eleanor Pringle: *Do you have any idea what time it is here?*

CP: *Where exactly is here? I thought you'd be working
from home as usual.*
EP: *I'm in America this week. New York. Delivering a
lecture.*
CP: *You didn't tell me.*
EP: *You didn't ask. Still tweaking my slides, so can't
possibly speak now. Not unless one or both of you is
dead or dying.*

Catherine wondered if the accident was serious enough to pass the 'dead or dying' threshold for a call. She thought not, and fell back on Liz who, despite her tendency towards bullying, was an always-on friend. After a moment's hesitation, she composed and sent a text that said:

Day two ruined by bad weather. Almost no progress. Fell into ditch at one point. Details later.

It was a stupid thing to do, a conclusion she reached only after sending an identical message to Brendan. Her worst fears were quickly realised. Liz responded with a reminder that Catherine was being paid to send tweets, not private messages. Brendan wanted to launch a full accident investigation and texted back a string of questions she couldn't possibly answer. It was more than she could deal with. She switched the phone off and dropped it into her bag.

She was still walking off the frustration when a taxi turned into the campsite. She watched it progress on a slow circuit around the network of bitumen lanes, and waved when it was obvious that Nick was in the back seat. When it stopped beside her he lowered his window and leaned out, grinning at her triumphantly – the returning hero demanding adulation for managing entirely on his own.

She felt for just a moment like slapping him. Imagining the crack of her fingers on his cheek, she wondered if this was the only way she might actually communicate her feelings to him.

As a penance, she leaned in and kissed him theatrically on the cheek. Then, stepping back, she said, 'Don't ever leave me in the dark like that again. When you're off somewhere on your own you can fall off a cliff for all I care. Get eaten by a shark, mauled by a lion. I don't want to know. I really don't. But when we're together you have to let me know that you're still alive.'

Stung by this reprimand, he replied, 'I would have called if there was a problem.'

'I was worried about you. You do get that, don't you?' Looking down at his leg, which was heavily bandaged around the knee, she softened and added, 'How is it?'

'Nothing serious.' His tired smile betrayed the lie. 'They did a scan and a string of other tests. Almost everything is where it should be.'

'Can you walk?'

He held up a pair of crutches. 'With these I could walk around France. Maybe we should drop the tandem and do the circuit on foot.'

She laughed at the absurdity of this. 'Seriously, what are we going to do now?'

'Well, I think we should get to the nearest hotel before the happy pills they gave me at the hospital wear off. Unless you'd rather we stay here.'

'A hotel? Give me five minutes.'

Walking anywhere, even across the pavement from the taxi to the entrance of the Hôtel Concorde, was almost too much for Nick. He was determined to do it alone, pushing Catherine away when she tried to help him from the car, but he struggled just to lift his leg and swing it onto the ground.

He took a halting step and paused, apparently entranced by the view across the road to Huelgoat's man-made lake. Without the crutches, and the eye-watering wince, the ruse might just have worked.

'For God's sake,' she said. 'Let me help you.'

'I'm going to do this under my own steam. If you want to make yourself useful, help the driver unload the gear.'

For the second time in less than an hour she wanted to hit him. As he shuffled into the hotel she was left again in the sole company of the expedition's equipment. This time it was only for a few minutes. The receptionist gestured to her from a lane at the side of the hotel, and together they pushed the tandem around to a storage room at the rear of the building.

She caught up with Nick in the stairwell, half a dozen steps below the first floor landing. He was resting with his shoulder against the wall, his head down, eyes screwed shut. His face was pale and creased with pain, and she decided that if he didn't move in the next few seconds she would overrule him and call for help.

Keeping her tone light, she asked, 'How are you doing?'

'Fine. Fine. Almost there. Is the tandem safe?'

'Safe. Dry. Tucked up in bed, and watching reruns of the Tour de France on television.'

'That's funny. I wish I felt more like laughing.'

'I know a lot of jokes. Have you heard about the man with only one good leg who couldn't bring himself to ask anyone, even the woman he claims to love, for help?'

'Don't start, Kate,' he said, edging up the stairs. 'Just let me get to where I'm going in peace.'

Their room was two doors along the corridor from the top of the stairwell. It was small but comfortably furnished and, crucially for Nick, had an en-suite bathroom a few metres from the end of the bed. She followed him into the room and watched as he eased himself onto the mattress, flinching as it sank more than expected under his weight.

Giving him plenty of space, she crossed to the window and

made herself watch the trees as they shifted in the breeze on the far side of the lake. After a while she turned and asked, 'So, what next?'

'I think I'm just going to sit here for a while. Maybe even for the rest of the summer.'

'What exactly did the hospital say?'

'I know it doesn't look like it but there really isn't much damage. Strained ligaments, nothing torn. They told me to stay off it for a few days. Then, when the swelling goes down, I should try to exercise it as much as I can to strengthen the muscles around the knee. I asked them if cycling would be good for it. They said yes.'

'I bet you didn't tell them you meant four thousand kilometres of cycling. Are you seriously suggesting you'll be able to continue?'

He looked darkly at her. 'I don't see why not.'

'You can't even walk from the bed to the toilet. How can you even think about going on?'

'I'm not an idiot. I'm just saying we should put off the decision for a couple of days. If the signs are promising we can take a stab at it. If not, well, we're not far from the ferry. What do you say?'

It was the one thing he needed from her, the suspension of her critical faculties at least until his own were fully functioning again. 'All right. We give it a couple of days.'

He smiled at her. 'And until we know for sure we keep this to ourselves. Agreed?'

She stiffened, debating whether to say anything about the text messages she'd sent. Realising that she was chewing her lip, she opted for a full confession. 'I texted Brendan and Liz from the campsite. I told them we had a slight accident.'

'Christ. What made you do a thing like that?'

'I was alone, out of touch with you. I didn't know if they were fitting you with a bionic leg, or airlifting you back to England.

You might have let me know what was happening.'

Deaf as ever to any criticism from her, he continued, 'I don't know which is worse. Bren's perfectly capable of organising a manhunt if he thinks we're hiding anything. And Liz is liable to dispatch a photographer to capture the moment Bren succeeds in tracking us down.'

'I didn't think about it until it was too late.'

'Well don't tell anyone else. Put your smartphone down and step away from it.'

Catherine nodded. Then, as she thought about it, she realised it was impossible.

Nick arrived at the same conclusion a moment later. 'I'll send him a message in the morning. Something neutral that says we had a slide in the rain, but a very soft landing. Which is entirely accurate.'

'I don't see how that's going to work. We'll be stuck here for a while, several days at least. If we can't explain that we should just tell him the truth now.'

Nick rubbed his face and let his arm trail over his eyes. Then he began to laugh. 'There's nothing I can say that would explain us being stationary. But you, on the other hand, might just help us get away with it.'

'Me?'

'That little delaying tactic back at Base Camp. It worked out pretty well for you then. Maybe you could come up with something similar and post it on your blog. A sudden panic about the trip that doesn't resolve itself for a couple of days.'

'I can't lie in the blog, Nick.'

'Then rearrange the truth a little. Exaggerate for effect. That's what you're good at, isn't it?'

He lifted his head a little. The strain somehow transmitted itself along the mattress and he squeezed his eyes shut in pain. Opening them again, he said, 'Kate, I really need your help with this. I can't let anyone at work know about the accident. Not yet. Not until it's clear that I can't go on.'

She stared back at him, wishing he wasn't asking so much. But there seemed to be no way out. 'All right. But let's wait until morning. If we haven't thought of anything by then I'll have a very public panic about cycling around France with you.'

He put his head on the pillow and closed his eyes, appearing to relax for the first time since arriving at the hotel. After a moment, he said, 'This has really fucked everything up for both of us.'

'Much as you'd like to, you can't control everything. On an adventure like this things are sometimes going to go wrong.'

'Amundsen, the man who beat Scott to the South Pole, believed that adventure was just bad planning.'

'You don't really believe that, do you?'

He shrugged. 'I'm beginning to wonder if there isn't something in it.'

Catherine crossed the room and took his hand. She leaned down and kissed him. Then she smiled and said, 'Well, from now on, every step you take, I'm going to be right at your side.'

He nodded, then looked thoughtfully at her. 'You know, I do want this trip to work for both of us.'

She squeezed his hand. 'I won't desert you, Nick.'

Satisfied, he closed his eyes. 'At least I've learned a new word today. The doctor told me. A cycling accident is *une chute*. I like the sound of it, don't you?'

'The sound of it, yes. The activity itself, not so much.'

5

From her seat at the western edge of the lake Catherine watched the sun rise over the centre of Huelgoat. The sky, cloudless and blue, cast a near-perfect reflection onto the glassy water which rippled only occasionally where the light breeze touched its surface. It was hard to believe that twenty-four hours earlier she and Nick had been struggling through mist and rain towards the accident.

Her extended walk around the town had been his idea, an invitation to leave him alone with the misery of his injured knee. They had spent a difficult night together, with every movement on the over-soft mattress amplified into a leg-stressing torment. By morning what he wanted most was to be on his own. Sleepless herself, she was more than happy to oblige.

She settled down by the lake to make a start on her next blog post. Writing to order, any topic, any length, any deadline, was the precondition for membership of her tribe. But the only newsworthy item from the last twenty-four hours still lay under a self-imposed embargo. In its place she had to spin a fiction about still being unready for cycle touring.

Eventually, an idea came to her, and she began to write: Tandem cycling has a well-deserved reputation as a graveyard for even the most robust relationships. It forces a couple to work together as a team, each constantly and utterly dependent on the other.

Many relationships survive only by stepping permanently away from the machine. Others, and I'm beginning to think it's just a tiny minority, thrive on the constant proximity, fusing themselves into something infinitely stronger.

It's all about trust. And the moment that best captures this is the start: two people, both straddling a finely balanced and heavily laden tandem, have to go from standing to moving without falling flat on their faces.

The stoker, and in a couple that's almost always the woman, clips both feet into her pedals and balances precariously on her seat. From that point onward she's totally at the mercy of the captain, who is holding the whole structure upright with just the force of his inner thigh against the top tube.

He's completely dependent on her too. A fractionally early rotation of her cranks will drive the tip of his saddle into his butt. If the timing is particularly poor, or if his seat post is set just a little too low, then it could be curtains for his manhood.

All of which brings me to the point of today's post. Yesterday we had a fall. Not life-threatening, but enough to severely dent my confidence (which is nothing compared to the dent hammered into Nick's rear). So we'll be staying in Huelgoat for a couple of days of much-needed technical practice.

When we've mastered the art of starting, when

trust has been fully re-established, we'll be ready to
head for the Loire.

Twenty minutes passed, all of them deeply absorbing. But she couldn't bring herself to publish a post containing such blatant fabrication, not without reflection. And that required a cup of strong coffee first.

She finished her circuit of the lake and continued into Huelgoat's central square, the Place Aristide Briand. Strolling along its western side, she began her quest for coffee, and was scanning a menu on the window of a crêperie when a voice behind her, mock-American, squeezed theatrically through a clenched jaw, said: 'Of all the crêpe joints in all the towns in France, she has to walk into this one.'

It was Steve. He was smiling at her, partly, she suspected, because his Bogart impression was so very good. He was still wearing his charcoal rain jacket, unzipped now to reveal a faded T-shirt, but had discarded yesterday's waterproof leggings for jeans. Taken completely by surprise, Catherine fumbled for a response until a fragment of Ilsa Lund's dialogue came into her head. 'No matter what happens, Steve, we'll always have Brittany. We didn't have it until yesterday, but now we've found it.'

When he nodded his appreciation, she laughed, a little too much, and had to hurry on. 'I didn't get the chance to thank you properly yesterday. Maybe I can treat you to morning tea.'

It was too early for the crêperie, but along the street they found a *salon de thé* where they ordered coffee and each chose a pastry from the display at the counter. Seated, they looked at each other again. His stare, intense and disarming, made her more than a little nervous. She tried to recall the aftermath of the accident, when they had been sitting on the wall together, and wondered if she had actually cried on his shoulder. She couldn't remember, but the thought made her reach into her bag for the comfort blanket of her smartphone.

'I don't know what we'd have done without you yesterday,' she began, as she pretended to scroll through her messages. Looking up, she added, 'Actually, I do know. We'd still be there now, waiting for Nick to think up a way of winching himself out of that ditch on his own.'

'How is he this morning?'

She told him about the pain he still felt with every movement of his leg, and of the official prognosis that he would soon be back to normal. 'I've got to be honest with you. It's a relief to be out of that room. He's devastated by what's happened. This trip means so much to him, to both of us. Now it's over practically before it started.'

'It's definitely over, then?'

'He says not, but today he can't even get out of bed. How is he going to ride around France?'

'Can't you just delay the start for a while? Go back home, let him get fully fit.'

'I wish it was that simple. There's a lot hanging on us doing it now.'

A waiter arrived with their drinks and pastries. Catherine used the interruption as an opportunity to change the subject. 'How about you. How long are you here for?'

'I go home – back to London, that is – on Thursday.'

'On the ferry from Roscoff?'

He nodded. 'I've been making my way north from Spain and detoured into Brittany to visit the stones at Carnac.'

He paused to attack his éclair with a fork. Catherine watched him demolish it and wondered if it was his first food in days.

'Sorry,' he said, misinterpreting her stare, 'I shouldn't go on about my good fortune with holidays. Not when you've had such a rough time.'

'No. Tell me more. It's a relief to be talking about anything other than tandems and knees.'

He began a diary-like narrative of his journey up the Atlantic coast, or as he described it: 'The way from, rather than to, Compostela. Somehow I always seem to end up doing the important things in life completely contraflow.'

He was a good storyteller, funny and engaging. Catherine felt she could listen to him all day and was disappointed when they found themselves outside in the square again on the brink of parting. They stood awkwardly, watching the traffic and the shoppers around them, neither wanting to be the one to walk away.

Eventually, he said, 'When we met I was on my way to take a look at the rock formations on the edge of town. Come with me. You can't stay in Huelgoat without writing something about *la grotte du Diable*.'

She smiled and nodded her agreement. They walked out of the square and crossed a small bridge where the overflow from the lake passed under the road. Beyond this, they turned onto a stepped path that followed the stream as it tumbled past gigantic granite boulders on its way to the floor of the forest.

When the path levelled he asked her a little more about how she had come to be on a tandem with Nick.

'This summer is the twentieth anniversary of his first major adventure. He'd just turned sixteen when he set off alone on a bicycle tour around France. A few months ago, over a very boozy dinner, a friend convinced him that recreating the experience with me along this time was a perfect way for us to spend some much-needed time together. That same friend, Brendan, thought that a tandem tour would sound romantic enough to suck me in.'

'Like in the old song.'

She nodded. 'A bicycle built for two. Combined with a Tour

de France it was the perfect angle for me to pitch to my editor. Just the right level of confessional journalism to fill the Saturday travel pages while the regular columnists are in their summer bolt-holes. So here I am.'

'And what happens to your column if you have to go home?'

'It will die a death. There is absolutely no news value in a blog about nursing back to health a fiercely independent, one-legged adventurer. Maybe I could squeeze a single article out of it but that's about the limit.'

Even to her this sounded mercenary. She turned to make light of it but Steve had fallen a little way behind and was staring at his iPhone. Assuming he was checking for messages, she continued a little way along the path and stopped by the riverbank where she sat on a tree stump and idly watched the water tumbling past the boulders.

When he caught up with her he held out his phone and she saw that it was open at the landing page of her newspaper's website. 'I thought you said you were a journalist.'

'I am.'

'There's no mention of the accident in your blog. Surely it's the most newsworthy event since you arrived in France.'

He was smiling but she took it as a direct challenge. 'Nick and I … We're still trying to decide how much we'll have to tell … It could affect both of our jobs if the truth gets out.'

It was stumbling and desperate but enough for him to realise that he should back off. 'Your secret's safe with me, Kate. I can see how you'd both be pretty keen to continue with the trip, if it's at all possible.'

'We are,' she replied, and realised that she meant it.

The exchange had broken the spell of the walk. It had also convinced her that she had to publish the post she had been drafting at the lake. Standing, she said, 'I should get back.'

She turned to go, then stopped and thought for a moment.

'Steve, will you still be around tomorrow?'

'I think so. I don't have to catch the ferry till the day after.'

'I could use some help with the tandem. To check it over. And maybe do a short test ride. If Nick and I do find a way to carry on we'll need to know that it's still mechanically sound.'

He smiled and replied, 'I'd love to. It sounds like fun.'

The restaurant at the Hôtel Concorde was already full when Catherine entered through the connecting door from the hotel's lobby. She scanned the room and saw Steve at a table near the front window. He was sitting with his back to her, staring out across the lake towards the setting sun.

She felt unaccountably nervous as she crossed the room, an unexpected sensation after the ease of their afternoon ride together. It had been the easiest and most enjoyable two hours she'd spent on the tandem, with a sense of fun she hadn't realised was possible on two wheels.

He turned when she was almost at the table and caught her trying to flatten a stubborn kink in her hair. A few weeks earlier, on a glacially slow news day, she had claimed space in the Lifestyle pages by volunteering to have it cut into an edgy, ragged, so-bad-it's-fantastic bob. The stylist, a gritty Albanian who was inexplicably trending for shabby-chic cuts executed with sheep shears, secateurs, anything but scissors, had created a sensational and highly regarded look. Unsurprisingly it was now in an advanced state of decay and had a half-life measured in minutes from its last blow-dry.

Preoccupied, she arrived at the table still undecided on whether she knew Steve well enough to kiss him on both cheeks. Thinking, *What the hell, I'm in France*, she leaned in but abruptly pulled away again when she realised it was unacceptably intimate. Embarrassed, she left the weird gyration unexplained, and slipped into her seat with a what-am-I-like roll of the eyes.

'I hope we haven't kept you waiting too long.'

'It gave me the chance to think through a job offer that came through late this afternoon.'

'Here in France?'

'No, back in London. I just sent a message accepting it.'

'That's great news,' she said, feeling instead an irrational sense of loss. She covered this up by signalling to a passing waiter. 'We must celebrate.'

Glancing back to the door, Steve asked, 'Nick is still joining us, isn't he?'

She nodded just as the waiter arrived. She ordered a kir for herself, a second beer for Steve and a very large whisky for Nick. 'Actually, he sent me ahead because he couldn't stand me hovering around him while he struggled down the stairs.'

'Maybe he's worried that every step he takes, every twinge of pain he reveals, will be mercilessly tweeted or blogged about.'

Catherine stared at him and tried to decide if the edge in his voice was real. The smile was still there but his eyes had suddenly lost their humour. 'You've been reading my latest blog post.'

'Which led me to your Twitter feed.'

'I'm sorry. Really, I am. But I'm under contract to create content all day long. With Nick out of action I had to get a bit creative.'

'Creative? It's a complete fabrication. You pretended that our walk yesterday and the tandem ride today were both with Nick. You somehow thought it was okay to take my words and have them come out of his mouth. And worse, you uploaded carefully cropped pictures of me ahead of you on the tandem and tried to pass them off as him.'

'I swear, Steve,' she replied, genuinely contrite, 'I won't do that to you ever again.'

After a moment, he relented. 'I just have this thing about social media. But I'm willing to forgive you as long as you turn off that tape recorder you've got running inside your head for the rest of the evening.'

She nodded and they found themselves staring deeply into each other's eyes. Catherine looked away first, in time to see Nick come into the restaurant. Compared to his efforts on the stairs he was making good progress on the flat. But every movement played painfully across his face, and many of the diners looked up from their food to watch his epic journey across the room. Their eyes stayed on him until he was resting on his crutches beside Steve, who rose to shake his hand.

'How are you holding up?' Steve asked.

'Put it this way,' Nick replied, as he slumped into a seat. 'I'm not planning on a stroll around the lake after dinner.'

When their drinks arrived he raised his glass. 'Thanks Steve, for everything. I really appreciate it.'

'I just did what anyone else would have done.'

'No, you've gone way beyond that. Today, for instance, you took a tandem ride with Catherine Pringle.' They all laughed, even Catherine, who felt there was more than a slight edge in his voice. 'It's hard to believe, isn't it,' he continued, 'that she spent every lunch hour at the gym for the last three months.'

She looked anxiously at Steve. During their test ride she had found herself telling him that the gym membership, a gift from Nick, had been used on only a handful of occasions. It was a secret she had kept from everyone else.

He kept her on the edge of her seat for a moment, smiling first at her and then at Nick. When he opened his mouth, she was certain he would take his revenge for the Twitter fiction she had engaged in at his expense.

'Actually,' he replied, 'I thought we were a pretty good match on the tandem. I'm hardly what you'd call a super-athlete.' Nodding at Nick's leg, he added, 'You can't claim to be one either right now. Are you any closer to a decision on going home?'

Nick finished his whisky, then cleared his throat. 'I can barely walk. I can't put any weight on my leg at all. I only got down here to dinner because I was desperate to eat one meal in this place sitting upright like a normal adult.

'But lying in bed for the last two days has given me plenty of time to think. I realised that you don't actually have to walk anywhere when you're on a bicycle. All you've got to do is sit on it and find a way to turn the pedals. If someone will carry me to the tandem tomorrow, I'd like to put that theory to the test.'

Catherine turned to him, wide-eyed. She was still lost for words when he added, 'Thanks for the vote of confidence. But I'm not going home without giving it one good try.'

The waiter arrived with menus and they turned their attention to dinner. After they had ordered, and the waiter had returned with bread and wine, Nick turned to Steve again. 'Kate tells me that you're about to head back to London.'

'I've just about run out of reasons to linger on this side of the Channel. And out of money too, if I'm honest. So it's back to the real world for a while.'

Catherine, who had heard all of this before, watched Nick closely during the discussion that followed. She could see that something was on his mind, but it was still a shock when he suddenly said, 'Steve, I was wondering if you'd be willing to stay on for a few days. I thought we might hire a car and get you to act as our support. Transport our baggage, that sort of thing. It's the only way I can see that will make this whole thing work.'

Steve hesitated, taken completely by surprise. In the silence, Nick added, 'We can't pay you but I can take care of your costs out of my travel budget.'

'If you cover my expenses and treat me to an occasional meal like this, I'll do it. I can't see what I've got to lose.' Realising that Nick hadn't talked the idea through with Catherine first, he turned to her and asked, 'What about you, though? I'd want to know that you were happy to have me around.'

She looked at Nick and saw just how much he wanted her to say yes. It annoyed her that he had made the offer without consulting her first. But she realised how indispensable to him she now was. 'I think it's a brilliant idea. It might just make the difference. So, I say yes. Let's do it.'

They turned back to Steve for his final answer. He grinned at them and replied, 'In which case, I'm in.'

He took out his iPhone and typed a short message into it. Then he passed it across the table to Catherine. 'Do me a favour, will you, and press the send button.'

She hesitated for a moment, then pressed it. As he took the phone back from her, he said, 'Looks like you just sent a message telling the agency I've quit my new job. I hope you know what you're doing.'

6

Huelgoat had always been an unplanned deviation, a temporary haven from the rain on that ill-fated second morning. Leaving it meant retracing their steps to the scene of the accident and continuing downhill past the campground where they had spent their first night in France.

Even though she was doing all of the pedalling Catherine found it unexpectedly easy. The only real struggle had been transferring Nick from his crutches to the captain's seat. His heavily bandaged left knee, still swollen despite three full days of bed rest, was too painful to lift over the tandem's top tube. Steve had found the solution, leaning the unloaded cycle almost to the ground so that Nick, clinging desperately to Catherine, could ease himself over it.

'Once we're moving I should be able to help a little with my good leg,' Nick had said to her during the short discussion on how they might get under way. 'Everything else is up to you.'

'And if we have to stop at an intersection?'

'I'll be concentrating on falling over gracefully. What will you be doing?'

'In that case we're not stopping for anything. From now on, it's crash through or crash.'

She had meant it too, but the first few minutes through the town passed without trouble. They lumbered up a short incline that would have been imperceptible in a car and barely noticeable if they had both been fit. Then it was downhill for more than a kilometre and it began to seem that the whole crazy idea might just work.

The thrill of getting the tour under way again soon evaporated and they lapsed into a deep silence, each focusing on their very different trials on the tandem. As her muscles tired Catherine struggled to keep the pedals turning. But seeing Nick ahead of her, working hard with his right leg while the left trailed loose from its pedal, she was determined to suffer in silence. Both were wary of stopping. The risk of another tumble, or of Nick jarring his leg, escalated dramatically during these moments. But inevitably the periods of rest grew in frequency and in length as the morning progressed.

Lunchtime came and went, and still they were nowhere near the midday rendezvous they had planned with Steve. It was late afternoon before they limped past the red-bordered road sign that announced the beginning of Carhaix-Plouguer.

Steve was waiting for them at a kerbside bar in the centre of the town. He helped Nick from the tandem and guided him to the nearest table. Then he turned to Catherine and raised an eyebrow to check that everything was all right. She managed a tired nod as she dropped into the seat next to Nick, who had already slumped forward and buried his face in his hands. Sizing up the situation, Steve took over and ordered for them.

'Cheers,' he said, when beers and croque-monsieurs were on the table. 'You've done a great job getting as far as you have.'

Catherine felt the effect of the beer and the food almost

instantly. Her body crept back to life and her spirits rose just enough to manage a reply. 'I don't think I want to move another inch. Maybe I could get myself as far as the back seat of the car, but that's about it. How about you Nick?'

Nick thought for a moment before answering. His face was drawn and pale and his brow was creased with pain. 'Stopping sounds tempting, I've got to say. I wish it was an option.'

'There's a choice of hotels on the edge of town,' Steve said. 'We could drop you there, then Kate and I could walk back and collect the tandem. After that, I'll drive on to Rostrenen, pack up the tents and bring them back here.'

Drowsy from the food and drink, Catherine took a moment to comprehend this. 'Do you mean you've already been to Rostrenen?'

He nodded. 'I thought it would save us time later if I went on and set up camp there. It's no big deal. I can collect the tents and be back in no time.'

'Sounds good to me. What do you say, Nick?'

He drained his beer before replying. The delay was ominous, and she was hardly surprised when he shook his head. 'Last time I checked, this was still a tandem tour. The clue is in the name, isn't it? If Steve's already set things up at the campsite, then we're going on. Stopping now will only make tomorrow or the next day even harder.'

'But it's pointless. At the pace we're managing it'll be midnight before we finish the ride.'

Looking directly at her, he said, 'My number one rule is: never make changes to a plan if you don't need to. Sunday was an example of that. If we'd stuck to our plan we wouldn't have been riding up to Huelgoat. There wouldn't have been a crash.'

She stiffened. 'Are you saying you blame me for us being on that road on Sunday morning?'

'No, I blame myself for giving in. It's just a fact that we

wouldn't be in this fix if we'd stuck to the plan.'

Livid, she pushed her chair back and stood up. She turned to walk away but Steve reached across the table and caught her wrist. It was as much of a shock as Nick's accusation and it stopped her dead. They stared at each other for a moment while she decided if he had crossed a line. But his eyes were imploring her to stay. He loosened his grip and she sat down again, trusting him for the moment.

'I've got an idea,' he said. 'It means the two of you spending an hour or so apart, but right now that looks like no bad thing.'

When they were both willing to listen, he continued, 'It's another twenty kilometres from here to Rostrenen. If you're determined to stay there tonight, then how about we make a temporary change of personnel on the tandem. Nick, you take the car and drive on to the campsite. Kate and I will follow on the bike. That way we don't fall any further behind the schedule. And you get the rest you need so that you can get back in the saddle tomorrow.'

Catherine smiled a thank you to him, then turned to Nick. 'Please say yes. I haven't got the strength to pedal us the rest of the way on my own. And you can't help me any more than you already have. It's our only option.'

The conflicting demands of resting and sticking to the plan played across his face. Eventually he gave in and nodded his agreement. 'All right. But this is strictly a once-only arrangement. If I can't do the trip the way I want to, I'd rather not do it at all.'

For Catherine, the ride east from Carhaix-Plouguer was a complete contrast to the pre-lunch struggle. Her only way of conserving the little energy she had left was to sit back and let Steve do most of the work. If he noticed, he didn't mention it. He was the perfect cycling partner: his legs were fresh, he was happy to encourage her with continuous small talk, and he had an infectious enthusiasm for every little detail of the rolling farmland they were travelling through. Most of all he was relaxing to be around.

As her energy levels flagged again she began to brood on the argument back at the bar. In the gaps between conversation Nick's words began to eat at her until she just had to bring them into the open. 'Do you think he really meant what he said back there? That he somehow blames me for the accident.'

Steve waited until they had crested the next hill before responding. 'It sounded that way to me. But you know him a whole lot better. What do you think?'

'He can be brutally analytical sometimes, especially when he's had an opportunity to brood. But it wasn't always like that. It's as if there's a dark cloud over him now that just won't seem to drift away. It rains on his every thought. Usually I can laugh it off but sometimes it just stings too much.'

'Maybe it's him you should be talking to about this.'

He was right and she thought for a moment about why it was easier to discuss with a stranger. 'We've kind of stopped having conversations like that. That's partly why I thought we should do this trip together.'

'So that it would either force you together or drive you apart?'

She tried to laugh the question off, but couldn't quite manage it. 'It sounds pretty stupid when you put it like that, doesn't it?'

'Not necessarily. I was just thinking that the accident looks like it's going to make all of that a little harder.'

'Maybe a shared hardship is just what we need to bond us together.'

She thought he would agree, even cautiously. But he didn't respond and suddenly her words seemed hopelessly naive. She let them drift away in the breeze, and put her head down, glad to have the distraction of turning the pedals and watching the bitumen glide past beneath her.

Arriving at the campsite, they found Nick lying on an air mat in front of their tents. Spread on the grass beside him were two Michelin maps and he was making shorthand notes in his notebook. Catherine knew these would be revised calculations on route and mileage. And, at that moment, she just didn't want to know.

'How are you feeling?' she asked, as she detached herself from the tandem. She lay on the ground and closed her eyes, relieved that her day's work was finally over.

'Much better. I took a long shower when I got here and it helped to loosen my leg. Since then, I've just been lying here doing a little reflecting on the day.'

She raised herself onto one elbow and looked at him. 'Anything useful come out of all that thinking?'

He shrugged and busied himself with his notes. As he did this Steve quietly picked up a towel and started towards the showers. They watched him go, then Nick passed her the second air mattress. It was a gesture of reconciliation and she rolled onto it with a sigh of gratitude. Turning onto her side, she watched him as he inspected the map. She decided against a confrontation and instead opted for something they could both agree on. 'We were incredibly lucky to find someone like him.'

Nick nodded. 'He did the right thing this afternoon when he suggested the switch. It would have felt like defeat to stop in Carhaix but I couldn't have done the whole ride. Given the situation I don't think it's cheating.'

'Neither do I.'

'And it will be good for us to have him around for a few days, if you know what I mean.'

She waited for him to expand on this but it was as far as he seemed willing to go. After a pause, she replied, 'I'll give you all the support I can, Nick. But we shouldn't make it any harder for each other than it needs to be.'

Looking up, he said, 'What I said earlier about the accident. It was the pain talking. You do know that, don't you?'

In other circumstances she would have reached across and placed a reassuring hand on him. But since the crash he was wary of the slightest contact in case it caused any pain to his knee. Seeing him brace against the anticipated touch, she abandoned the idea. With it went most of her hopes for using the journey to rebuild the physical intimacy they had shared at the beginning of their relationship.

Rolling onto her back, she watched a cloud drift across the sky. More to herself than to him, she said, 'You've done amazingly well to get back on the tandem again. But I don't have limitless capacity to bounce right back when you push me away. If you keep me at arm's length for long enough, I might just get used to staying there.'

She felt him take her hand. 'Kate, please just give me some time. Every day will be better. And we have a whole summer before us. South of the Loire everything will be different.'

Catherine wanted to look at him, but couldn't. She closed her eyes and hoped that what he had said was right.

7

With its head-high hedging and meandering cul-de-sac lanes, the campsite at Josselin resembled an elaborately constructed maze.

All that Catherine wanted to do after a third full day of cycling was roll to a stop and fling herself to the ground. But first she and Steve had to find Nick. They knew he would be in the remotest corner of the campground – that much was a given. But this particular site had been conceived by a landscape designer with lone-wolf tendencies, and they had to check almost every twist and turn before they finally cornered him in his chosen lair.

Even then they almost missed him. Their tents were completely obscured by a long-wheelbase Land Rover that had been parked across the one open side of the *emplacement*. As they turned in she realised why the dark green vehicle looked so very familiar. Sitting opposite Nick in front of the tents, his mass of rust-red hair stirring in the breeze, was Brendan Stillwater.

He turned when the cicada rattle of the tandem's freewheel announced their arrival. 'It's a huge relief to hear that sound,' he said, through a thin smile. 'It's the first real evidence I've had for days that this is still a fully functioning cycle tour.'

He walked across to Catherine and hugged her. Then he stepped back, and added, 'And you must be Steve. The new, and evidently indispensable, third member of the team.'

'I wouldn't put it quite like that,' Steve said as they shook hands. 'I'm just the driver. And an occasional extra pair of legs.'

'From what I've just been hearing that's something of an understatement.'

Catherine could see that Brendan was determined to make them suffer for leaving him out of the loop. She glanced at Nick, looking for a signal that an abject apology might be in order. But he just smiled vaguely and said, 'Bren has invited us all to dinner.'

'To celebrate what you've accomplished so far,' Brendan added, as he crossed to the driver's door of the Land Rover.

'That's very good of you,' she replied. 'Coming all this way. Just to take us out for a meal.'

'It's my pleasure, Kate. There's a lot more I could have done too, if only I'd known how things were. But we can discuss that in more detail while we eat.'

As they watched him drive away, she asked, 'How did he find us?'

Nick shrugged. 'I didn't want to give him the pleasure of telling me. I'm sure he'll make it pretty clear at dinner that he's always at least one step ahead of us.'

With his easy manner and natural talent for organisation, Brendan had managed at short notice to reserve the best table at the Hôtel Restaurant du Lion d'Or. And he had chosen for himself its best seat, just to the side of the restaurant's picture window. A glance to the left offered him a clear view across the river to Josselin's medieval château. And to his right he had a commanding view of the dining room. There would be no catching him by surprise, Catherine reflected as she followed

Nick and Steve across the restaurant.

Brendan seemed to have recovered most of his humour since leaving the campsite. He made a great show of helping Nick into a seat and, when they all had an aperitif in their hands, proposed a toast. 'Here's to travel and the unexpected adventures that make it all worthwhile.'

They touched glasses and drank but it did nothing to relieve the tension. This only eased when Brendan drained the last of his Ricard and turned to Nick with the question they had all been waiting for. 'Time to put your cards on the table. Just how bad is the knee?'

Catherine expected an evasive response, an attempt at humour, or a denial that the problem existed. But the reply was swift and honest. 'Bren, it's completely useless. Every morning I set off thinking I might possibly last a full day on the tandem. But after an hour or so the joint starts to swell. Eventually I have to stop and let Steve take over for the last twenty or thirty kilometres. If it wasn't for him the last three days would have been a complete waste of time.'

The waiter arrived with menus and they turned their attention to dinner. When they had ordered, Brendan made an elaborate perusal of the wine list and selected a Haut-Médoc. 'May as well pull the stops out. Crookie insisted on paying for everything tonight.'

Catherine leaned over to Steve and explained. 'Aidan Cruickshank. The main man at Cruickshank and Spears.'

'Your boss?' Steve asked Nick.

'Brendan's too. Bren is the senior consultant in our travel division. His job is to stay one step ahead of simpletons like me.'

'He's exaggerating, of course,' Brendan cut in. 'I'm no more than a glorified storyteller who offers the occasional word of advice. Advice that people increasingly tend to ignore. But the job title was irresistible. Head of Adventure. Not bad for a washed-out wanderer with a dodgy heart and a few too many broken bones.'

During the entrée he gave Steve a potted history of the company. 'Cruickshank and Spears organises expeditions, mainly for scientific or research purposes. They started back in the early 1800s and quickly made themselves the go-to people for naturalists or explorers who needed to go up the Nile or along the Zambezi. It grew from that into a global operation. When Aidan took over from his father a decade ago we expanded rapidly into the bespoke leisure market. All of this looked like a pretty good move until the financial crash in 2008. People suddenly stopped spending large amounts of cash on expensive adventure holidays. Now we're adjusting to the times – adventure on a tight budget, value for money. Exactly the kind of experience Kate and Nick are supposed to be having right now.'

'By the way,' he continued, 'when I called Crookie before dinner, I didn't tell him anything about the crash. Or about there being a stand-in who is doing at least half the riding. No offence, Steve, but your contribution isn't exactly what Cruickshank and Spears had in mind from a marketing point of view when we sponsored this little fiasco.'

He refilled their glasses and signalled for another bottle. Then he turned serious again. 'Nick, how far are we behind schedule?'

'At least three full cycling days. We should be across the Loire by now.'

'And tomorrow. How far would you get, supposing Steve didn't take over partway?'

'If it's completely level, I could manage fifteen kilometres. But that's pushing it.'

'So at this rate, in a week you'd be two weeks behind schedule. In another week, a full month. We just don't have that sort of time, do we?'

The waiter returned to clear the entrée plates. It gave Nick an opportunity to avoid an answer. 'Right now, just planning and executing an expedition to the loo is on the outer limit of my capabilities. But if I start right away I should be back before the next course arrives.'

Catherine passed him his crutches. He hobbled upright and began a very slow passage across the room. When he was out of earshot Steve leaned close to the others. He said, 'I've never understood why the schedule's such a big deal to you all. Can't you just delay the whole thing till next summer?'

'It has to be this summer or not at all,' Catherine replied. 'Twenty years to the day since he first cycled around France. That first adventure meant everything to him. Missing the chance to repeat it is not an option.'

She turned to Brendan, wondering how much else they should say. She watched him toy with his glass until he had made up his mind. Then he leaned in and quietly added, 'The anniversary is important but there's a lot more to it than that. Nick's last expedition was a total disaster. Crookie sent him down to the headwaters of the Amazon with a couple of potential investors. Russian businessmen, supposedly. Mafia according to Nick. If half of what they boasted about is true they were pretty dangerous customers.

'It was supposed to be a couple of weeks of kayaking, a little bit of gentle white-water stuff – you know, show them what C&S is capable of – then back home via London so they could give the business a much-needed cash injection. The thing is, they fell out with each other from day one. One thing led to another, the party split and one of them went off on his own. Ended up getting himself killed in circumstances that have never been fully explained.'

'None of this was Nick's fault,' Catherine broke in. 'But he was in charge and Aidan blames him for losing control of the group. And for scotching the chances of investment capital when the whole thing fell apart. So, he's on a kind of probation with Aidan now. The last chance saloon.'

Brendan nodded at this. He added, 'In our line of work, confidence – luck, whatever you want to call it – is everything. If you lose it, or the punters begin to think you have, it's time for a career change. So I dreamed this trip up to make Nick look like he still has what it takes. No Russians, no guns, no white water. Just France and a tandem tour. Easy enough that a complete novice could manage it.

'Who knew that a crash would happen on day two. Now it's going to be all about repackaging this to look like a roaring success. And somehow keeping him in a job.'

'How are you going to do that?' Steve asked. 'Apart from anything else, he seems to be his own worst enemy.'

Brendan smiled. 'He didn't use to be. Whatever happened down in the Amazon was the straw that broke the camel's back. The question we have to answer now is: can he actually carry on and complete the trip by the first week in September? And if that's a yes, or even just a maybe, then how do we get to that point from here?'

'Why is September so important?'

'Because he's scheduled to fly out to Africa in the first week of September. He's got to finish the tandem ride, successfully, and be fit enough to lead a film crew and a team of entomologists along the Niger by the end of August.'

'So,' Steve said, looking at Catherine. 'No pressure, then.'

'No,' she replied. 'No pressure at all.'

When Nick returned it was obvious they had been talking about him. He swallowed most of a glass of wine, then said, 'Well, Bren, you've seen me in action now. And it's not a whole lot prettier on the tandem. What would you do if you were in my shoes?'

Brendan mulled over a response while their main courses arrived. Then he gestured with his fork towards the château. 'Looks pretty impressive, doesn't it? A solid example of fourteenth-century architecture.'

The light was fading and the sky was a little overcast, but the floodlights had come on, warming the stonework of the château's curtain wall and its cylindrical fairy-tale towers. It was the kind of setting that made Catherine glad she was in France, and she found herself feeling sad that there was so much more out there that she probably wouldn't have the chance to see.

'The thing is,' Brendan continued, 'it's just a facade. Most of the original was demolished by Richelieu during the Huguenot Wars.

'It's a bit like your tour really. From a distance it looks like the genuine article. There's a tandem, with two people riding it. Not always the same two, but that hardly matters right now. Meanwhile, Catherine is pumping out social media updates that give the impression everything is completely on the level. But behind the facade there's nothing much there. You're deceiving yourselves if you think you can complete a circuit of France by the end of August.'

'I'm not giving up,' Nick insisted. 'You don't quit a week into a trip. It just isn't done.'

He looked at Catherine for support and she surprised herself by siding with him. 'A week ago I would have said just go home. But now I'd feel cheated if we had to stop.'

Brendan paused long enough to let the inevitability of failure sink in. 'There's only one way to make this work,' he said. 'I'm going back to Roscoff tomorrow to catch the afternoon ferry. And Nick is coming with me.'

He held up his hand to stop them interrupting. 'Kate, you and Steve will continue the ride as far as the Loire. While you do that, Nick will see a specialist and get some intensive physiotherapy. He'll be back almost before you miss him.'

In the silence that followed he studied their faces, clearly enjoying the effect of this bombshell. Nick was first to react. 'I like it. But there are a host of practical problems to solve. How on earth could we cover up my absence for so long? And how are they going to carry Steve's equipment on the tandem as well as ours? He'll need his own tent for a start.'

'Wait a minute,' Catherine said, shooting him a dark look. 'It's a bit soon to start worrying about the accommodation. I haven't even said I'd stay if you go back.'

'But you will, won't you. For me. For both of us.'

'I don't like it. Granted, it's a way for me to keep my column. And with Steve on the tandem we'd certainly make up the lost time. But it falls too far on the wrong side of dishonest.'

Brendan bristled at this. 'It's nothing more than an extended version of what you've been doing for the last three days.' He took out his mobile phone and pushed it across the table to her. 'But if you're worried about honesty, call Liz Madison now and tell her you've been living a lie since the crash. While you're at it say that you're coming home early but want to keep your column in the paper for the rest of the summer.'

Catherine let the phone sit in front of her, angry that he was pushing so hard. She was also annoyed that Nick seemed to have sided with Brendan so easily. 'Okay, I admit I'm no saint. But that doesn't mean it's right to continue with a half-truth.'

'Make the call then, Kate. You'll feel better when you get it off your chest.'

She turned to Nick, and he finally came to her rescue. 'Bren, we don't need to decide this tonight. Why don't you come out to the campsite in the morning. We'll let you know then. Okay?'

Catherine realised that she had one last card to play. 'We haven't heard from Steve yet. Maybe he's had enough of us already.'

Steve shrugged. 'I'm in for another week whatever your decision. I enjoy being on the tandem and we can catch up on a lot of lost distance. As for the sleeping arrangements, I'm easy about that. We're all adults with a serious job to do. I can sleep on my own under the stars so long as it's dry. Or in a hotel room if someone's willing to pay for that.'

Nick was about to argue, but Brendan held up his hand. 'Look, let's leave the practical details to me. That's what Base Camp is for.' Softening his tone, he added, 'Come on, Kate. Say that you'll at least think about it overnight. We're all counting on you.'

Catherine hesitated, then pushed his phone back across the table. 'Okay. We sleep on it and make the decision in the morning.'

8

A few kilometres into the ride from Josselin, Catherine realised
that moving on without a rest day was a major mistake.
Emotionally it made perfect sense – staying where they were for
a second night would have felt like marking time. But it was her
fourth riding day in a row and she struggled right from the start
just to turn the pedals.

With Nick ahead of her on the tandem it would have been
impossible. But he was long gone. There had only ever been one
realistic option. When Brendan arrived at the campsite after
breakfast, Nick was already packed and ready for the drive back
to Roscoff. Waving him off Catherine had been struck with a
sudden premonition that she wouldn't see him again in France.
It felt achingly real and she had only just suppressed the urge to
run after the car and beg him to return.

Fortunately her new partner fitted perfectly with her own
riding style. They had an almost identical natural cadence, the
holy grail of tandem cycling. They both wanted to change gears
at the same time and to stop for food and drink as if they were a
single organism. It was still a stop-go day, full of rests and short

bursts of cycling, but they talked constantly and encouraged each other when the going was tough.

They also had the unexpected pleasure of arriving early at a campsite for the first time, and marked this achievement by sharing a bottle of wine with their picnic dinner. After the intense physical effort of cycling, the first glass of the full-bodied red went straight to Catherine's head. She caught herself again and again laughing hysterically when either of them said anything remotely funny. It was only when the light began to fade and her thoughts turned towards bed that she realised why the humour had been so forced. The time when they would have to crawl into the tiny tent together was fast approaching.

Nick had still been adamant at breakfast that there was plenty of room on the tandem for two entire sets of camping equipment. When he wasn't looking Brendan had quietly stowed Steve's tent in the back of the Land Rover. It was purely for practical reasons – another five kilos of equipment was the last thing they needed – and Catherine wasn't about to argue. But it had added an extra dose of nervous energy to an already exhausting day.

She could tell that Steve was aware of it too. He was still his laid-back, unflappable self, but the faded and torn T-shirt he usually changed into at the end of each day had disappeared, replaced by a fresh one of exactly the same design. Written across the front of his chest in bold gold lettering was the slogan *Aestivation Zone*. She tried to ignore this sudden raising of the sartorial bar but the wine eventually loosened her tongue. 'Why do all your shirts have the same words on them?'

'It's a legacy of my stint as a male model in China.'

Catherine burst out laughing. 'Oh, come on.'

'It's true,' he insisted, looking hurt that the explanation seemed so unlikely. 'I was talent-spotted at a railway station in Wujiang by a clothing manufacturer who was trying to break into the Western market. More accurately, it was my then girlfriend they spotted first. But when they found out there were two of us, a male and a female, they were delighted.

'All we had to do was model their range of T-shirts and sleepwear for a new English language catalogue. It was the easiest day's work I've ever done. We literally didn't have to get out of bed. They gave us a hundred dollars cash in hand each and an enormous crate of T-shirts. Absolutely everything had this *Aestivation* logo written across it. Sophie and I didn't get the point of that at the time – it was only later that we realised it had something to do with hibernation.'

Catherine still had no idea if he was telling the truth, but the story had her hooked. 'So how did it work out between you in the end? You and this Sophie.'

'Between us I'd estimate we still have nearly a dozen unused T-shirts.'

'I meant *between* the two of you.'

He shrugged. 'It turned out that the box of T-shirts was all we had in common. We went our separate ways a few months later.'

'And is there anyone now?'

'Yes,' he replied, turning uncharacteristically serious. He swallowed the last of his wine then half-looked at her. 'It happened quite recently and I really don't want to jinx it by telling you more. Anyway, I honestly don't think she knows I exist, not in that sense. So if you have any tips on how a good-natured sort like me, a man with the obvious physique of a catalogue model, might present himself in the best light, you will let me know, won't you?'

'I'm not sure I know you well enough yet to offer that sort of advice.'

She was sorry as soon as she said it, particularly the use of *yet* which implied an intent she hadn't been conscious of. The line seemed to hang between them while they cleared away the picnic and made ready for bed. Catherine got into her sleeping bag first and made a show of checking her phone for messages. For once there was nothing and any thought of using it as a prop had to be abandoned.

When he crawled into the tent a little later his knee struck her on the ribs. Full of apologies he wriggled into his sleeping bag and they tried to settle. But it was a warm evening and they struggled to share the tiny space without their bodies coming into contact. After a while he began to laugh.

'What's so funny?' she asked, both irritated and amused.

'This must be the last thing you imagined when you set off for France. Here you are, sleeping with another man, and no one can ever know.'

'Steve, get your facts straight. I'm sleeping next to you, not with you.'

This made him laugh even more. 'If fact-checking is your idea of pillow talk then the journey along the Loire is going to seem very long indeed.'

'Imagine what this is like for me,' she replied, 'lying here with all this material slipping through my fingers. I can't even tell my best friend because she's also my editor. Even if I could, I wouldn't. She's never been convinced about me and Nick as a couple. This would set her off all over again.'

Neither of them knew where to take this. They retreated into an awkward silence that became impossible to break. For a while Catherine lay beside him, overtired but unable to sleep. The situation was absurd. She had come to France to be with one man and now found herself lying inches from another, listening to the rise and fall of his chest, feeling every movement of his body. The thought drove her from the tent and she sat disconsolately in front of it, picking at the remains of a chocolate bar.

After a while he joined her. She broke off a square of chocolate and passed it to him.

'It's odd, isn't it?' she said, after a long silence. 'Suddenly being alone together all day and all night.'

'There doesn't seem to be anywhere to hide on a tandem, or in a two-man tent. But I don't mind if you don't. Most of the travelling I've done recently has been on my own. I'm enjoying having someone else to share the experience with, even if it's only for a few days.'

Deciding it was safer to change the subject, she asked how he had started travelling.

'I'm a born traveller, almost literally. My mum and dad did the full-scale Europe tour that lots of Aussies did in the seventies. When they got home again they couldn't settle and took off in a camper van for a trip around Australia. I was born in Darwin and spent my first couple of years in campsites in the Northern Territory.'

'So you got the travel bug early.'

He nodded. 'I didn't really start on my own till after university. My dad practically manhandled me onto a plane. I think by then he regretted the sedentary lifestyle he'd settled into. He was completely obsessed about me finding my own way in life instead of accidentally slipping into his. He told me to go off and find my own equivalent of Shangri-La.'

'I guess you're still looking, given that you're here.'

'It turns out that finding it isn't as easy as it seems. But I've begun to realise that how you go about looking for it is what really matters.'

When she smiled at this, he asked, 'What are you thinking?'

'Just that I wish I could write about you in my column.'

'Maybe one day I'll let you. But only if I retain full editorial control. And only if you answer an equal number of questions about yourself.'

'Like what, exactly?'

He shrugged. 'I've just told you about my family. Maybe you could start by telling me about yours. For instance, are you following in the family tradition with the work you do?'

'God no. They wouldn't dream of penning an article for a newspaper, certainly not one so far down the food chain as mine. I don't think they're all that comfortable with one of their offspring doing it either. Writing doesn't count to them unless it's been through at least two rounds of peer review.'

'Peer review?'

She laughed. 'My parents are academics. Mum is the historian. The quickest way to her heart is to take a strong and clearly argued position on the contribution of the Carolingian Renaissance to the survival of Western civilisation. Dad is rarely seen in daylight hours outside of his study. He's a professor of English literature, an expert on Jane Austen, which he seems to think is an excuse for channelling completely the character of Elizabeth Bennet's father.'

'Does he have five daughters all in need of a husband?'

'As a matter of fact there are only two children,' she replied, suddenly a little embarrassed. 'I'm the only girl. And, as you know, I'm not exactly in need of a husband. So that's where the analogy ends. It's also just about all I feel like sharing for free. There might be more but not until you decide to let me write about you in my blog.'

'You drive a pretty hard bargain.'

'Information is just the currency I deal in.'

He smiled. 'I'll let you know when I've got something to trade.'

At the end of their third day together they reached the Loire. It was a major milestone, the end of the first phase of the tandem tour, and a cause for celebration. After setting up camp on an island in the middle of the river they walked into Saint-Florent-le-Vieil for dinner. On a small rise on the southern bank of the river they paused and looked back at the broad expanse of water, watching it ripple in an evening palette of silver-greys brushed with an occasional stroke of orange or red.

Enjoying the sunset, Catherine turned to Steve and smiled. 'I never thought I'd hear myself say this, but I'm beginning to think that I can actually call myself a cycle tourist.'

'Glad you came this far?'

'Yes. And I don't want to stop. Now that I've discovered I can do it.'

As they stared at each other there seemed to be a mutual realisation that it was something they could only have achieved together. With Nick, Catherine would have been very much the junior partner. Every accomplishment would have been judged against his standards and, more likely than not, found wanting. Steve was an equal. They complemented each other and were a stronger unit because of it. She realised that she would miss him when he was gone. The thought made her want to wrap her arms around him and, if he responded, to kiss him and see where it led.

His eyes told her that he felt exactly the same. Lost in the moment, they were drawn towards each other but, before their lips touched, Catherine somehow found the strength to pull away.

Turning her back, she said, 'I'm sorry.'

Confused, he backed away and faced the river. 'I thought you wanted to.'

'I did. I still do. But it would be wrong. For this to work we can never be anything more than friends. I have to know that you can accept that.'

After a while, he nodded. 'Then let's agree, if it ever comes up, that we both were carried away by the moment. It won't happen again.'

'Agreed,' she replied, more to herself than to him. 'It was something about the moment.'

To move them on she looped her arm through his and steered him towards the village. 'Come on, partner,' she said, with excessive bonhomie. 'I'm going to buy you dinner.'

As they climbed towards a restaurant in the upper village she took out her smartphone and tried calling Nick, first on his mobile, then at their home number in London.

'Still nothing?' Steve asked, when she put the phone back in her bag.

'I'm so angry with him. I know I shouldn't let it get to me, but I'll never understand why he can't just pick up the phone and tell me how he is.'

'Well, if I were you, I'd try calling Brendan. He's more likely to answer and much more certain to tell you what's happening.'

She knew he was right. It was also true that subconsciously she'd been avoiding this, that calling Brendan was an admission of defeat in her never-ending communications stand-off with Nick. She rang Base Camp and got an answer on the second ring.

'Bren,' she said, cutting across his greeting, 'is he there?'

'He's up in London. Been there for a couple of days.'

'So he's still alive then.'

Brendan chuckled. 'As far as I know.'

'And his knee. Will we be able to carry on?'

'All the advice we have says yes. It may take a few weeks before he's doing a full day on the tandem, but in a month he should be almost back to normal.'

It was good news, but she was more angry than she had imagined. Mostly it was with Nick, but partly with herself because of what had almost happened at the riverbank with Steve. Lowering her voice, she said, 'Bren. Why is it so hard for him to just tell me what's on his mind?'

'I don't know, Kate. All I can do is make him feel guilty enough to call you.'

She was torn. It shouldn't be necessary, but it was the only way to be certain of hearing from him. 'Okay. But make it sound like it's your idea. Otherwise, he won't.'

She started to end the call, then added, 'I thought it would be different between us when we were on the road. I thought that if I met him on his territory he'd be more open with me.'

'I suppose, after the accident, he feels that things are slipping out of control again. I don't think he can see anything beyond that.'

'Did he tell you this?'

After a pause, he replied, 'Not in so many words. But I can read between the lines. I know what it's like. It took me about a year to get over the loss of my fingers. Some people would say my guitar playing still hasn't recovered.'

She laughed. 'I'm not willing to wait a year. And I hope he realises he's not the only act in town.'

They had just returned to the island campsite when Nick's call came through.

'I'm not a hundred per cent sure I recognise that voice,' Catherine said, after his tentative greeting. 'Are you by any chance Nicholas Farne, the one-time traveller and very nearly ex-partner of the journalist Catherine Pringle?'

'I'm sorry for not calling sooner.'

'I hope so, Nick. I really do.'

'I retreat into myself too much at the moment. So far that I sometimes wonder if I'll ever find my way out again. But you shouldn't read anything into it.'

'Anything else in the script Brendan gave you?'

She was determined not to be the one who broke the lengthy

silence that followed. Eventually, he managed to say, 'I know I'm hard to be around right now. But once I'm back, and get my leg working again, things will get better. They have to.'

'Please, Nick,' she said, her mind returning to the moment with Steve on the riverbank, 'just get yourself back here as soon as you can. I really do need you here.'

'I have two more days of physio. I'll be back with you the following day. Where will you be on Saturday night?'

She opened up the map and traced the route. 'Probably Azay-sur-Indre. But we won't decide for sure until Friday night.'

'Azay sounds good. It means I can take over the riding on Sunday and we can cover the thirty kilometres along the Indre to Augmont.'

She had forgotten about the château at Augmont. 'Are we still doing that? I didn't think there was time now.'

'Claire Augmont got in touch again yesterday. She still wants us to come. Sunday is the day of the château's annual medieval fair. When she heard you're looking for material to write about in the column, she said she's got something perfect for you. They had a journalist lined up for it but the arrangement fell through.'

'Sounds intriguing. Maybe I should call her for more details before I say yes.'

'What is there to know? Claire's one of my oldest friends and she's asked for our help. Can't you just say yes for once without launching an inquiry?'

'All right. It's decided. On Sunday we go to a medieval fair.'

'Is Steve camped nearby? I'd like to talk to him.'

'He's not far away.' Catherine walked back to the tent and passed the phone to him. He raised his eyebrows, but she just shrugged and turned away. She picked up her toiletry bag and crossed to the toilet block.

As she brushed her teeth she brooded on the call with Nick. It should have been enough that he had called, and a relief to know that he would soon be back. Instead it had descended into an argument over administrative practicalities. Staring at herself in the washroom mirror, half-dimmed in the light from a dying fluorescent tube, she decided that waiting for Nick to close the distance between them was a loser's game. She had to stir things up, force him to respond. It crossed her mind that the week she'd spent with Steve might be a catalyst. A blog entry that Nick would interpret as a threat might be a step in the right direction. It needed further thought and she decided to let the idea simmer overnight.

Steve was pacing beside the tent when she returned. He asked, 'Do you already know what he wanted to ask me?'

'I think I'm about the last person likely to know what's going on inside Nick's head.'

'He was sounding me out about staying on a little longer. He says he'll be able to do the riding again, but not with a full load. The idea is that he brings his car over and I use it to transport the gear, just like in Brittany.'

Catherine couldn't help feeling relieved. 'It's a great idea. How long can you stay for?'

'Ten or twelve days. That should be enough to get the tandem down to Saint-Émilion. He said that if you're not there by Bastille Day, there's no point in going any further.'

My Tandem Tour de France
By Catherine Pringle

Day 15, Saturday 02 July
Azay-sur-Indre

I don't know how it happened, or where exactly, but at some point on our journey along the Loire I stopped being a tourist on a bicycle and began my transformation into a cycle tourist.

It's nothing to do with the distance covered – 560 kilometres in 10 riding days is hardly the stuff of Tour de France legend. But there is a kernel of change in me, one that I'm struggling to fully understand.

For one thing I've stopped actively resisting the experience. I can't believe that Catherine Pringle is saying this but she actually looks forward to her daily ride. And she loves being part of a small (and decidedly eccentric) band of travellers, people who are out in all weathers with all their worldly possessions strapped to the frame of a touring cycle.

They come in all shapes and sizes and in a wide range of nationalities, with the exception ironically of the French who wouldn't dream of weighing themselves down with anything more than a bidon of water and an energy bar.

No classification system can adequately capture the cycle tourist in its most extreme incarnation. I'm talking here about expedition cyclists, a breed sighted only rarely in a country as civilised as France. You can spot them a mile off when they're still a dark and lumbering speck on the horizon.

Expedition cyclists don't go anywhere in a hurry. They don't have to. Their entire life is with them on the bike, conveniently within reach of an outstretched hand.

Which means they always have time to stop and talk. And when they do you can see in the face and the eyes that they've done some serious travelling. There's the faraway look, the outdoors set of the face and, behind the facade, a catalogue of untold stories that they'll never share because the experience was for them alone.

It leads me to wonder: what kind of cycle tourist will I turn out to be? A light-touring speed-junkie? An epic adventurer? Or something in-between. The thing is, it's not something you get to choose. You have to wait and see what the journey turns you into.

Transformations like this can happen quickly. An example is the change in our team. I now trust the man in front of me in a way that I'd never have imagined ten days ago.

In Huelgoat I wrote about being afraid to balance on the pedals, afraid to trust him to keep me and the tandem upright. Now, I've stopped thinking about it. A dozen times a day I place myself entirely in my captain's hands.

I'm developing a bond with this strange man in front of me, a bond that will be hard to break, even if we are apart. It could never have happened without spending the last week on the tandem together. I'm so grateful that this journey has given me the opportunity to discover it.

Roscoff to Azay-sur-Indre

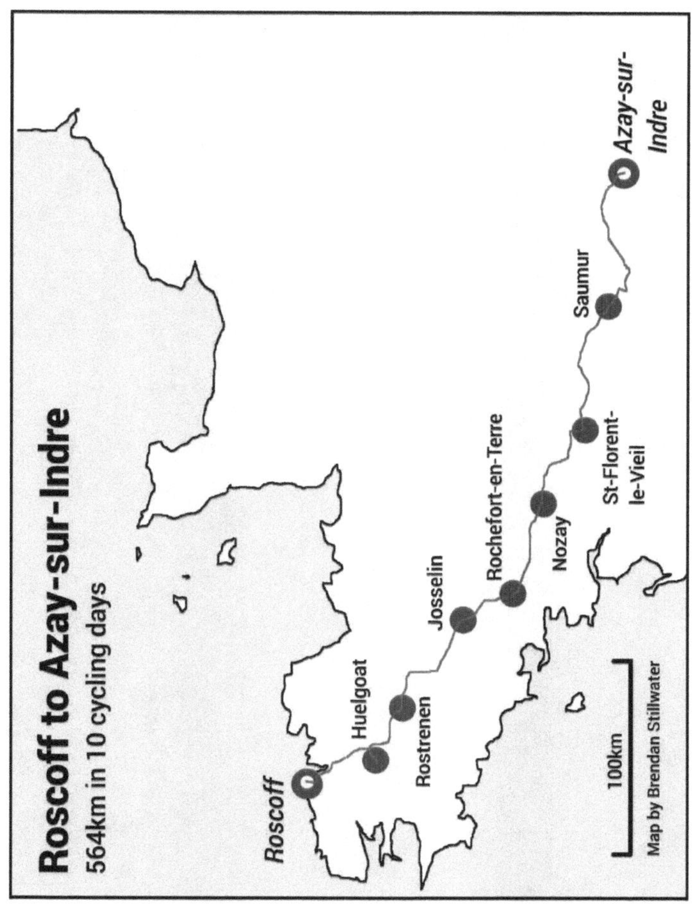

South of the Loire
everything will be different

9

With its towering donjon and brooding curtain walls, the château at Augmont looked more like a fortress than the Renaissance palace of Catherine's imagination. It dominated the valley of the Indre, hanging above the river on a sheer outcrop that had been visible for almost an hour. But with Nick back on the fully loaded tandem, progress towards it was painfully slow.

When they eventually arrived they were greeted warmly at the château's main entrance. Instead of joining the throng of visitors, many in medieval costume, who were milling in front of the ticket office, they were directed across the drawbridge into the outer courtyard to wait for Philippe d'Augmont's personal assistant. After a short delay they were approached by a young woman in a loose-fitting woollen overgown and voluminous wimple. She was chattering into a walkie-talkie and a mobile phone at the same time. Both conversations were hampered by the heavy folds of cloth from her headdress that swirled constantly across her face.

'Bonjour,' she said, when the conversations had finished. 'You are Nicholas and Catherine, no? My name is Nathalie. The

Augmonts have asked me to look after you this afternoon.'

'I had no idea there would be so many visitors,' Nick said, looking at the snooded and kirtled throng filing across the drawbridge.

'This is our biggest year ever. All day there will be medieval-themed events. Tours of the château, jesters and jugglers, archery, and fireworks tonight. And, of course, this evening's banquet. Both of you will be honoured guests at the top table. This is a thank you for giving your time as the journalist today, Catherine.'

Catherine looked at Nick, who shrugged blankly back at her. Turning back to Nathalie, she said, 'I'm only doing my job.'

'But it is a special role, no? The Augmonts always do this for those who make a major contribution to the afternoon's programme.'

Nathalie's walkie-talkie squawked and she turned to begin another conversation into it. Catherine heard her say something about the arrival of *les Anglais*. The discussion concluded with a long string of *oui*'s and final *d'accord*.

Turning back to Catherine and Nick, Nathalie said, 'Follow me, please. We will secure your bicycle, and then I will show you to your room.'

Even with the collapsible walking stick he had brought back from England, Nick found the narrow stone staircase that led to the château's upper floors heavy going. He lagged several spirals behind the others, ignoring the urgent pleas from Nathalie that they had to hurry. Eventually the stairs opened onto a wide, stone-walled corridor, and she guided them into a small chamber that was dominated by a heavily upholstered four-poster bed. Above it, oak beams supported an elaborately inlaid ceiling. Three of the walls were draped with tapestries, each depicting a scene from a medieval hunt. The final image showed a stag in its death throes, cornered and harried by a pack of hounds.

Catherine thought it hideous and wondered how she would sleep in a bed that faced such a horror.

'Please make yourselves comfortable,' Nathalie said, opening a small arched door that led into an en-suite bathroom. Pointing to a low velvet sofa directly under the dying stag, she added, 'Claire asked me to find suitable costumes for both of you. Please dress in them as quickly as possible. I will return for you shortly.'

While Nick showered, Catherine inspected the clothes laid out on the sofa. A red doublet and hose with a matching feathered cap were carefully arranged on one side, and on the other a simple skirt and blouse with a cross-lacing bodice. She tried a linen coif that had been left on the dresser, then discarded it in favour of the red-feathered cap from what she took to be Nick's costume.

'I don't think much of the ensemble they've dug up for me,' she said, when he limped back into the room.

'They won't want you in anything too elaborate at this stage,' he replied. 'Given that you have work to do.'

She was about to ask what he meant when he quickly added, 'I expect they'll have you in all sorts of places, doing interviews and so on. These old castles are incredibly dirty places.' He turned and looked at her. 'I'm just guessing. Anyway, you should get into the shower. We don't want to hold proceedings up.'

When she returned he was already dressed and leaning out of the window, watching a troupe of jugglers and troubadours entertaining in the courtyard.

'Maybe you should start down now,' she said. 'I can easily catch you up before you get as far as the courtyard.'

'Good idea. I don't think I can stand to have Nathalie snapping at my heels all the way down.'

As he made his way slowly to the door she picked up her smartphone and took a picture of him in costume. It was a relief, after a week of snapping headless or very distant shots of Steve, to have concrete evidence that Nick was still part of the tandem tour. She uploaded the image onto her blog with a few lines of text about the arrival at Augmont. As she finished she realised guiltily that photo opportunities were what she had missed most about him while he was gone. The thought made her feel so bad that she decided to be especially nice to him for the rest of the week.

Alone, she dressed in the skirt and blouse, and was struggling to lace herself into the bodice when Nathalie returned. As she helped with the costume, Nathalie said, 'We must hurry. Philippe has put the next stage of the entertainment on hold until you are ready.'

They descended by a larger, more formal staircase that opened into a wide corridor on the ground floor. From there, Catherine followed Nathalie into the château's Great Hall, a long, oak-lined chamber dominated by an elaborately ornamented hammer-beamed ceiling. In the spaces between the Gothic arched windows a variety of armour and weaponry decorated the walls. The hall's chequerboard stone floor was almost completely hidden under row after row of long wooden tables. At the far end of the room, on a raised stage, was another table; this was draped in gold-embroidered cloth, and arranged with high-backed oak-framed chairs. Catherine imagined this was where she and Nick would join their hosts later.

Nathalie pointed to a harlequin-costumed man who stood just in front of the stage at the far end of the hall. 'That is Philippe d'Augmont.'

Catherine watched as he spoke in rapid French to a small cluster of men in medieval costume. Even with his slight stoop he was easily the tallest in the room. He also seemed the most out of place. His face, long and pale with eyes that were sad and

heavy, marked him as a world-weary bureaucrat. The feathered
cap and the blazing red and yellow embroidery on his coat did
nothing to dispel the impression of a man who had accidentally
become entangled in the wrong century.

Nathalie's walkie-talkie squawked and she turned away to
take the message. After a short conversation she touched
Catherine on the arm and whispered, 'I must go down to the
kitchens. A minor crisis over the roasting of the venison.'

She pulled a stocky, armour-clad youth from the crowd and
whispered to him. Then to Catherine she said, 'This is Luc. He
will introduce you to Philippe.'

'Wait, Nathalie. What happened to Nick?'

'Claire took him out to the viewing platform in the courtyard.
He will join you later. *Bonne chance*, Catherine. Philippe will look
after you now.'

Catherine followed her new guide into the mail-clad group.
He caught the attention of Philippe d'Augmont and spoke softly
into his ear. As the message was delivered Philippe's face
brightened. He turned to Catherine and shook her hand
vigorously. 'Thank God you are here at last. Everyone, this is
Catherine Pringle, our journalist.'

Catherine was surprised to receive a warm round of applause.
She was still wondering what it could mean when Philippe
gestured to a short, heavy-set man with a thick moustache who
stood next to him. 'This is Pierre Grimaud, the mayor of our
local commune.'

Grimaud shook hands with her. 'It is so good of you to take
part in today's entertainment. We raised a thousand euros last
year for our local charities. With a larger than usual crowd today
we can't fail to do better.'

'I hope it goes well for you,' she replied.

Beyond Grimaud stood a taller man wearing spectacles.
Tapping him on the chest, Philippe said, 'And this is Alain

Duval, the manager of our local bank.'

'Pleased to meet you, madame,' Duval said, as he shook her hand. 'How good of you to step in when Julie took ill.'

'It's nothing. I'm only too happy to represent the fourth estate. But I have to confess I don't know exactly what's expected of me.'

'Oh, there's no need to worry,' Grimaud cut in. 'All you have to do is sit next to Alain and me. And look like you're enjoying yourself. Everything else will be taken care of for you.'

He winked knowingly at Duval and they began to chuckle. Puzzled, Catherine started to ask what he meant but Philippe cut her off. 'Please. We are seriously behind schedule.'

Duval whispered to her, 'Just follow me. Grimaud will come after you. We can fill you in once we are all seated. There will be plenty of time to talk then.'

The party crossed the hall to its ceremonial western doors. Outside they descended a short flight of steps to the internal courtyard where a dozen men in chain mail, carrying pikes and shields, were lined up in two ranks. Philippe guided his guests through a space in the nearest rank and arranged them in single file between the guards. When he was happy with their positioning, he said, *'Bonne chance, mes amis. Ça commence!'*

He spoke into a walkie-talkie and immediately a fanfare of trumpets sounded from the roof of the château. The gates ahead of them opened and, at a signal from Philippe, the procession set off, moving to the steady beat of a drum through the archway and into the swell of tourists in the outer courtyard.

Everywhere she turned Catherine saw countless smartphones, video recorders and cameras, all of them directed at her, their flashes cutting through the late afternoon light. Overwhelmed, she lifted her eyes above the crowd and took in the details of the courtyard. It covered a roughly rectangular space between the core of the château and its outer curtain walls. Every centimetre of the cobbles was filled with a crush of medieval peasants, including a tiered wooden stand that had been erected in front of the inner wall. She scanned the faces in the stand for Nick. If he was there she couldn't see him.

The procession halted against the outer curtain wall and turned to face the crowd. Another flourish of trumpets sounded, then Philippe raised his hands and gestured for silence. Catherine understood nothing of the speech that followed, except for its ending, when he pointed to her and her two colleagues in the sandwich between the guards, and accusingly bellowed, '*Politique! Banquier! Journaliste!*'

The crowd responded to each word with a mixture of mock jeering and whistling. It seemed to Catherine that they might easily harden into a mob, but the good-natured smiles of Grimaud and Duval on either side of her belied this impression. Philippe finished his speech and the trumpets sounded again. As the flourish died away the rank of guards behind her moved aside and she saw for the first time the low wooden frame of the château's stocks. She realised with a sinking feeling that she wasn't there to report on the afternoon's entertainment, she was about to play a major part in it.

'Is this what it's all about?' she asked Grimaud, as a pair of guards took her by the arms.

'It's perfect. No? Who could be more hated than the three of us – a banker, a politician and a journalist. We stumbled across this little scheme in 2009. It never fails to part people from their money.'

She stopped struggling and looked at him in amazement. 'I don't understand. People are going to pay just to watch us sitting in the stocks?'

'Of course not. Those baskets next to Philippe are full of eggs. He charges four euros for every half-dozen. And for the next two hours we are going to let people pelt them at us.'

The guards settled Grimaud, Duval and then Catherine onto the stone bench behind the stocks and guided their ankles into slots on the lower beam. The upper beam was then lowered and an elaborate show was made of locking it to the base with a pair of rusty padlocks. Catherine wriggled on the bench, trying to get comfortable. Warily, she faced the crowd which had formed an elongated semi-circle a dozen paces from them. For the most part it was silent now, nervously anticipating the action that would follow.

'This wasn't explained to you?' Duval asked from her left.

'No, it certainly wasn't.' A suspicion was forming in her mind that Nick had been holding something back.

'It's too late to stop now. Think of the money you are helping to raise.'

After a brief frenzy of egg buying, Philippe stepped into the crowd and took the arm of a stocky middle-aged woman who was encased in a grey woollen gown and wimple. He persuaded her to follow him across the courtyard until she was standing about ten metres from the stocks. With an egg in her hand she turned and, to the delight of the crowd, eyed Catherine and her companions with a theatrical menace.

'That is my wife,' Grimaud said to Catherine, 'the Lady Mayor. By tradition she throws the first egg.'

'This is a tradition?'

'Oh yes. For five years now. More than enough for a tradition to form.'

Madame Grimaud rolled up the sleeves of her gown, took aim and threw her first egg in a slow underarm trajectory. It rose in a high arc and sailed gently across the gap, splattering onto the cobbles well short of their feet. On her next try, she shot high and wide. The crowd laughed and took up a chant to encourage her aim. She tried repeatedly, but only hit home with her final egg which looped across the gap and landed on Grimaud's lap.

Laughing, he said, 'The agreement is that she is supposed to miss. But this year, unfortunately, it looks like she has started a new tradition of her own. Who can you trust, if you can't trust your spouse, eh?'

Catherine was still mulling this over when she took her first hit, an egg that smacked onto her shoulder with a sulphurous stench. She gasped as she realised the eggs were rotten. Despite an enthusiastic wriggling and weaving she was hit several times in the next few minutes. Eggs continued to come for the next hour and soon her head, shoulders and upper body were covered in a sticky, yolky, smelly goo.

The crowd's interest waned only with the announcement of an archery display outside the château's walls. Catherine, assured by her two companions that they were making a mint, relaxed and tried to let the rest of the experience wash over her. She began to draft in her head the outline of an article.

As the crowd thinned she saw Nick sitting in the middle of the viewing stand. He waved and gave her a mock round of applause, then turned and spoke to the woman sitting next to him. When Nick had finished speaking, the woman nodded, then stood and crossed the cobbles. She was fine-featured, slim, with hazel eyes and shoulder-length auburn hair. Wearing blue jeans and a simple T-shirt, she appeared to be the only person in the courtyard not in medieval costume.

Arriving in front of Catherine, she smiled and said, 'Would you like a little water?'

'Yes, please.'

'This is such an outrageous way to treat a guest,' she continued, after passing Catherine a bottle of mineral water.

Catherine laughed. 'It's not so bad, except for the smell. I'm assured we're making wads of money for a local school.'

'Hah! If it was money they wanted I could have donated a sackful. Chocolate money, too, if the children prefer that.'

'Well, if you want to donate something now, the local custom seems to be that you buy a half-dozen eggs first.'

'God no. There's been enough of that already. Nicholas asked me to give you a message. He said he is very proud of what you're doing. You're being a great sport.' She held up Catherine's smartphone and added, 'He also wondered if you were missing this. He would have sent it over earlier but didn't know if it was egg-proof.'

As she took the phone Catherine looked over at the viewing platform and wondered again how much Nick had known in advance about the egg-throwing event. 'Please thank him for me,' she replied. 'And tell him that I will probably break his one good leg if I find out he knew any more about this afternoon's entertainment than I did.'

The woman smiled. As she turned to go, she said, 'I'm not sure that's a message a stranger should deliver. But instead, if you'll let me, I'll buy you a proper drink later.'

'Wait,' Catherine said, realising there was something she needed help with. 'Would you mind taking a couple of pictures for me. I almost forgot to record this for posterity.'

'I would have thought it was something you'd rather forget,' the woman replied, as she took the phone. She framed and took a range of pictures, close-ups and group shots with Grimaud and Duval.

Catherine spent a few minutes selecting the best, one that included her two companions. All three of them were smiling defiantly through the yolky goo that had dried onto their faces. Perhaps because of the technology-rich peasantry milling in the courtyard, she saw nothing odd about opening the Twitter app and writing:

> *Couldn't send an update before. I've been locked in*
> *the stocks all afternoon. #norespectforjournalists*

Then she opened a new blog post and began to write:

I've always had a healthy disrespect for fancy dress. It's fine for children's parties – I'm not that much of a killjoy – but I've always felt that adults who do it, particularly in large groups, should be given a respectably wide berth. Today I've finally realised just how right I was ...

As she wrote, the courtyard filled with a large group of Chinese tourists.

'They are here for the banquet,' Duval explained. 'Philippe has scored a coup to get the Augmont experience onto their tour schedule. Grimaud and I were hoping they wouldn't get here until the two hours were up. They'll all get a complimentary throw now.'

The newcomers were fully clothed in medieval costume. With cameras flashing, and to much merriment, they took turns at pelting eggs across the courtyard towards the stocks. Then they drifted away for a tour of the château behind a guide holding a yellow umbrella.

The two hours were finally over. The guards released Catherine and the others. It was a relief to be able to move her legs again, and to wipe the egg from her face. She shook the hands of Duval and Grimaud, and they agreed to have a drink together later before the banquet. Then she walked across the courtyard, pointedly ignoring Nick, and climbed the staircase to their room.

10

Despite the assurances that her formal role in the château's entertainment had come to an end, Catherine waited upstairs until a few minutes before the banquet was due to start. She almost left it too late and was hurrying down to the Great Hall when she encountered Nick stumping towards her up the lowest spiral of the staircase.

'I was just coming to check that everything is all right,' he said tentatively.

'The action of a guilty man, perhaps?'

'I don't know what you're talking about.'

'Maybe you'll feel better if you just tell me right now how much you knew about this afternoon's fun and games.'

If she'd been ahead of him on the stairs she might have cornered him into an answer. But he just turned his back and started the painful process of shuffling down the last spiral. 'We're holding up the start of the banquet,' he said, over his shoulder. 'And I don't need an argument right now. This place is giving my leg hell.'

At the bottom of the stairs she got level with him and gripped his forearm. 'Just be straight for once. You knew all about it, didn't you? For God knows what reason of your own, you set me up.'

He pulled his arm free. 'Stop. You're being childish.'

'You knew, and you let me sit there and take it. How could you do that to me? How could you?'

He was about to answer when the oak doors across the hallway opened. Catherine turned and saw that a dozen faces, including those of the Augmonts, were staring out at her from a private antechamber adjacent to the Great Hall. After an awkward silence, Claire and Philippe d'Augmont detached themselves from the other guests and swept across the flagstoned floor to greet them. Like Catherine they had changed into more elaborate costumes for the banquet. As the lord and lady of the manor, theirs were more extensively embroidered in gold and silver thread than the finely textured, but simple, woollen gown she had chosen.

Claire, dark-haired and hazel-eyed and a good deal shorter than her husband, reached Catherine first and kissed her on both cheeks. Philippe, following close behind her, was obviously more relaxed than Catherine had found him during their last encounter. He smiled and said, 'We must thank you again for this afternoon, Catherine.'

Wondering just how much they had heard through the door, she shrugged and replied, 'It was nothing.'

They escorted her into the antechamber and signalled to a waiter, who offered them all champagne. For Catherine it was the best moment of the day. She had been desperate for alcohol since coming in from the courtyard, but had more urgently wanted to hide away on her own. She drained the glass, handed it back to the waiter, and took another.

Claire then took Catherine by the arm. 'Now, I'm wanting to know just how you've managed with only three good legs between you.' Her voice, even after a decade at Augmont, still retained most of its native Irish lilt. 'Nick tells me you're doing most of the work on your tandem. He always was a lazy one.'

'It's not so bad really,' Catherine replied. Then, smiling sweetly at Nick, she added, 'Somehow we seem to have muddled our way south of the Loire. Some of the time it actually feels like there's an able-bodied man sitting in front of me. But only some of the time.'

Everyone laughed, Catherine a little more than Nick, who looked worried about what she might say next. They had agreed before arriving at Augmont not to mention Steve, who had taken the car north while they were at the château. Looking around the medieval crowd in the room, she suddenly wished that she had gone with him. The simplicity of being at leisure in the twenty-first century seemed infinitely preferable to the medieval antics required of visitors to Augmont.

Philippe excused himself and went off to the kitchens for a final check of the banquet preparations. Turning to Catherine and Nick, Claire said, 'Come and meet the rest of the people you'll be at the top table with.'

They began with Grimaud and Duval and their respective wives. After a few minutes of comradely humour about the trials of the afternoon Claire moved them on to the other guests. Last among them was the woman who had reunited Catherine with her smartphone earlier. 'And, of course, both of you have already met Karina Balchoffer.'

'Hello again,' Karina said, extending her hand to Catherine. 'This time you are in a position to shake hands.'

'Thank you for the water this afternoon. It was a lovely gesture.' Karina was still dressed in jeans, and had added only a long velvet cloak as a concession to the period. Tugging at the wimple that hung irritatingly around her own face, Catherine added, 'I see that you've escaped the requirements of this evening's dress code. I wish I'd known that was a possibility.'

'I always check the rules very carefully. Dressing up is not exactly my idea of fun, and it's only encouraged, not compulsory. Besides, my darling husband more than makes up for me in this case.'

Karina touched the sleeve of the broad-shouldered giant beside her. He was dressed in leggings and a tunic of Lincoln green. On his back he had a full quiver of arrows and his right hand rested on the point of a longbow. He broke off a conversation he was having with Duval and turned to face them.

'Catherine,' Karina said, 'this is my husband, Werner.'

Werner Balchoffer pulled off his feathered cap and bowed elaborately. He was handsome, with a strong face and a generous smile. As he completed his bow he took Catherine's hand and kissed it theatrically. She felt the smile on her own face widen into a grin.

'I'm pleased to meet you, Catherine,' he said. 'Karina has been telling me how you have become the heart and soul of your little tandem tour.'

'She's too kind. I must congratulate you on your costume. I would never have expected to meet Robin Hood at Augmont tonight.'

'I see you are a real connoisseur when it comes to fancy dress. I took some trouble to be the best-dressed man in the room.' He stroked his moustache, which was a perfect match for his white-blonde hair, then ran his thumb and forefinger around the corners of his mouth into the goatee beard on his chin. 'I ordered the facial hair from a theatrical wig maker in Paris. It's good, isn't it? And I had the longbow shipped across from England last night. Every banquet should have at least one outlaw at the top table in my opinion.'

Turning to Nick, he said, 'And you, of course, are the famous Nicholas Farne. Traveller, explorer and adventurer. I almost feel like I know you already.'

Catherine watched Nick's eyes light up as the two men shook hands.

'I've done some travelling myself,' Werner continued. 'But all of that is behind me now.'

He glanced over at his wife and smiled warmly. She added, 'Werner has recently become a film-maker. Only German language so far, so you will not have come across his work.'

'Claire told me a little about it,' Nick replied. 'I'm delighted to meet you Werner.'

Catherine watched the two men click – it was so extreme that she almost heard the snap of invisible fingers above their heads. A glance at Karina confirmed that she had noticed it too.

'Come on,' Karina said, taking Catherine by the arm. 'Let's leave these boys to tell adventure stories to each other. I promised to buy you a drink earlier. Perhaps we can chase down another glass of champagne instead.'

Two glasses later, a trumpet flourish brought Philippe back into the antechamber. He joined Claire and they led their guests in pairs through an archway onto the raised stage at the end of the Great Hall. Joining the tail of the procession, Werner escorted Catherine, while Karina strolled beside Nick, who limped slowly across the platform like the comic relief in a Shakespearean tragedy.

At a signal from Philippe, the banquet began. Lute music filled the hall and a wandering troubadour strummed his way between the tables. On the stage servants passed down the top table, bearing platters that were heavy with roasted meats, poultry and vegetables. Wine flowed into silver goblets and Catherine, already light-headed from the champagne, began to feel that her experience of the Middle Ages had vastly improved since mid-afternoon.

As they ate, Werner and Nick began an intense discussion

about travel experiences they had in common. Quickly tiring of this, Karina leaned across the table to Catherine. 'Are you really feeling no ill effects from your incarceration this afternoon?'

'Amazingly, none whatsoever. I don't think I'll be eating eggs for the next few weeks but, other than that, I'm feeling much better already. This wine is helping to wipe away the remaining memories.'

'Fine wine is almost my favourite luxury.'

'Almost?'

'My number one is chocolate, of course. If you are a Balchoffer that is the only permitted answer.'

Catherine stared at her new acquaintance but there was no clue to her meaning. Karina saw this and laughed. 'Perhaps the House of Balchoffer is not so well known in England as in the rest of Europe. We are makers of the finest and most sought-after bespoke chocolate products in Germany. The world even.'

Catherine nodded, slightly embarrassed that her limited knowledge of the chocolate world had been so easily exposed. Karina dismissed this with a gesture of her wine goblet. 'Sometimes I too wish I'd never heard of it. But in a family-run company you can't escape your destiny. For the last three years I have been the chief executive of the Balchoffer chocolate empire.'

Overhearing this, Werner leaned in and put his arm around her. 'As we like to say, there is only one thing better than making chocolate money, and that is making the real thing from chocolate.'

It was obviously a well-worn joke between them. Karina turned and kissed him on the cheek. 'My darling Werner. Where would you be without our chocolate money?'

'I would still have you, my sweet.'

In another couple, the darling this and my sweet that would have been too much, but with the Balchoffers it seemed natural and genuine. Catherine watched them stare into each other's eyes as though they were the only people in the room. How long, she wondered, might it take for a little of their magic to rub off on her and Nick? She glanced at him and watched as he massaged his knee. When he lifted his head, he saw her looking at him, but his thoughts appeared to be elsewhere. He turned away and followed the progress of the wandering minstrel.

A few courses later the tables were cleared to make room for hefty platters of cheese and fruit. Nick stirred beside her. 'I've got to get up and move my knee before it stiffens. I'm going to take Werner across to the stables to show him the tandem.'

As they left, Karina said, 'If I wasn't so certain that my darling loved me so very much, I would be feeling a little jealous right now.'

Catherine laughed. 'They seem like quite a fit already.'

'This is just as Claire predicted. I'm glad she urged us to stay on so they could meet.'

'You didn't plan to be here?'

'Tonight we should have been in Toulouse. The day after, Carcassonne. But this is one of the few weeks a year when Werner is completely in charge. When that happens, I find myself expecting the unexpected.' Standing, she added, 'You know what, Catherine. I'm not going to sit here all night waiting for my man to come back to me. Let's get out of here too. We can walk out onto the battlements and find the best view for the fireworks display. Philippe somehow got a little money from Brussels to pay for it, some kind of Tourism and China fund. We can watch all that lovely EU money go up in smoke together, no?'

They made their way out of the banqueting hall, detouring to the kitchens for Karina to liberate a bottle of champagne. Then they climbed to the roof of the western range of the château. Karina seemed to know her way very well, and as they came out onto the roof, Catherine asked her about this.

'Werner and I come to Augmont every year. I met Philippe years ago in Brussels. We were both at a trade conference and became friends. But today is the first time one of our visits coincides with the medieval fair. I prefer the place a little more intimate than I've found it today.'

'I only have today to go by, but from where I was sitting, I'd opt for something a little quieter too.'

Karina laughed and handed Catherine a glass of champagne. 'Tomorrow should be very different. If you are staying on.'

'We shouldn't really. We're so far behind because of the accident. But every day that passes gets us a step closer to Nick being fit again.'

'Are you really going to ride all the way around France? He can't even go up the stairs properly.'

'It's actually easier for him on the tandem than off. And he said he would do it.'

'I know what that means. Werner was the same. But now he channels that determination into his film-making.'

The first rocket shot up from the terraced gardens below them. It burst overhead in a shock of green that trailed across the evening sky. The display that followed seemed like the perfect end to the day. And when it was over, Karina and Catherine linked arms and descended back into the château, then crossed the courtyard and made for the private wing. They climbed the spiral staircase with Karina in the lead.

When they reached the top, Catherine said, 'Thank you Karina. I mean, for being a friend this afternoon. And for this evening.'

'It was a pleasure.'

'Perhaps I'll see you in the morning then.'

'Of course. Absolutely no one is going to manage an early start tomorrow.'

Their room was so high in the château, and the walls and doors so thick, that Catherine could well have slept through to lunchtime. It was a deeper sleep than any she'd had since taking to the tent. When she drifted into consciousness, it was initially into a cosy, memory-free state. She knew who she was, but not where, and was happy with that limited knowledge for quite a while. The trouble came when she opened her eyes and tried to move her head – a sharp pain stabbed at her temples and spread rapidly across her forehead. Her eyeballs hurt when they moved. Her mouth was dry and her tongue swollen and rough.

Slowly she remembered the night before and the drinking that had begun at the reception before dinner. She touched her temples, massaging them gently in the hope that this would make the journey to the bathroom seem possible. When she was sure she could, she peeled back the heavy covers, eased her bare feet onto the cold stone floor, and walked slowly across the room.

Fifteen minutes under a hot shower revived her a little, and she felt strong enough to examine herself critically in the mirror. Her towel-dried hair sat limply over a pale and drawn face. She dragged the grown-out fringe away from her eyes and leaned in close, peering at the tiny red-crazed patterns around her pupils. 'Why,' she asked accusingly of the face in the mirror, 'did you let me drink so much champagne last night?'

She wrapped herself in a bathrobe, lingering for a moment in the luxury of it. Looking at herself in the mirror again, this time swaddled in a layer of rich white towelling, she wondered how much equipment would have to be sacrificed from her pannier to make room for such an indulgent item. It was a hopeless thought and she dismissed it, returning to the bedroom to look for something to wear.

Nick was awake, and had made it across the room as far as the velvet sofa. He was slumped forward, his head in his hands, directly under the tapestry depicting the dying stag. Taking pity on him, she asked, 'So when did you get in last night?'

'I don't really remember. I'm surprised you didn't hear me, though. I fell over something as I came into the room. Funny thing is, it didn't seem to hurt at all.'

'Maybe the answer to all your worries is to ride around France anaesthetised by large quantities of champagne and red wine.'

He was sitting upright now and slowly massaging his forehead. 'That wouldn't be enough of a cure. I distinctly remember still feeling my knee until the moment we started on Philippe's brandy.'

'We, being you and Werner.'

He nodded. 'And Philippe towards the end. Werner challenged us to an archery competition after the fireworks. The man's a natural athlete, no matter how much he drinks. He wouldn't let us quit until we had shot a full quiver each. And emptied the brandy bottle. Which probably wasn't such a good idea after everything else we drank.'

She watched as he struggled onto his feet and gingerly tested his bad leg. There was still plenty to resolve with him about the egg-throwing event, but she had enough sympathy left to postpone the argument. 'I'd recommend a long hot shower. That and a large quantity of coffee should just about make us feel human again.'

'Go down to breakfast if you like. It's going to take me an age just to hobble as far as the shower.'

She was about to protest but the idea of coffee was too tempting. 'All right, I'll see you down there.'

Catherine took her coffee out onto the Augmont family's private terrace and sat in the sun overlooking the château's grounds. The formal gardens extended from the moat to the river in three descending tiers. Two figures, both women, were strolling arm in arm a few hundred metres away. Squinting into the sun, she recognised Claire and Karina and waved, hoping they would join her. But they turned again and disappeared through a gap in the hedges that separated the garden from the meadows leading down to the river.

She heard a rattle of crockery behind her and turned to see Werner crossing the terrace towards her. 'Good morning, Catherine,' he said, a broad smile on his face. 'I hope you slept well.'

'Very well, thank you. But I'm afraid I indulged a little too much last night.'

'As did we all. I may call you Kate, no? Nick said it would be all right.'

'Of course.'

'I'm thinking, actually, that I might use Käthe instead. I like the sound of that even better. And you remind me of a Käthe I once used to know.' He sat opposite her and rested his tray between them. It had two of everything: bread, croissants, eggs, cheese, meat and fruit. Lost in his own memories for a moment, he seemed about to tell the story of the original Käthe. But his eyes came into focus again, and he asked, 'You have eaten already, Käthe?'

When she shook her head he pushed the tray towards her. 'Then we must share all of this. The best cure for what we put ourselves through last night is a hearty breakfast.'

She could see that he was going to insist, and nodded. 'Perhaps a little fruit, then.'

She chose a slice of melon and found that the sweet, cool fruit was just the right start. He watched her eat, which unnerved her enough to try distracting him with conversation. 'You and Nick must have been up into the wee hours.'

'I think about three in the end. You girls could have joined us, you know. We were only talking about adventures we had in common.'

'I think I would have exhausted the conversation a whole lot earlier if we'd been limited to that topic.'

'You are the partner of an adventurer, but one who stays at home, no? I'm not making light of this. My darling Karina would no more go down the rapids than I would attend one of her business summits.' He laughed at the mental image he had created. 'But we still have common ground. She makes a point of travelling with me several times a year. And this trip is one of them.'

'I can't imagine Karina roughing it.'

Werner laughed. 'Roughing it isn't exactly how I'd put it. Karina doesn't mind going away with me so long as there's no appreciable difference to being at home. I talked her into a safari trip in the Serengeti a couple of years ago. We looked like something out of *King Solomon's Mines*. You know, with a line of bearers stretching behind us back to the horizon.'

'What about this trip? I don't see a squad of assistants standing in the shadows.'

'This time it's just yours truly. I'm scouting locations for my next film project and she has agreed to camp with me while we are in the south. But our friends have a little joke about Karina-style camping. They call it Übercamping. You Brits would probably think of it as glamping but Karina turns up the luxury a few extra notches on that.'

Nick limped onto the terrace. Catherine waved and went over to carry his coffee. 'You're not a moment too soon,' she whispered. 'I thought it might be just me and Werner for the rest of the morning.'

Nick laughed. 'I can think of worse fates than that.'

'Sounds like you know him pretty well already.'

'It's just one of those things. When you're on the road you sometimes meet people and just know you're going to have everything in common. It's like that with him. I don't really care what he's talking about, I could listen to him all day.'

She looked back over her shoulder and realised that for the rest of the day she was going to face stiff competition for Nick's attention.

Over a leisurely breakfast Catherine actually found herself listening to a robust debate on the merits of various styles of outrigger canoe. Werner and Nick, it turned out, had strong and differing opinions on the subject and were soon embroiled in a heated argument. She was happy to laze on the terrace and half-listen. Cycling for a living had given her a new appreciation of the moments when she was sitting absolutely still, especially when they were accompanied by a dose of morning sun.

Claire and Karina returned to the terrace a little later and the three women steered the conversation back to the tandem ride.

'I've been reading your blog,' Claire said to Catherine, when she thought the others weren't listening. 'How do you decide what to put in and what to leave out?'

Catherine glanced at Nick and saw that he had suddenly tuned in, despite an apparent interest in something Werner was showing him on a laptop. The decision to leave the accident and his injury out of the blog still made her uncomfortable, but on the road they hadn't actually encountered anyone who admitted to being a reader. Not until Claire.

'It's not so hard really,' she replied. 'There's always something each day that stands out more than others. My next post will certainly mention eggs.'

'I did promise Nick you'd get something different to write about,' Claire said, laughing. Then she asked the inevitable question. 'But here he is, stumping around like a war veteran, and you haven't mentioned it in print. Having a crash must be an everyday occurrence to you if it doesn't make it to the top of your topic list.'

'I started to write about it. But it seemed unnecessarily intrusive on Nick. He was suffering and I didn't want it to be broadcast to the world. Now that he's on the mend it doesn't seem so important any more.'

The explanation seemed to work. Claire smiled and said, 'Well, if I'm ever trapped in a burning building with you, I'll certainly remember to be the one screaming for help.'

While Claire and Karina moved on to talk about chocolate, Catherine stole another glance at Nick. He met her eyes and smiled his approval, then turned back to study the screen on Werner's laptop. Catherine tried to keep up with something Karina was saying, but her mind went back to Huelgoat and the fact that she had, in a sense, been lying by omission to Liz and all of her readers. There was no way now that she could write about the accident, and in the absence of that, she couldn't write about Steve and what his contribution meant to her.

Nick must have seen the look on her face. 'Catherine, is everything all right?'

'Fine. Just too much to drink last night.' She felt instantly guilty that she had covered up her thoughts on lying with yet another lie.

'Werner has just suggested we all ask Philippe for a tour of the castle's dungeons. Would you like to come?'

She shook her head. 'No, I think I'll sit out here for a while and do some writing.'

'I was thinking,' Werner said to her, 'that I might borrow Nick for a few hours. I want to take the kayaks out on the river. That's something he can do sitting down. And this will excuse Karina from that duty. She hates kayaks worse than camping.'

With Werner and Nick gone, Catherine had the opportunity to raise the issue that had been burning in her mind since the previous day's entertainment. Turning to Claire, she said, 'I just need a little background on yesterday's entertainment. For the blog.'

'Of course. Alain just texted me to say that we raised more than 2,000 euros yesterday. And Karina has just offered to write a cheque for another five hundred.'

'That's great news. The thing is, I was wondering how much detail you gave Nick about it before we arrived.'

'Well, I did give him a quick summary on the phone. And I sent him the pictures from last year and a link to the article by last year's journalist.'

'Pictures,' Catherine said, trying to keep her tone neutral.

'Yes. I have to say, I didn't think you'd volunteer once he'd shown them to you. But we're so grateful you did. It made everything so much easier for us.'

'Volunteer?'

Claire saw the look on Catherine's face. 'He didn't show you the pictures, did he?'

'No.'

'Well, that's a little naughty. But to be fair, I was busy telling him about Werner too. Maybe we should have a word with him together when he gets back. Make him sorry, and all that.'

'No, Claire. It really doesn't matter. I'm more than used to him keeping things back.'

Wondering what she would have done if she had been asked to take part, she added, 'And I would certainly have volunteered anyway.'

11

The Café des Sports was the perfect location for a late-afternoon rendezvous. Standing in the centre of Abzac, its kerbside tables offered uninterrupted views along the main routes into the village. A pair of plane trees gave just the right amount of shade from the sun. There was even a low wall near the kerb to rest the tandem against.

Catherine and Steve had made better than expected time during the afternoon section of the day's ride. Their reward was a wait of more than an hour in Abzac, with no indication of how much longer it would be until Nick arrived for the day's final changeover with Steve. Catherine checked her phone regularly for messages but it was clear that wherever he was he would only make contact when it suited him.

While they waited they sipped on their beers, trying to make one drink last the rest of the afternoon. Steve fiddled with the cycle computer and made a series of calculations on a paper napkin. 'At the end of today,' he said, when he had finished, 'you will have ridden more than seven hundred and fifty kilometres in France. Not bad for someone who wasn't expected to stick at it for very long.'

'I think that will have surprised more than a few people.'

'Like Liz, for instance? And everyone else at your work?'

'Definitely. She's full of admiration. But I was thinking of my mum and dad too. They were pretty confident I'd be home in a fortnight. Much more of this and they'll begin to wonder if I really come from the same stock after all.'

'They're not good travellers then?'

Catherine laughed at the thought of this. 'It's more than that: they've always seen it as a total distraction. Anything, anything at all, that threatens to get in the way of their research has been systematically weeded out of their lives. We used to have holidays, but it was more like a long weekend at the seaside, or a week with our grandparents. Even then, either mum or dad, sometimes both of them, would stay behind to get on with their work. That's just how it was.'

'And you thought you'd inherited this lack of interest in travel.'

She nodded. 'But it seems it was more a case of nurture rather than nature.'

'What about their academic genes. Did you inherit any of them?'

'Hardly. I managed to scratch out a basic degree in English Literature, but it was literally nothing to write home about when my father was already a subject specialist. I don't think that would have mattered if I hadn't drifted into tabloid journalism. Now I've gone even further beyond the pale and become a long-distance traveller. Like I said, they're really going to wonder if I didn't get mixed up with their real daughter back in the maternity ward.'

'Sounds like you're a little worried you won't fit in any more.'

'You might want to ease up on the analysis there, Professor Freud. I just want them to feel proud of me and what I do. Even if it's not something they'd choose to do themselves, I'd like to think they admire the way I've taken this on.'

'Kate, I'm sure they already do.'

'Thanks for saying that.' After a pause, she added, 'What about your parents? You weren't tempted to follow in their footsteps?'

He laughed. 'My dad would hate it if he thought I was following him in any way.'

'What if you decided that what you wanted was exactly what he has?'

'He'd think I was taking the piss. Have you ever heard of a place called Nimbin?'

She shook her head.

'It's a village in northern New South Wales, not far from the Queensland border. It was a pretty big deal in the late 1970s, a magnet for anyone looking for an alternative lifestyle. Mum and dad pretty much fit the bill for that, so they bought a couple of hectares not far from it. Dad's a carpenter by trade. He built the house I grew up in, mainly out of materials other people were throwing away. It's a one-off, pretty weird even by local standards. But at the time it all seemed very normal.

'The whole front wall of our house is built out of discarded doors. Dad still thinks that's funny, especially when he gets a first-time visitor to the place. He's got a webcam now covering the approach to the front of the house. When a stranger mounts the stairs onto the verandah, dad is on to them straight away and invariably yells, 'Come on in! The door's open!' Then he sits back and watches the fun. Only one of the doors actually opens at any one time, but he's forever changing which it is. I sort of grew out of that slapstick approach to humour in my early teens, right around the time my first girlfriend started coming over after school. But that just made him worse.'

'That's what parents are for, isn't it. To make sure you don't look too cool around people you're trying to impress.' She thought of her own father, who had delighted in publicly critiquing his daughter's undergraduate efforts at serious literary criticism, often sharing them with colleagues or dinner guests. It was, she could see now, a key step in her journey towards the humorous, self-deprecating confessional journalism she excelled in.

'Growing up around my dad wasn't all bad,' Steve was saying. 'About a kilometre down the back paddock he built a yurt he retreats to every other week for a few days. It gives us, and him, some breathing space. He loves it down there. But he'd be pretty bloody suspicious if I suddenly turned up in the yurt next door, and tried to convince him it was my very own idea of Shangri-La.'

'Is that why you're travelling the world then? Looking for a yurt of your own.'

'You could put it like that,' he said. 'I'd even settle for a house with just one front door.' Then, looking at her pointedly, he added, 'There are worse reasons for committing yourself to long-distance travel, if you ask me.'

'What do you mean by that, exactly?' she asked, turning as a car approached from the direction of Montmorillon. It was a four-wheel drive, chocolate-brown with heavily tinted windows. She lost interest as it pulled in to a parking space behind her. She turned back to press Steve for an answer, but stopped when she heard approaching footsteps.

'So, there you are Käthe.'

She turned and saw that it was Werner. Startled, she managed to ask, 'What are you doing here?'

He narrowed his eyes and smiled. 'And this, I suppose, is Steven Munro. The secret weapon with the two legs.' He held out his hand to Steve and added, 'You've heard all about me already, I expect.'

Steve shook Werner's hand and gave the expected reply. 'Oh, yes. You're the first thing Nick told me about when we met up again after Augmont.'

'I'm mighty glad to hear that.'

He sat down and gestured to the waiter. After ordering a round of beers he turned back to Catherine. 'Karina and I were also in this neighbourhood today. We bumped into Nick and invited him to lunch.'

'Quite a coincidence.' She pulled down her sunglasses and raised her eyebrows to make it clear she didn't believe in chance where Werner was concerned.

'You never know what surprises life will throw at you, eh?' he replied, grinning sheepishly. 'Anyway, we got to talking and delayed him a little more than we should have. Too late to make it worth him riding today's final leg on the tandem. I felt responsible, so I insisted on coming here to apologise.'

'That was good of you, Werner.'

'I know.'

'I'm still trying to take in the chances of you and Karina bumping into Nick.'

He held up his smartphone. 'That's what these things are for. Nick and I have been texting each other every day since Augmont. You didn't know?'

'Apparently not. So where is he now?'

'Shopping with Karina. The plan is that we all meet up at the campsite in Confolens. Then I'm going to cook you cyclists a special camping dinner, Balchoffer style.'

'Sounds good to me,' Steve said, strategically taking over from Catherine. 'It's a pretty easy ride from here. Forty minutes at most.'

'I'd offer to drive you there but I know that's not in the rules. I can surely take some of your load for you, though.'

'You can take it all if you like. All we need are our helmets and a little water. With the prospect of a meal at the end of it, we'll make pretty short work of the remaining distance.'

They finished their drinks, then helped Werner stow their gear in his car. As he left, he promised them the best campsite meal they'd ever eaten.

Alone, they rode quietly out of the village. After a kilometre, Steve broke the silence. 'All right. I can tell you're totally pissed off.'

'Totally is an understatement.'

'What I can't work out is what's got you the most upset. Is it Werner, or the fact that Nick didn't bother to tell you they were still in touch?'

'Nick, of course. I just don't know what he's going to do next. If you'd told me a couple of weeks ago we'd communicate less on the tandem than when we're thousands of miles apart, I would have laughed in your face.'

'Would you like to hear my opinion?'

'I'm not sure. Am I going to agree with it?'

'You'll never know if you don't take the chance.'

'All right, Dr Munro. What's your professional opinion?'

He didn't answer right away and for a while she thought she'd been too sharp. She made up her mind to apologise but, over the crest of the next rise, found that there was no need. He had just been waiting until they were freewheeling downhill.

'If you're sitting comfortably,' he said, 'I'll tell you what I think. I've known you both for about a fortnight. Which isn't all that long to form an opinion. On the other hand, sometimes it doesn't take any time at all to see right to the core of a situation. To me, Nick is almost completely and utterly self-contained. He doesn't need other people, not in the same way that you or I do. I'm not saying I dislike him, it's just that I don't see the man I've met as ever being part of a set. And, if I'm being really honest, I can't quite see how the two of you ever got hooked up together in the first place. Or how it's lasted as long as it has.'

Catherine's simmering frustration with Nick boiled over into anger at his stand-in. 'Shut up, Steve. Just leave it alone.'

'I thought it might help, coming from an outsider.'

'Look, I want to stop. The tandem, I mean. Just pull in now. I've got to get off.'

He braked and guided them off the road. As soon as they were stationary she slipped her leg over the top tube and walked away along the road, relieved to put a little distance between them. She knew she'd invited him to say whatever he wanted, but the back seat of a tandem after a couple of beers didn't feel like the best place to explore her relationship in detail with an opinionated amateur psychologist.

Five minutes alone on the grassy verge was long enough to cool off and she retraced her steps. Having overcome the initial shock, she couldn't resist wanting to know what else he had to say. 'When you give an opinion, you don't mess around, do you?'

'I'm sorry. I thought you'd want me to be completely straight with you.'

'I did. I do. I just wasn't expecting it, that's all.'

Standing face to face with him she felt too exposed. 'Maybe if I'm sitting behind you again, I might be able to explain.'

When the tandem had lumbered back to life, she began, 'Nick and I met through work, about two and a half years ago. Liz sent me to interview him after he came back from a cycle ride along the Silk Road. He was giving a talk to promote his first book. He was so engaging and full of enthusiasm about what he'd just done that I just fell for him there and then. We had dinner three times in the next week. In a month he'd moved into my flat and it's been his London base ever since.

'To this day I can hardly talk about it with Liz. She thinks I made a huge mistake, wishes she'd sent anyone else along to interview him that day. I think she's totally wrong. I'd just come out of a long-term relationship that ended badly. Things were going nowhere for me at the time, and I loved that first six months with Nick. Everything about it was so easy and uncomplicated. Including the sex.

'But something inside him has changed over time. I didn't notice until last year but he was slowly fading away from me. Bren and I like to blame everything on the Amazon trip but it started well before that. It was the last straw, though. He came back from there a different man, unwilling to share anything. Now he never spends more than a couple of nights under the same roof, prefers to eat alone, often sleeps in the spare room. He spends more time now with his diary than he does with me.'

They rode on in silence for a while, then she added, 'Maybe I'm the problem. He doesn't seem to want me or need me to be around. And I can't seem to bring things back to how they were.'

When he didn't respond, she said, 'Say something. Anything you like. I'm ready this time.'

'All right. Since you asked, there is something that's confusing me just a little. So far on this trip I've encountered two very different Catherine Pringles. The first really loves to laugh and does things on a whim because it's either going to be fun or funny to write about. The other is tense, frustrated, bordering on cranky. She's chasing hard to catch up with something but doesn't seem to be getting any closer to it. Mostly, but not always, I see that version of Kate when Nick is around. I'm wondering which one you think is the real thing.'

'How should I know? Maybe there's another Kate, one that hasn't been completely dreamed up inside that thick skull of yours.' She realised how this sounded and laughed. 'Okay, I'm sorry. I guess that was proof the cranky one is dominant.'

'It wasn't a fair test. I started you on a topic guaranteed to get a reaction. Let me ask something a little more straightforward.

You said earlier that you and Nick live together.'

'We do. Whenever he's in London, anyway.'

'How often is that?'

She hesitated, then decided on the truth. 'Just a couple of nights a week now. In the last three months before France he spent most of his time with Brendan at Base Camp. The rest he split between his sister up in the Lake District and an old friend from school who runs a retreat in Wales.'

Steve said nothing, leaving her with the realisation that, to anyone else, it wasn't living together at all. Grateful that he hadn't pressed for the details of her almost non-existent sex life, she hurried on. 'You said earlier that Nick couldn't be part of a set. What about the two Kates? Pick whichever one you think has the most going for her. Do you think she's not cut out to be part of a relationship either? Is that the real problem here?'

He was silent for a while. Then he laughed and replied, 'You know what? Dr Munro just went off duty.'

She started to punch him on the shoulder then thought better of it. 'You started this whole discussion. It isn't fair to stop now. I want to know what you think.'

'And I'm not ready to tell you. It's all getting a little too abstract for the simple mind you kindly pointed out I'm lumbered with. If you like I could book you in for another session next week. Once I've had the chance to think it through at my own pace.'

The campsite at Confolens was on the eastern bank of the Vienne a kilometre north of the town. At first there was no sign of Nick's car, or their own tents, but as they rode further into the campsite, closer to the river, they saw that their pitch lay in the shadow of a high-ceilinged, vertical-walled marquee. It was the colour of milk chocolate and was stamped with an enormous House of Balchoffer logo on the sides and across the roof.

Werner was standing in a covered porch at the front of the structure, arranging a six-seater teak table in the centre of the wooden decking floor.

'Oh my God!' Steve said, as they took in the extent of the Balchoffer pitch. 'That's not a tent, it's a house. You could hold a wedding reception in there. They've even brought their own trees.'

Werner had finished with the table and was dragging a pair of potted palms towards the front of the deck. As they freewheeled past he waved and called out, 'There you are at last. We'd begun to wonder if you'd decided to run off on your own together.'

'No,' Catherine replied, wishing that the possibility had occurred to her in Abzac. 'It just took longer than expected. Sitting around for so long in the middle of a ride stiffens up your legs.'

Nick had put his head out of their own tent when he heard her voice. 'They can't be anywhere near as stiff as my leg, I can tell you.'

He was in an unusually good humour, and she was so pleased to see this that she almost decided to forgive his failure to appear in Abzac. 'It's a lucky thing you had the company of friends to help you forget your troubles.'

'Amazing luck, wasn't it,' he replied, giving nothing away about who might have instigated the reunion. 'Werner just about has things ready for the barbecue. He'll make a start as soon as you both finish your showers.'

When they assembled at the dinner table Werner was piloting the Balchoffers' six-burner gas barbecue. 'I had it especially constructed to my own design. Compact, lightweight, almost indestructible. They say you could cook for a regiment on it, something I'm tempted to try one day.'

With the gas lit he went back to chopping salad. Catherine

offered to help but he fended her off with a long-bladed chef's knife. 'No, it's my job. Actually, when we're camping, all jobs are mine. That's the deal we have, isn't it my sweet?'

Karina, who was sitting at the end of the table with some paperwork and an iPad, looked at him over the top of her glasses and smiled. 'Correct as always, my dearest.'

'Now,' he said, opening the mini refrigerator, 'tell me what you'd like to drink. We have a wide selection of beers, and the usual spirits and mixers. Personally, I'd recommend a very special Pineau des Charentes we picked up yesterday on a short excursion down to Cognac.'

Catherine chose the Pineau. Nick and Steve opted for beer. When they all had a drink Werner raised his glass to them. 'I welcome you all to camping Balchoffer style. Tonight you will share with us the best camping experience that chocolate money can buy.'

They touched glasses, and Karina added, 'We have a trailer full of spare equipment. If you need an extra mattress, or pillows, anything at all, just say the word.'

Catherine burst out laughing. When the others stared at her she had to pretend that the Pineau had caught in her throat. Cycle touring on a tandem meant abandoning absolutely the concept of extra. It was almost comical to encounter a couple who were unaware that such limits existed. Still, she reasoned, there was no point in rejecting the German gift horse. She was going to fully enjoy the evening and return to her spartan existence in the morning.

After the aperitif Werner put the finishing touches to the entrée, a Roquefort salad with warm croutons and lardons. He had two bottles of Bordeaux breathing on a side table and poured everyone a glass.

As they ate, Karina asked Steve: 'So where were you hiding when Nick and Catherine were at Augmont?'

'I wasn't hiding exactly. I had free use of the car for a couple of days and decided to make the most of it. I started in Tours, then drove over to Blois and on to Orléans. It began as a château tour, but by the end I was in Chartres taking in the delights of the cathedral. Then it was back on Tuesday morning to meet up with Catherine and Nick.'

'And back onto the tandem it seems?'

Steve glanced at Nick but decided there was no point in trying to keep secrets from the Balchoffers. 'Only today. The first two days south from Augmont Nick stuck it out on the tandem. But three whole days in a row is still too much for him, so I offered to do the hilly stretch near Abzac this afternoon. We would have swapped back for the last fifteen kilometres but I guess you tempted him away with a better offer.'

'I think he realised that he wasn't up to another couple of hours on the tandem,' Werner said, getting up to put the steaks on.

'Enough,' Nick said. He waved both hands over his head. 'Stop talking about me as if I wasn't here. I just couldn't ride any more today. End of story. Next topic.'

His tone was so sharp that everyone stared at him. Instead of an apology, he looked at Werner and said, 'Tell Kate and Steve about your new project.'

'I'm planning a series of six 30-minute programmes on historical walks in the Cathar country. This is a scouting visit to look for locations. From here we go down to Saint-Émilion then south into the foothills of the Pyrenees.'

'The Cathars,' Steve said. 'That's twelfth century?'

'Correct. More precisely, mid-1100s through to about 1300. The whole Languedoc region too. Very roughly, from Toulouse across to Albi, and then south to Foix and Carcassonne. There are perhaps twenty or thirty viable walking routes and I aim to find the six that are of the most interest.'

'Why the Cathars in particular?'

'Every journey needs a theme. I'm sure you've already discovered that. It's possible to reach an objective without one but it's so much easier, and also so much more interesting, when there's a thread holding it all together. With the Cathar country there's something on every level. First there is the rugged beauty of the landscape itself. Then there are the Cathar castles, magnificent but sad ruins perched on the highest and sheerest cliffs.

'Finally, there's the sad, terrible history itself. The brutal persecution by a church that was determined to stamp out the merest hint of heresy.'

The monologue brought a reflective mood to the table, which he punctuated by delivering the steaks onto their plates. He sat down, refilled everyone's glass, and added, 'A toast to journeys with themes.'

As they drank Catherine wondered about the theme of their own tandem journey. It had started as an attempt to put mortar between the separate bricks of her relationship with Nick. But she was spending so much time with Steve that she was beginning to think she knew, and wanted to know, him more. She looked across the table and saw him staring back at her. They were developing an uncanny ability to know each other's minds and she was certain he was thinking the same thing.

'What about you?' she asked him. 'Do you prefer journeys with themes?'

'Werner's right. Travelling without a theme is just aimless wandering. I found that out in my first year away from Australia. I went to all the tourist destinations in South-East Asia, but after a while everything and everyone started to merge together. I filled my social media pages with pictures of me in front of everything. And it just didn't add up to a damned thing. I was looking for something without knowing what. But it takes a little while for your own theme to become obvious. The trick seems to be in recognising it.'

'Perhaps,' Werner added, 'the theme of your ride is becoming one of the injured knee. Will you complete your journey despite the knee, or not?'

'I don't agree,' Catherine replied, a little too hastily. 'Not entirely, anyway. For me, it's also about achieving goals. You and Nick – when he's fit, anyway – wouldn't see the idea of a cycle ride around France as much of a challenge. But I do. And there are plenty of everyday people like me who would too. It's come as a surprise to me just how good it can feel to take on a physical challenge and succeed. Even the camping is good, especially the Balchoffer variety.'

'Well said, Käthe,' Werner said, raising his glass to her.

After coffee, cognac and a box of Balchoffer chocolates, Karina excused herself, saying she had some emails to respond to before the morning. Werner watched lovingly as she disappeared into the marquee. 'She calls this her after-dinner chocolate time, the hour before bed when her team get a little nudge about making the House of Balchoffer that little bit better tomorrow morning. Sounds a little harsh but she's a good boss and they would do anything for her.'

He chuckled and added, 'Which gives me precisely one hour to talk. I want to know every detail of your route down to Saint-Émilion. With my special knowledge of the region I bet I can make some real improvements.'

Catherine could think of nothing worse than revisiting their plans, or having Werner improve on them. She announced that she too was turning in and made her way, a little unsteadily, to bed. While she waited for Nick she tried to decide which Kate he was going to find when he got there. She really wanted it to be the first, the one who loved to laugh, the one who was surprised and thrilled to be entwined with the Balchoffers again.

This Kate was also determined to try one final act of seduction, an all-or-nothing effort to overcome the barriers that lay between them. She began a transformation of the tent into a cycle tourist's best shot at a stately pleasure-dome. Anything remotely tinged with the labours of the road – shoes, socks, cycling shorts – was ejected as far into the night as possible. Equipment, tools, spare parts for the tandem followed suit. Then she zipped the sleeping bags together for the first time since the accident.

The inside of the tent still had a staleness about it that she couldn't pin down. She masked this with a liberal sprinkling of scent. Satisfied, she attacked the problem of mood lighting. A naked flame, a major hazard inside a ripstop nylon shell, was out of the question. She considered and dismissed the LED light from her head torch: strapped to her forehead it was comically unalluring. This left only the soft glow from the lowest setting on her smartphone screen. She tried it but could only laugh at the ghoulish hue it gave her naked body. She switched it off and waited in the dark.

An hour passed, then most of another, and the twin voices of Werner and Nick next door showed little sign of abating. Eventually she had to dress and make an urgent dash to the toilet. The Kate who returned was the other Kate: tense, bordering on cranky, spoiling for a fight. This Kate didn't bother undressing, she wrapped herself in the sleeping bag and flicked aimlessly through the stale e-book collection on her smartphone.

When Nick eventually crawled into the tent she was almost asleep. The smell of brandy was overpowering but she roused herself and tried to help him as he struggled into the sleeping bag. Inevitably his bad leg caught in a fold of material and he swore under his breath.

'Christ,' he slurred, when he was finally horizontal. 'Why did you zip them together? I'm not a fucking contortionist.'

'I thought it might be a good idea,' she replied coldly. 'Clearly I was wrong.'

By the time he had worked it out, she had turned onto her side and had her back to him. 'God,' he whispered, 'I'm an idiot … sorry … too much to drink … didn't think.'

'No,' she agreed, 'you didn't.' When it was clear that nothing sensible would follow, she added, 'Go to sleep. We can talk in the morning.'

'In the morning,' he replied, his breathing settling towards a brandy-fumed snore. 'Can't talk … Werner … plans.'

12

Catherine woke to the steady drumming of rain on the roof of the tent. She rolled over and tried to ignore the urgent need for a trip to the toilet. After a few minutes she was forced to admit defeat and wriggled out of her sleeping bag.

From the toilet block she dragged herself to the nearest shower. She stood with her head under the nozzle for a quarter of an hour until her stiff muscles began to relax and the concrete in her head softened into a working slurry. Afterwards, she dried herself in front of the mirror and dressed in the same cycling clothes she'd worn the day before. It was an act that extinguished the tiny amount of *joie de vivre* she'd been able to muster.

On her way back to the tent she encountered Werner, who was riding into the campsite on a folding bicycle. Despite the soaking rain he was dressed in shorts and a T-shirt. His eyes were hidden behind a pair of aviator sunglasses, but she just knew they would be bright to the point of sparkling.

'Good morning, Käthe!' He caught up with her and dismounted. 'I love it when it rains like this. Perfect for clearing the head. I was afraid all of you would miss it entirely.'

'You looked after us too well last night. I don't think the tandem team will get very far today.'

'Well, why don't we wake the others up and come to a decision on that over breakfast. I'm just back from the *boulangerie.*'

As they walked back to the Balchoffer marquee, he said, 'You know, I'm extremely interested in that man you're travelling with.'

'Steve?' she asked, completely puzzled.

'Nick, of course.' He tilted his head back as though he had sniffed something behind her mistake. 'We've been talking a lot, Nick and me. I've got to warn you, I have it in my mind to steal him from you.'

She stopped and stared at him. 'You're not thinking of proposing to him, are you? Because the way I feel this morning, I'm inclined to say you're welcome to him.'

'That's a good joke, but my darling Karina would have something to say about that. He and I are pretty good together, that's for sure, but not in that way.'

'Then what?'

'I think I could use a man with his talents to help me develop an English language version of Walking the Cathar Country. I need to talk this through with him, flesh the whole idea out a little. Maybe it's just as well I got you all a little bit drunk last night, eh? A late start today gives me just the opportunity I need.'

Karina waved to them from the Balchoffer tent. 'Good morning, you two. Come in out of the rain.' She stepped off the porch to double-kiss Catherine, then shepherded her under the awning. 'The coffee is ready. And, *natürlich*, there is also hot chocolate from the House of Balchoffer. You haven't experienced it yet, I don't think.'

The chance to quiz Werner further was gone and Catherine sensed that he wasn't ready to talk more openly about it yet.

The conversation at breakfast turned immediately to the prospect of cycling in the rain. Catherine had absolutely no desire to go anywhere and she could tell that Nick felt exactly the same. But neither of them was willing to take responsibility for the decision. Steve, who was showing himself well attuned to the meaning behind their silences, solved the problem for them.

'Today looks like a bit of a washout,' he said. 'By the time we drag all the gear down, dry it off and stow it away, most of the morning will be gone. You don't have to say anything. I'll take your silence as agreement.'

Catherine and Nick looked at each other and nodded.

'Excellent news,' Werner said. 'This gives me an unexpected opportunity to get my head together with Nick. And that means getting ourselves back into the kayaks. I do some of my best thinking out on the water.'

Nick brightened considerably at the idea. On another day Catherine might have been annoyed, but the truth was that a few hours on her own sounded like a luxury. She retreated to her sleeping bag and began her next article for the Saturday edition of the paper.

It was easy work but the realisation that the completed draft contained at least three fabrications made her pause. Everything she wrote seemed to add another spiral to the fiction she had trapped herself in. An inadvertent slip, a reference to Steve or mention of Nick's injury, was bound to happen eventually. When it did she would be exposed as a liar. She thought she could just about live with herself – it was arguable that the deceit was well intentioned. But she doubted that Liz would be nearly so forgiving. To mitigate the risk she decided to start a private log that matched the real events on the tour against the fictional version she was reporting. Showing it to Liz at the end of the tour, maybe even offering to publish it in one elaborately crafted über-confession, might recover the situation.

By late morning the sky had lifted and tiny flecks of blue were showing through thinning clouds. Catherine had finished her work and was ready to seek out company.

In the next *emplacement* Karina was sitting with Steve on the porch of the Balchoffer marquee. They were side by side at the table, with Steve whispering conspiratorially in her ear. His hand was resting on her shoulder and, when she threw back her head and laughed, Karina lifted her own hand and squeezed his appreciatively.

Catherine was instantly jealous. It was irrational but she couldn't help it. The ease between her and Steve was something she looked on as special. Seeing him behave in a similar fashion with another woman was too much. The hand on the shoulder, an intimacy he had never come close to sharing with her, was even worse. It took an effort of will to stop herself from storming over to interrupt them. Instead she made a show of lazing in front of her own tent, her way of proving she didn't care quite as much as she had first thought. She wasn't a Sophie or any of the myriad other women he'd already mentioned in tales from his travels.

After a while Steve stood and stretched. He spoke a final word to Karina and they laughed again. Then he crossed to Catherine. 'I thought I'd take a walk into Confolens. Do you feel like coming?'

'I'd rather not. I think I'll just laze here for the rest of the morning.'

Her tone was petulant and she could see that he was puzzled, but she wasn't interested in explaining. She watched him go and was both pleased that she'd said no and suddenly angry with herself for feeling instantly lonely.

She decided to join Karina on the Balchoffer porch for coffee. She badly wanted to know about Karina's private moment with

Steve but a direct question was impossible. Instead, she began, 'I could really get used to the kind of camping that you and Werner do. Every detail is taken care of.'

Karina shrugged. 'That's just the deal we made. And it pays him to make sure I'm happy when we're camping. You see, his film work is almost entirely funded by a subsidiary of the House of Balchoffer. Even on a trip like this I'm still the boss.'

'The Cathar Country Walks project. You're funding that too?'

'If I have to I will. But there are limits to what I can put into it right now. The Balchoffer board is having one of its periodic family spats. My dear cousins won't agree right now to fund more than fifty per cent of what Werner needs. So we're looking frantically for someone else with deep pockets. Would you like to give a donation, perhaps?'

Thinking back to the earlier conversation about Nick, Catherine smiled. 'I think it's possible that Werner's already asked me for one.'

'A donation? I don't understand.'

'Sorry, just a bad joke. Tell me something, Karina. On your business card, it says Dr Karina Balchoffer. That's not the medical kind, is it?'

'God, no. I am literally a Doctor of Chocolate. You can look this up if you don't believe me.'

'You mean an honorary one?'

Karina gave a disgusted click of the teeth. 'I assure you it was the real thing. The only thing I've ever done that was completely outside the control of my family.'

She got up and refreshed their coffee. 'Balchoffer Schokoladenfabrik has been a family-run business since 1848 when Willi Balchoffer opened his first chocolate shop in Munich. These were troubling times with revolution in the air, but it turned out to be a boom time for drinking chocolate or coffee. Willi passed a flourishing business on to his eldest son

Rudi a few years later, starting a tradition that the eldest child takes over from their parent. If the eldest is a woman the convention is that her husband also takes the Balchoffer name. This ensures that the next generation will always be a Balchoffer.'

'Werner doesn't strike me as the type to meekly go along with that.'

'The name change? It's more common than you might imagine. And there are compensations. In his case it meant he could play at being the adventurer and now a film-maker. In previous generations there have been a few aviation pioneers, and a racing driver who almost won a Grand Prix. Chocolate cars. Chocolate aeroplanes. Chocolate travellers. All good marketing.'

Catherine nudged Karina back to the original question. 'You were telling me about becoming a Doctor of Chocolate.'

'Yes, of course. I am the last of my particular strand of the Balchoffers. And it's pretty fair to say that I resisted my father's attempts to bring me into the business. I wanted to do research, something in science or engineering – it suited my temperament, and my strengths. But my father made it absolutely clear where my responsibilities lay. And I could see how much it meant to him that I follow in his footsteps.'

Catherine thought of her own father, and of her ill-judged foray into his field of academic expertise. She knew that it could have been worse. She might have chosen history and suffered more at the hands of her mother.

'We made a compromise,' Karina was saying. 'He agreed to the extra years at university provided I did something to advance the science of chocolate production. So my thesis topic was: *Temperature-determined plasticity in thin-walled chocolate structures*. Sounds better in the German of course, but then every thesis does. Basically, I built a prototype process that uses a type of 3D-printing technology to manufacture very thin-walled chocolate structures. The technique allows you to make literally anything you like out of chocolate.'

Catherine didn't know what to say. 'Weren't you sorry to leave all of that behind after the effort you put in?'

'I rarely think about it now. My father took ill suddenly and I was soon up to my neck in trying to keep the company afloat through the eurozone crisis. I used to think I could only be good at one thing, and that I should stick to it. As it turns out I'm rather good at making money too. Life is funny like that, isn't it? One minute you're certain there's only one thing that will make you happy; the next, you can't understand why you wasted so much time clinging pointlessly to it.'

'Doesn't it worry you that somehow along the way your ideals might have been compromised just a little?'

'Not in the least. I'm free to choose what I do. We all are. If something stops working for me I just walk around it and try another path. Werner taught me that attitude.'

'Supposing it was something more complicated than just your work. What if it was Werner? Would you walk away from him, or stay and work things out?'

Karina leaned back as she considered a response. 'The question is absurd. My relationship with Werner is beyond question.' She turned to look at Catherine and added, 'Have Werner or I given you the impression we are something less than completely in love?'

'Not at all. It was just a clumsy way of asking what your secret was.'

'Maybe it's easier to understand if I give you a little example. In October he has his fortieth birthday. We always do something special for each other. But forty – that requires a little extra effort, right?'

When Catherine nodded, Karina continued, 'So I think I've come up with something he's never going to forget. I'm going to take him up in a light aircraft and the two of us are going to go skydiving from 4,000 metres. It still terrifies me every time I think about it. Normally I can't stand being more than a couple of floors off the ground. But I'm already fifteen jumps towards my freefall qualification. I just want to see his face when we go out that door together, the only two people in a completely empty sky.'

Karina smiled at the thought and added, 'Werner and me, it works between us because we're willing to do anything for each other. Isn't this the same with you and Nick?'

Catherine hadn't seen the question coming. She tried to nod, but couldn't. With a thin voice, she replied, 'I've done everything I can think of to make it work. I came to France for him, kept things going while he got treatment in London. Nothing seems to be enough.'

'What about the things he does for you in return?'

She thought of the gifts he had recently given her, from the gym membership all the way through to the head torch. The most extreme was the heart rate monitor he still insisted she wear on the tandem. She considered making a joke about the charts he kept of her daily vital signs, spinning it into an affectionate concern for her well-being. But she couldn't make herself do it. A direct comparison to the magic of the Balchoffers was a game she and Nick were always going to lose.

Sitting still was suddenly too much for her. She had to be up and walking off her troubles. Ignoring Karina's plea for her to stay, she rose and made for the path that led towards the river.

Next morning, the journey south from Confolens began with an easy stretch along the right bank of the Vienne. Nick and Catherine were accompanied by Werner who had produced from the cavernous trailer attached to his car a mountain bike that had been extensively modified for road use. He cycled beside the tandem a little ahead of Catherine and level with Nick and, in a detailed monologue, outlined the design modifications he had personally supervised.

When the conversation turned to documentary film-making Catherine fell into a sulk. It irked her that Nick, normally so quiet on the tandem, was always so animated around his new comrade. She also wondered at the direction the tour was taking. She had imagined, after his return from England, that they would by now have reverted to a team of two. Instead they had swollen, seemingly permanently, to a touring party of five.

Her mood didn't change until La Péruse, about twenty kilometres south of Confolens, when Nick decided that he'd done all the cycling his leg could manage for the day. He called Steve and arranged a handover. Werner decided he would stop too and they drove off together, waving back at the tandem. As the car rounded the first bend Werner put his head out of the window and shouted, 'The last ones to Montbron are losers!'

Steve turned to Catherine and said, 'There's a branch in the road just over the next hill. If we go left we'll be on course to meet up with them at the end of the day. Or we could go right and just see how the rest of our lives turn out.'

'Don't tempt me. Why can't it be like it was on the Loire? Just riding the tandem all day long seemed more than enough then.'

'It will get better again. Once you've detached from the Balchoffers, and from me too, you and Nick will find a way to make it work.'

'I hope you're right. In two days it will be a month since I left home. But we'll still be only a quarter of the way around France. This whole thing feels like it's hanging by a thread.'

'Have you talked with him about what will happen after Saint-Émilion?'

She shook her head. 'He's in denial. He seems to think he's magically going to get better. I don't even know how to approach the subject any more. Anyway, I'd be lucky to catch him alone. He and his new best friend are practically inseparable.'

'There's always a way around every obstacle, you know. You just haven't thought of it yet.'

She pulled down her sunglasses and stared at him. 'You sound exactly like a guru I once interviewed.'

'Which I'm going to take as a compliment.'

'He didn't particularly say anything earth-shattering. But there was something about the way he said it that seemed to help. At the time, anyway.'

He laughed. 'Well why not try interviewing me now. Maybe that will help too.'

'All right, mister guru, seeker of Shangri-La with a single front door. Tell me, what should I do?'

'Let's find a place to sit first. We need to be perfectly still to think this through.'

He took her hand and guided her into an open field. They sat facing each other on a patch of meadow, then he pressed the tips of his fingers together and held them under his chin. His eyes closed and he let his head rock gently from side to side. When he opened them again they were deep, dark pools, fixed like limpets on hers. The sudden mood change almost unnerved her. She wanted to laugh but knew it would spoil the performance.

'Sometimes,' he began, his voice slower and deeper than usual, 'there are simple solutions to your problems right within reach of your fingertips. It's just a question of seeing them for what they are. Why don't you start by telling me exactly what it is you think you want. For instance, would it make you happy if the trip ended right now?'

'I'd kill for a weekend at home sleeping in my own bed. That's normal, isn't it, after a month away. But giving up entirely seems like total failure and I don't feel ready for that.'

'Then don't do it.'

'But we can't go on as we are. I'll go insane. Plus, we'll run out of time.'

'Make your own plan. Set your own goals and make your own demands on everyone else. Stop feeling that Nick is the only one with the right to control the agenda. Shake off the hangers-on. And just get back to the simplicity of riding a set number of kilometres every day with a single partner. That's what you've enjoyed the most from the last month.'

He was right: it was all about the simplicity of cycle touring. But she couldn't tell him that what she enjoyed most were the segments of each day she rode with him. 'That little trick you just did with your eyes. Where did you get that from?'

'I told you I grew up on the fringes of an alternative community. Gurus used to come and go like travelling salesmen. My mother fell under the spell of one in particular and went off travelling with him for nearly a year. They let me tag along for the summer holidays on a trip up the north Queensland coast. Along the way I picked up a few of his little tricks for looking all-seeing and all-knowing.'

'Regardless of the tricks, what you said makes a kind of sense. Maybe you are a bit of a guru, after all.'

He shook his head and for a moment looked genuinely sad. 'Not really. Otherwise I wouldn't be roaming the globe looking for something I'm never going to find.' Forcing a smile on his face, he added, 'Getting back to your situation, Catherine Pringle. It's clear to me that you already know what you want. You just haven't found the nerve to grasp it yet.'

13

A month of travelling, constantly in the company of others, was a burden that Catherine could no longer cope with. She needed time alone, time to reflect on all that had happened since crossing the Channel. Saint-Émilion, the end of the southern leg of the journey, seemed like the perfect place for this to happen.

She began to plot her escape almost as soon as she woke at its lakeside campground. Peering through the flap of the tent, she saw Werner sitting a few yards away on the porch of the Balchoffer marquee. He had one of his video cameras on the table in front of him and was fitting a lens to it. When he saw her he lifted the camera and zoomed in for a close-up. It was the wrong thing to do, on the wrong morning. She picked up the nearest soft projectile, a string bag filled with unwashed cycling clothes, and threw it at him. While he dodged out of the way she made her way to the amenities block.

Two showers a day was ridiculous but it was the only few minutes of total privacy left in her day, the one place where she could be reasonably sure of uninterrupted thinking time. It was so private and quiet that she stayed under the hot water until her skin was blotched from the heat.

As she towelled herself dry she examined herself in the mirror and noted the small external changes that had come over her in the last month. Despite the endless application of sunblock, a thousand kilometres on the tandem had brought a light tan to her face, arms and legs. She liked it, except for the abrupt T-shirt line around her neck and upper arms. Even with constant exercise, she suspected she had lost only a little weight and would be lucky not to gain some given all the food and drink that a day on the tandem seemed to excuse. But her arms and especially her legs had a tone that she'd never felt in them before. She liked the feeling of it. Except for a general exhaustion and regular aches and pains, she almost felt a glow of fitness.

Smiling to herself in the mirror, she angled her smartphone so that only her neck and upper arms were in the frame. She took a selfie and attached it to a tweet with the text:

*One-quarter of the way around France and already
my #Tshirttanline is coming along nicely.*

In seconds her phone was vibrating madly, a sign that the tweet had attracted more than the usual attention. She studied the picture again and realised that she had come dangerously close to showing a little too much breast. It was safe, but only just. A new tweet about the risks associated with selfie photographs came into her head and she started to type it. Partway through she realised what she was doing and stopped. Staring critically at herself in the mirror, she said, 'You know what, Käthe? If you and Twitter don't take a little break from each other, one of you is going to end up doing something you'll regret.'

Returning to the Balchoffer marquee for the communal breakfast she remained silent, hoping it would be obvious that she just wanted to be left alone. It seemed to work until Nick switched on his phone for the first time in days and saw that there was a message from Brendan. Summarising it, he said, 'Cruickshank and Spears have couriered a new batch of camping equipment out to us for review. They want me to collect it from Bordeaux and send back everything we have now.'

'Well, it seems to me we should make an expedition out of this,' Werner replied. 'There's room in my car for five, so why don't we all drive down this morning, have lunch and collect the new gear. What do you say?'

'Sounds good to me,' Nick replied.

'I'm in too,' Steve added. 'I'm getting a little itchy for a day in a city.'

'Count me out,' Catherine announced, with a harshness that surprised everyone, including herself. She tried to soften the effect a little by adding, 'I'm going to be bad company today. Why don't the rest of you do it without me.'

'But we want you there too,' Werner said. 'It's our last day together as a group. We'll make sure you have a good time when you get there.'

'Look Werner, you just don't want me around today. Okay?'

He held up his hands in surrender. 'Hey. No problem, Käthe. We can be back early, so you won't miss out on a little bit of love from us.'

She wanted to tell them not to hurry back on her account. Instead, she added, 'There is one thing you can do for me. Can I borrow your folding bike to ride up to Saint-Émilion?'

'Are you sure you really want to? On your day off the tandem. Maybe I should drive you up there.'

'Werner. Please. Just tell me I can have the bike.'

An hour later she had waved them off and cycled the three kilometres uphill to Saint-Émilion. Almost as soon as she arrived she felt whole again. It was like playing truant from school combined with taking a sick day from work. Leaving the bicycle locked to a street sign, she visited a bookshop and found that it had a small selection of English language paperbacks. She told herself she was only browsing, that buying was a luxury she couldn't afford in terms of weight and bulk. But e-books just didn't have the tactile comfort of paper, and eventually she left the shop clutching two chunky paperbacks.

She wheeled the folding bike along cobbled streets into the Place de l'Église Monolithe. There was a choice of cafés and she made for one with tables in the shade. Sitting with a *grand crème* and a pastry, she lost herself in one of the books. At noon, when the chimes struck in the bell tower across the square, she moved next door to a brasserie and ordered *omelette frites*. It was her first encounter with eggs since the medieval day at Augmont, and she found that it had been long enough to forget the smell and taste of the eggs that had worked their way into her every crevice that afternoon.

After lunch she felt ready to rejoin the world again. Scrolling through her messages, and putting most of them in the ignore-till-later category, she came across one from Steve. It read:

> *Just to let you know we're back from Bordeaux and will be in Saint-Émilion soon. We agreed that if we see you we'll pretend to be strangers unless you give a sign that you feel like being around us again.*

She smiled. It would have been his work to make the others agree that she needed some space.

She did see them too, in various combinations, over the next hour. First there was Karina, who was on her own. When she saw Catherine she ducked with exaggerated speed into a souvenir shop. Shortly after that, she encountered Steve – he gave her a wide berth on the Rue du Marché and they passed each other without a word. A little later she saw Werner and Karina but this time they truly didn't seem to notice her.

Eventually she decided that whatever point she was trying to make was no longer necessary. The tour might be unravelling, possibly taking her job with it, but she was still in France and wanted to enjoy whatever time remained in the company of friends. On her next circuit through the Place de l'Église she saw Karina sitting at a table with her iPad and a glass of wine. Catherine waved and went over to join her. They double-kissed then she signalled to a waiter and ordered a soft drink.

Karina laughed when it arrived. 'You're in the centre of Saint-Émilion and you're drinking Orangina. Surely there must be some sort of local by-law against that.'

'I expect we'll be indulging in the local produce later. Tonight will be our last dinner together, after all.'

'Perhaps. Things seem to be a little bit up in the air now. I might be going up to Paris on my own for a few days, and then home.'

'I thought you were going down to the Cathar country with Werner.'

'So did I. But he tells me suddenly that I am surplus to requirements.'

'I hope that's not the way he put it.'

Karina smiled. 'Not exactly. He always takes care to coat a little sugar around it. And because I know that the sweetness is real, I don't mind so much. How about you? Have you talked with Nick about when you will go home?'

'You're still assuming that we are going home.'

Karina looked confused by this response. 'Forgive me, Kate. Maybe I misunderstood the situation.'

'Did Nick say that we were?'

The waiter passed their table and Karina ordered another glass of wine. When he had gone she glanced down at her iPad again and appeared to become absorbed in an email. Catherine wasn't fooled. 'Karina, you're trying not to answer the question.

Did Nick say it was decided?'

'He seems to think so. And being the one with the injury, the decision is his, isn't it?'

They were joined a little later by Steve, and shortly after that by Nick and Werner. For the rest of the afternoon and into the evening they acted as they had done for days, pretending that they might go on forever as a party of five. But throughout dinner Catherine was conscious that Nick had told the others something in Bordeaux, something that he should have shared with her first. It hung in the air, waiting for someone to bring it into the open.

In the end it was Werner who raised it. 'So Catherine. What will be the lasting memory you take home from your time in France?'

She could see that he knew he was picking at a scab. Before answering she glanced at Nick but he was staring down at his wine glass, swirling it perhaps a little more violently than intended. Precious drops of Saint-Émilion splashed onto the tablecloth.

Turning back to Werner, but directing her words to Nick, she said, 'There have been so many, I hardly know which to choose. Perhaps the day Nick staggered from the hotel to the tandem and we rode out of Huelgoat. With help from Steve we made a start when it would have been easier to quit and go home. I was proud of us that day.

'But the most complete experience I've had of cycle touring was the week Steve and I spent riding along the Loire. Everything felt right. I'd be grateful for anything that even approached that again.'

She stopped abruptly, afraid of what might come out if she kept going. She swallowed too much wine, almost choking on it, and was relieved when Werner broke the silence with a burst of applause. 'Well said, Catherine. Well said.'

Steve and Karina took up the applause, leaving only Nick who was still staring gloomily at his wine. Catherine decided to press him. 'Your turn, Nick. Don't think about it, just be completely honest.'

'You want the honest truth?'

'No holding back.'

'The whole thing has been unremittingly awful. Everything I hoped to achieve this summer went into a ditch on the second day in France. So if you want my highlights, then there's only one – our first day. We did a reasonably competent job together. We could have built on that. And you surprised me. I don't mind making a little confession: after the first night at Base Camp, when you did that little delaying trick, I asked Brendan to find me a solo touring bike. Just in case you decided to pull out completely.'

'You did what?' She didn't know whether to be angry or impressed. It seemed he knew her – the old Catherine, anyway – better than she'd realised.

'I thought it was a reasonable precaution to take. The irony is that I'm the one who brought this tour to its knees. Pun intended.'

He stopped to refill his glass. Catherine held her breath. She was afraid of what he might say next, but still she wanted to hear it. 'And since that first day?' she pressed. 'Isn't there anything you'd think of as a highlight?'

'Not in the sense we're talking about. I'm doing a job of work here and that's all. From a personal point of view we've had the chance to meet the others. But what else is there? The whole thing has been a nightmare.'

Hearing this she realised just how far apart they were. Their experience of the last month had been so different that she could see little hope for a shared view of what might lie ahead. She wanted to push him further, to ask directly about the two of them, but in front of the others it was too embarrassing. It would have to wait. Instead, she asked, 'Did Brendan buy that solo touring bike for you in the end?'

'Yes. It's back at Base Camp.'

'Would he still ship it down here if you asked him to?'

'The last thing I need right now is a solo touring bike.'

'I was thinking of me using it, not you.'

She said it so lightly that it seemed like a joke. Werner, followed by the others, began to laugh. It broke the tension and, after a moment, she joined them.

'You know, Käthe,' Werner said, 'if you need a new tandem partner, why not choose me? We could eat up the miles together. I know we could.'

She laughed even more. Whether he was serious or not wasn't clear, but the idea was ridiculous. 'Werner, there's nothing I'd like more. But you already have Karina and Nick competing for your attentions. I don't think I could stand to come last in a three-horse race, not so soon after losing one where there was no competition at all.'

A crowd had been gathering around them in the square for some time. The waiter, when he came with the bill, explained that a fireworks display celebrating the eve of Bastille Day was about to begin. He gave them directions to a point higher in the town where they would get a clearer view, but only if they hurried. They made their way up to the vantage point, reaching it just as the first rockets burst white over the tower of the church.

By silent agreement Catherine and Nick remained apart. She linked arms with Karina and they strolled ahead of the men, weaving through the growing crowd, making small talk just as they had on the night of the banquet at Augmont. When the first volley of rockets burst above them Catherine turned and stole a glance at Nick. He was standing a few metres to her right and was staring darkly at the sky. If he regretted any of what he had said, it wasn't obvious. She felt her eyes welling with tears and looked down at the cobbles, hiding her emotion from the others.

She wiped her eyes and looked up towards the fireworks again. As she raised her head she saw that Nick was watching her. She pretended not to notice, turning instead towards Steve. Very deliberately she leaned towards him and put a hand on his shoulder. Surprised, Steve smiled at her and put his arm casually around her waist, the first time in a month they had been so close. With Nick still watching, it was exactly what she wanted. She thought about adding a kiss too, but it would have been too much. She settled instead for half-resting her head on his shoulder until the fireworks had come to an end.

At breakfast the following morning Nick surprised her with an invitation to have lunch with him in Bergerac. During the hour they spent in the car together they made more small talk than in all of their time together on the tandem. It was like stepping temporarily into a parallel world, a warm and unexpectedly companionable state. But all the time she knew that it was a very deliberate and mutual effort to delay the coming confrontation until they were stationary.

Arriving in the *centre ville* just on noon, they found a restaurant with outdoor tables and ordered from the *menu du jour*. The waiter brought them bread, water and a *demi-pichet* of white wine. Hidden behind their most reflective sunglasses they faced each other, neither knowing how to begin.

Eventually Nick said, 'I think we've delayed the inevitable as long as we can. It's time to bring this charade of a journey to an end.'

It was out at last. She had known it was coming – in a practical sense it was the only thing that his injury would permit. But it still shocked her to hear him admit defeat so openly. It made her feel a concern for him that she had almost forgotten she could have. 'It must be very hard for you to say that.'

'You'd think. But look at what we're doing. Sitting around, eating and drinking again. I hate it but it's all I'm good for since the crash. I just don't want to go on like this for another couple of months. It's not what I came here to do.'

'What if we settled for something less? We could continue slowly to the Mediterranean. That way we could at least say we rode north to south.'

He shook his head. 'Kate, you're only making this harder.'

She knew he was right but couldn't quite let it go. 'How are you going to break this to Brendan?'

'I called him yesterday from Bordeaux. He wasn't happy, but he's trying to come up with a way to help me smooth it with Aidan Cruickshank.'

Aware that she was unlikely to succeed when Brendan had already failed, she gave up. They focused on the entrée, the silence between them a tacit acknowledgement that the trip was over.

When their main courses arrived she turned the conversation to practicalities. 'If we're going home, I guess we should make a start tomorrow.' When he didn't respond, she added, 'Or the day after, if you'd rather.'

Still he said nothing, and she asked, 'What is it that you're not telling me?'

'I'm not going home right away. I've had an offer of work for the next couple of weeks and I'm going to take it.'

She stared back at him, wondering how he could possibly have received a job offer in the last few days. Then it hit her. 'Werner.'

'He wants me as a consultant on the English language version of the documentary. I'm going south with him to scout for locations and select the six walks that we want to cover in detail.'

'That's your real reason for quitting, isn't it?'

He managed to look a little embarrassed. 'It's not that simple. I can't play a full part on the tandem. It hurts me every time I change places with Steve and watch the two of you ride away, able-bodied, happy, almost eager to be making an escape. Then Werner comes along with this offer. Thinking about the possibilities for me in it, I'd be crazy not to accept, wouldn't I?'

'Does he really think you've got a shot at being part of this programme?'

'He's been talking to some contacts in the UK. We might even get into other English language markets. He's been very persuasive and it's flattering. I don't feel I can say no.'

Catherine finished her main course while she considered her own options. There was no way she could face tagging along on the Cathar expedition. Werner hadn't asked for her and she would have said no even if he had. That only seemed to leave taking the car and heading back to London.

'Go home, Kate,' Nick insisted, when he realised she was still brooding. 'It's your only option.'

He reached across the table and put his hand on hers, a gesture that she might have welcomed a few days earlier. Now it triggered an anger in her that she struggled to control. As it bubbled to the surface of her skin she realised that she didn't care any more about finding a solution for both of them. He had an answer that worked for him alone. She was going to do the same.

'I can think of at least two possibilities for me,' she said. 'I could get Brendan to send down that solo touring bike you mentioned last night. It would be ironic, don't you think, that it was me using it rather than you.' She could see that this hit home. 'I'll do it too if I have to. But I think I've got a better idea.'

'Which is?'

'I'm going to go on with the tandem. I'll ask Steve to do it with me.'

Nick sat back, stunned. 'You and him on the tandem? Just the two of you, the whole time? You've got to be kidding.'

'I'm deadly serious. And here's another little surprise for you. You're going to keep paying his expenses out of your Cruickshank and Spears travel budget.'

He took his sunglasses off and stared at her. 'Do you think I'm stupid? There's no way I'm going to pay for you to ride into the sunset with the first able-bodied man you happened across in France.'

'Oh, grow up. You're not the only one capable of maintaining a professional distance on a tandem.' She stopped and stared hard at him, thinking through the implications of what he had said. 'Are you somehow jealous of him? Is that why you don't want him around me?'

Nick drank down his wine, all the time staring along the street, avoiding her eyes. Softening his tone, he replied, 'He's likeable, easy to get along with. Who wouldn't want to be a little like that? But my feeling is, he's got no staying power, no grit. He's a wanderer, a dreamer. I've come across plenty like him on my travels. They have no purpose, no goals. One choice is just as good as another. They make and break relationships on a whim. In the end he'll disappear over the horizon when you least expect it.'

'Well, I trust him. Completely. And he's the only option I've got for keeping the summer alive. From where I'm sitting right now, sharing a tandem with a wanderer and a dreamer looks infinitely preferable to sitting behind a clinically-minded professional.'

'He's not getting a penny out of my budget. I need that money to go down to the Cathar country.'

'Werner can pay for you out of his pocket money. He's got

plenty to spare. It's either that, or I send an anonymous email to Aidan Cruickshank telling him the real reason you've quit. Your choice.'

He stared at her while he thought it through. Then he leaned back and laughed. 'You're something else, harder even than me when you want to be. But you know what? I think you've hit on something brilliant. The trip with Werner won't last more than two weeks. I can take my chance on the Cathar project then join you in Avignon for the ride north together. Aidan doesn't even have to know I'm gone.'

'Wait a minute. We can't carry on as though this didn't happen. Letting you back on the tandem would be my decision. Mine alone.' She wondered exactly what she was saying, whether the tandem ride was coded terminology for anything larger. It seemed at that moment that it was. 'The way I feel right now, it would take some pretty clever talking on your part to bring me round.'

He continued to stare at her while he considered this. She knew that he wanted to keep arguing, that paying for Steve to stay with the tandem might be too much for him to stomach. It seemed to take an age, but eventually he capitulated. 'All right. Have it your way. A couple of weeks apart might be a good thing for both of us. But that seat on the tandem is mine. I'll find a way to persuade you I'm the right person to go north with you.'

She nodded, sensing that it was better for now to leave it at that. He had conceded a lot, given her a means of continuing. 'Does Steve already know that you're going off with Werner?'

'He heard us discussing it in Bordeaux yesterday.'

'Then I'd better call him as soon as possible. In case he's made plans to find his own way home.'

'And if he says no?'

'He won't. Unlike you, he actually seems to enjoy being on a tandem with me.'

My Tandem Tour de France
By Catherine Pringle

Day 27, Thursday 14 July
Saint-Émilion

Bastille Day, symbol of revolution and the sweeping away of old regimes. A day of unity, celebration and common purpose. And, as it turns out, a day when we challenged and toppled our own *Ancien Régime*, a mindset that's been acting as a drag on this tandem tour for far too long.

In 18 cycling days since we rolled off the ferry at Roscoff we've covered only 960 kilometres. Almost, but not quite, a quarter of the target distance. But there's still a long way to go, another 3,000 kilometres, and a rapidly shrinking number of days still available.

The cause? Too much of the good life: good food, good wine and good company. It's beginning to take its toll. And, I have to confess, it's almost entirely my fault. It's summer, we're in France, and I've been insisting we enjoy ourselves just a little too much.

At a crisis meeting in Bergerac today we agreed that things will have to change. It was lunchtime by the way, and yes, we were eating from a fixed menu at a restaurant of my choosing. There was a small quantity of wine too, white wine, which I'm pretty sure doesn't count when it's consumed at lunchtime. Does it?

I know what you're thinking – this all sounds very Marie Antoinette. Which is exactly how the discussion began to make me feel.

Between the entrée and the main course, Nick unrolled his

precious schedule, a document he treats with a religious reverence. It tells us where we should be and what we should be doing on every day of the remaining two months.

Twice a day, morning and night, it's taken out for worship, and to calibrate our actual performance against the perfection that only a pair of tandeming saints might achieve.

He showed me where we should be by now. And it really wasn't good news. The schedule had us more than 500 kilometres to the south-west. Almost enough to put me off my main course.

Until then, I was a non-believer. I didn't want to be on a tour that needed plans to keep it on track. But I can see now how wrong I was. On a long-distance journey, one with limited time, there's nothing more necessary than a plan. And, like any recent convert, there's a pretty good chance that I'm going to be fundamentalist about it from now on.

But it has to be a plan that belongs to both of you, or it's not going to work. That's the major change we've both had to come to terms with.

We've had our moments on this trip, not all of them fit for publication even in a blog as confessional as this. But today we turned a corner. At last we understand each other perfectly. Every minute of every day from now on, the man ahead of me on the tandem will be my equal in a perfectly balanced partnership. I want him sitting in front of me. And he wants me there with him.

The old cycling order has changed. Heads have rolled, and there is no turning back. *Vive la Révolution! Vive le tour!*

Azay-sur-Indre to Saint-Émilion

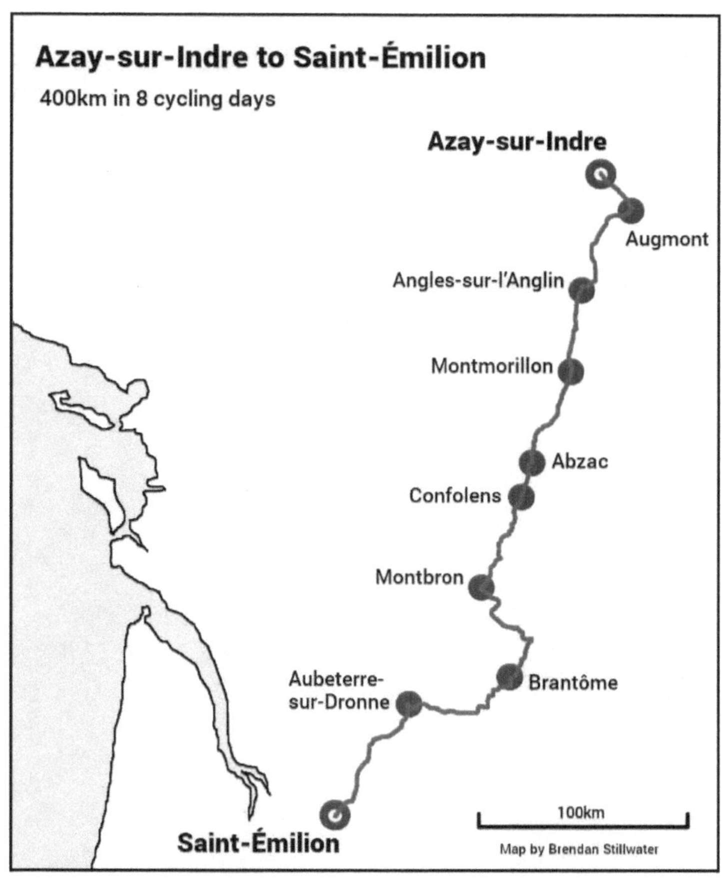

Careless lips

14

The early morning sky was brightening into a perfect summer blue as Catherine and Steve slipped out of Saint-Émilion and descended onto the plain of rolling vineyards to its south. The air, cool and invigorating, invited them on and they lifted their pace, racing towards the Dordogne.

It was easy cycling. Soon they were across the river and riding along its southern bank. As the vineyards gave way to agricultural fields, a patchwork of broad-leaved tobacco and deep green artichoke, Catherine reflected on her parting from Nick. Even by their own standards it was the strangest yet. After two years of his constant coming and going she was used to the peaks and troughs of emotional energy that flowed between them. Leading up to a departure he invariably withdrew as his focus switched to the job ahead. She had struggled with this in their early days but over time had found herself adopting a complementary attitude.

On the final night in Saint-Émilion the detachment had become extreme, as if some strands of the elastic that held them together were stretched to breaking point. Their new tent, chosen by Nick from the Bordeaux shipment, was a low-ceilinged graphite-grey tube. It felt like being in an upended sardine tin, one that she was sharing with a particularly odd fish.

In the morning they had eaten a last communal breakfast with the others. The discussion was frosty, restricted to practical arrangements, and it had left her desperate to be on her way. When the meal was over and the packing complete they had parted, almost without another word. In one sense it followed exactly the template of their standard farewell. But there was something deeper this time – they were both moving on, no one was staying behind.

After lunch the pace on the tandem eased. The morning's explosion of energy had been spent and the route was harder, passing through the rolling hills of the bastide country in an endless succession of climbs to hilltop villages and sharp descents to valley floors. It sapped their strength but they held to an unspoken agreement that they finish the day as far as possible from Saint-Émilion.

A hundred kilometres was more than enough. Resting in the shade of Villeréal's medieval market hall, they found directions to the nearest campsite. A final downhill plunge took them into the valley of the Dropt and they were soon, for the first time since the Loire, setting up a simple pitch for two.

The evening meal was a world away from Werner's elaborate cuisine. As she lay on an air mat beside a simple picnic of bread, cheese and salad, Catherine felt the first glass of red wine deepen her exhaustion. She sagged a little further into the mat and had to force herself to make conversation.

'Thanks, Steve,' she managed, eventually. 'For saying that you'd stay on with me.'

He held up his wine glass and touched it to hers. 'Yesterday I was packing to go back to London. Tonight I'm still part of this extraordinary adventure. I'd like to think of this as a new start, something that exists only in the present, with no before and no after.'

'I like the sound of that. No before and after. We do whatever it takes to make this work.'

'Yes. Whatever it takes.'

As they ate he reached for the large-scale map of the south of France and spread it on the ground between them. 'Suppose you weren't following someone else's plan. If you could do anything you wanted in the next week, what would that be?'

'I've only just published a blog committing myself emphatically to the existing schedule. I can hardly retract that a day later.'

He threw his head back and laughed. 'Humour me a little. Suppose for a moment that no one really expects Catherine Pringle to stick dogmatically to anything she writes. What if everyone just wants her to do what makes her happy?'

She ignored the dig at her principles and leaned over to study the map. With so many kilometres of catching up to do, her first thought was to follow the straightest possible line from Saint-Émilion to Avignon. Then her eye wandered across the map to the north-west. Tracing an alternative route through Périgord Noir, she said, 'I've always wanted to visit the prehistoric sites along the Vézère valley – see the cave art at Font-de-Gaume and Lascaux. There was no way I could fit that in while Nick was on the tandem. But now … '

She looked up, deciding suddenly it was exactly what she wanted to do.

He smiled and nodded. 'On one condition.'

'Which is?'

'For every detour you choose I get to add one of my own.'

'All right. Tomorrow we begin with a cultural diversion to the Vézère. We stay at les-Eyzies-de-Tayac and explore the Cro-Magnon sites.'

He pulled the map towards him. 'Then we recross the Dordogne and turn west to the pilgrimage site at Rocamadour.'

'After that, south to Albi for the cathedral and the Lautrec museum.'

'And finally, a journey along the Tarn and through the Cévennes. No traveller should cross the south of France without following in the footsteps of Robert Louis Stevenson and his donkey.'

As he passed the map back to her their hands touched briefly. On the tandem they bumped and brushed against each other all day long, but this was different. Embarrassed, she pulled her hand sharply back and made a deliberate show of folding the map. She was suddenly aware that they would be sharing a tent again – a smaller, narrower one than in the Loire. Something, and not just the tent, had changed.

Disconcerted, she tried to cover her feelings with humour. Mimicking Karina, she said, 'I think, my darling, that we really need to leave the donkey out of this. Things are complicated enough already.'

Laughing, he replied, 'Well said, Käthe. You know, together we really are going to be quite a team.'

It was only the second time he had used the diminutive that Werner liked to tease her with. Maybe it was the tiredness, or its combination with a large glass of wine, but she realised that she didn't mind at all when he used it. She turned her head to conceal a smile.

Catherine drifted awake on their first morning in the Vézère valley with the unfamiliar feeling of having all the time in the world to do whatever she pleased. Ahead lay a mostly cycling-free day, the tandem touring equivalent of a Sunday, devoted to prehistory and culture. It happened to be a Sunday too, the fifth since coming to France, and her mind lingered for a moment on the pleasure of waking on Sunday mornings in her own bed in London. The memory of snuggling next to a snoozing partner drew her a little closer to the body beside her and she looped an arm around him for extra comfort.

Still with her eyes closed she listened to the early morning sounds of the campsite: birdsong in the trees above the tent, the footsteps of early risers on the gravel paths, a muffled conversation nearby. It was still cool enough to enjoy the extra body heat from her companion. She pressed a little closer and he stirred slightly. His hand closed around hers, squeezing it gently. It was the slightest of gestures and she smiled to herself before his breathing became heavier again and he settled into a deeper sleep.

A thought that she couldn't quite take hold of made her open her eyes. The grey vault of the tunnel tent surrounded her, her own side flooded with light from the rising sun. She took in the form in the sleeping bag next to her, dimly aware that something wasn't quite as she had imagined. The vital clue was the hair, fair and slightly wavy instead of short and dark. With a jolt she realised that it wasn't just any Sunday in London. She wasn't lying next to Nick. Her arm was fixed securely around Steve.

She began to peel herself away, to put some distance between them in case he woke. Then she realised how deeply asleep he was. Slowly she lifted her hand and put the tips of her fingers into the fine curls at the back of his head. When he still didn't stir she leaned across and kissed his neck just below the hairline. It was crossing a line, betraying a trust, but it was also something she couldn't stop herself from wanting to do.

Embarrassed, she struggled out of the sleeping bag and crawled as gently as she could from the tent. Outside she squatted in the entrance and reached for her towel and toiletry bag. Looking back through the flap of the tent she saw that there would be no immediate consequences. He was still fast asleep.

In the shower she tried to understand what the kiss meant. It would have been easy to blame a semi-conscious mind but there was more to it than that. Maybe all the talk of doing whatever it takes had awakened something deep in her psyche. The thought niggled at her for the whole time she was under the water. And when she came out and looked at herself in the mirror, big-eyed and anxious, she still didn't have an answer. Or even a route map for finding one.

She knew at least that she wasn't ready to face him. Leaving a quick note, she started for the centre of les-Eyzies. On the bridge over the Vézère she paused and stared into its dark, blue-brown waters. Safe in the knowledge that no one could hear her, she said aloud, 'Käthe, you really need to get a grip. It was just a kiss. And he was asleep the whole time.'

She found a bar in the main street and ordered breakfast. While she ate she worked through the messages on her phone. It started as a comforting distraction, but lurking at the bottom of the list was a new message from Liz that almost made her choke on her coffee. It read:

> *Just been catching up on your blog posts for the last*
> *week. Can't understand the reference to Nick's knee.*
> *Call me any time Sunday.*

Linking to the blog, Catherine scanned through the text of the last few entries. She found the reference in a short post she'd written on the last afternoon of the ride into Saint-Émilion. It was explainable, a one-line reference to them almost falling from the tandem when he had put too much weight on his injured knee. But a phone call with Liz was out of the question. She knew she wouldn't survive even a gentle grilling.

She opened the private log she was now keeping and documented the error. Then she added a short description of the moment when her lips had touched Steve's neck, ending with the words she had spoken aloud on the bridge over the Vézère.

As she wrote, a text message arrived. It was from him, asking her where she had disappeared to. She gave directions then switched off the phone and began to toy with it, spinning it on the table as she watched the early morning passers-by on the street.

She was still doing this when he strolled into view. There was just time to slip on her sunglasses before he waved and came over to sit opposite her.

'Have you been here long?' he asked, after signalling to the waiter.

'I don't remember really. You didn't notice that I was up and about?'

'When I'm asleep you could be playing a tattoo on my back and I wouldn't know a thing about it.'

'Maybe I'll try that sometime. Just to see if it's true.'

'Be my guest,' he said, through an impenetrable smile. 'In the interests of science, of course.'

He ordered breakfast then leaned back and gazed at the sky. It was an almost featureless blue with just a few lazy strokes of high-altitude cloud. 'It's beautiful this morning. Suddenly everything feels very different.'

'Maybe because we're further south.'

'It's more than that. I can't put my finger on it exactly. Do you feel it too?'

She ignored the question and turned away, maddened that she was unable to read a clue in his smile or his words. It was possible that he had felt the kiss on his neck and was deliberately toying with her. On the other hand he was probably just being his carefree self, casually passing comment on a perfect summer's morning.

When his breakfast came she watched him pour coffee then butter a shard of bread. He looked up suddenly and caught her staring at him. 'Is everything all right, Kate? You seem a little … anxious.'

'I'm just the same as ever,' she said, emphatically tucking a strand of hair behind her ear. It fell forward again and she yanked it back into place. For the first time in weeks, how she looked seemed to matter and the backcountry phase her hair was growing through made her want to turn away. 'Nothing has changed.'

'Well I'm glad that's sorted.'

She tried laughing but it sounded forced, idiotic, and she realised just how irregular her breathing had become. She wanted to tell him exactly what was on her mind, or better still to lean across the table and kiss him properly. But she couldn't do it. The casual intimacy that seemed to exist between them was a sign that there could easily be much more. But she couldn't put from her mind the strange moment she had seen him share with Karina at Confolens. That too had looked like real intimacy, but to him it must have been nothing more than a friendly gesture. The risk of over-interpreting his words and gestures was just too great and, if she got it wrong, their friendship might be permanently soured. They had survived one misjudged moment on the banks of the Loire. A second could make life on the tandem impossible.

She wanted suddenly to be away from the table, for them not to be sitting facing each other. 'Since we're already on this side of the river we could walk along to the caves at Font-de-Gaume.'

'Let's do that. It sounds like a nice change of pace. A Sunday morning stroll to a 20,000-year-old gallery.'

'It's my idea of a perfect Sunday,' she continued, aware that she was beginning to gush. 'In London at this time I'd be making plans for a visit to a museum or an exhibition. Nick, of course, wouldn't dream of going, not unless it involved a ten-mile walk to get there. So if you'd rather not come I'm quite used to doing things like this alone.'

'It sounds perfect to me,' he replied. He stared at her closely, obviously puzzled by her manner. 'We can forget about the tandem for a while, and just relax like two normal adults.'

They walked side by side along the road to the visitor centre at Font-de-Gaume. A French-speaking tour was just departing and they followed it into the cave complex rather than wait hours for an English one. Catherine was soon separated from Steve, who stepped aside in the first passage to let a family group move closer to the guide and found himself bringing up the rear.

After fifty metres, when the passage opened into a large chamber, the guide turned and gestured for the group to gather around him. Catherine moved aside hoping to rejoin Steve but in the crush they missed each other again. She listened as the guide explained that they were now in a part of the cave known as the Rubicon, on the threshold of the decorated gallery. Most of his words washed over her. She lifted her eyes toward a shadowy fold in the ceiling of the cave and found herself thinking again about the early morning kiss.

She realised just how important it was, that it was driven by something that had been building in her for weeks. She was on the edge of taking a radical step and hoping that he would respond. It was exciting but felt full of risk.

'*Madame!*'

She turned and saw that she was alone with the guide. At the far end of the cave, where the new chamber began, she could see Steve and the rest of the group waiting for her. The guide smiled and, in English, said, 'Please, you must cross the Rubicon to continue the tour.'

She hesitated, grasping the words and their resonance. In that moment she decided she had to go ahead and reveal her feelings to Steve, but she would do it gradually so that there was every opportunity to watch for a reaction and step back if he showed no interest. Nodding to the guide, she walked to the other side of the Rubicon. When she reached Steve she smiled and threaded her arm companionably around his. He looked a little surprised but said nothing, gave no hint that he thought anything of it. None the wiser, but pleased that the first tentative step had been taken, Catherine strolled beside him into the decorated chamber.

Later, as they cycled north along the Vézère to Montignac, she reflected on the strange closeness she now felt to the man in front of her. With his back just inches ahead of her she was acutely aware of everything about him. Between his shoulder blades a tiny patch of sweat had formed. She leaned a little closer and inhaled deeply, searching for the faintest trace of his scent. When he half-turned to speak she straightened, noting the gestures with his hands as he pointed to something that had taken his interest at the side of the road. She forgot about the ride, lost any sense of where they were, her mind narrowed its focus to him.

When a dragonfly landed on his back she let it hitch a ride for a while, unsure if she wanted to risk touching his back. In the end she couldn't resist the opportunity and brushed it away, leaving her hand on his T-shirt just a little longer than she needed to.

She was acutely aware of being physically close to him and of wanting to be closer still.

Her struggle to deal with the real and fictional versions of the journey intensified the next morning at Lascaux. The visit was a progression through an intricate copy of the original cave structure, exact in every detail down to the painted images of bison, reindeer, bear, horse and mammoth. The reproductions were splendid, still an intense experience, in some ways more beautiful than those she had seen the day before. But there was something missing, an absence of the emotion that had accompanied her across the Rubicon at Font-de-Gaume. She realised that, in the end, standing in the actual cave where the images had been created 20,000 years earlier added a dimension of reality that elaborate copies, no matter how carefully produced, could never match.

Outside, during an early lunch at a shaded picnic table, she tried to craft a few sentences comparing Lascaux with Font-de-Gaume. Distinguishing between reality and an impostor was easy, she decided, only when you already knew which was which. If she had been led blindfolded into both caves, the emotional experience when she opened her eyes might have been quite different.

Twice, as she wrote, Steve caught her staring at him. Each time, hidden safely behind her sunglasses, she smiled and carried on with her work until she had found a viable hook to start her post:

> The nature of reality is not a topic that ordinarily springs into the mind on the stoker's seat of a tandem.
>
> Deep thinking of any kind takes an almost permanent back seat to more basic, everyday concerns. My mind rarely gets further than worrying about eating, drinking and getting over that next hill. Which is entirely reasonable, in my opinion. It's pretty hard to focus on anything much at all when the gradient gets steeper than seven per cent.
>
> I know what my critics are thinking. I'm pretty sure two of them in particular are already desperate to point out that deep thinking isn't something I've burdened myself with very much at all, never mind on a tandem.
>
> Picture the scene at a breakfast table in a house

not far from one of our major universities: chief critic number two – you know who you are, dad – is scrolling on his iPad through the latest instalment of his daughter's tabloid magnum opus. He skim-reads a couple of paragraphs into this post, tut-tutting no doubt at the loose grammatical construction, until he encounters something that almost makes him choke on his muesli.

After a short chuckle, he looks across the breakfast table at chief critic number one – from now on, let's call her mum – and says to her, 'Catherine seems to be saying that the gradients in France are preventing her from focusing her mind on the deeper questions in life.'

'That's pretty rich,' she replies. 'We all know she's a soufflé-light thinker. And she gets distracted by the merest puff of wind. What was it her philosophy tutor said? "Catherine would struggle for depth at the bottom of a mineshaft."'

They're both wrong of course, always have been. I'm more than capable of deep thinking, it's just that I prefer to deploy it a little more sparingly than they do.

'Kate, dearest,' critic number one is now saying directly to me, 'you've just proved me right. Look at what this post is supposed to be about, and ask yourself why your father and I are even in it. Puff? Wind?'

There is, as it happens, a light breeze drifting across the picnic area as I write this. But coming back to the point: this detour along the Vézère valley is having a profound impact on me. I hope one day I'll be in a position to explain it more clearly, but for now let me just return to the nature of reality.

Visits on successive days to two of the Vézère's most stunning sites have triggered extremely different reactions in me. Font-de-Gaume allows the visitor into the original chambers where Cro-Magnon humans created spectacular cave paintings some 20,000 years ago. Yesterday was an intensely emotional day for me. I felt close to something then, something I'm not yet able to put into words. I could almost reach out and touch it, grasp at an opportunity that was going to change my life.

Lascaux, on the other hand, left me cold. I should perhaps add that this is probably my fault and not the cave's. On the surface it was stunning, more beautiful than Font-de-Gaume. But it lacked emotion. Behind the elaborate facade it was just a fake, a copy of reality that I would have settled for if I hadn't seen the real thing at Font-de-Gaume ...

She stopped and looked up again, resting her eyes on Steve.

He caught her this time and asked, 'What is it? You've been acting a little strange since yesterday.'

'Have I? It's nothing. I don't know really.' It was an embarrassingly poor attempt at passing herself off as normal. She felt she had to go on. 'I suppose I'm just happy I got the chance to do all of this.'

'I understand. I feel the same. Meeting you and Nick ... I don't really believe in fate, but it's beginning to seem to me that when I stumbled across you in the rain on that road in Brittany ... I don't know ... that it happened for a reason.' He seemed embarrassed to have revealed this thought, and immediately made light of it. 'Of course, I'm always on the verge of a life-changing discovery. But I usually end up no further forward.'

They finished eating and rode away from Lascaux. As they cycled along the western bank of the Vézère she touched him on the back and said, 'You will let me know, won't you.'

'What?'

'When you've figured that reason out.'

'Oh that.' He laughed and added, 'I'm a bit slow about some things. I don't know if I'll work it out at all. But if I do, I promise you'll be the first to know.'

'Thanks Steve.'

Slipping into his mock Werner again, he replied, 'You're welcome already, Käthe.'

15

Catherine dreaded every minute she now had to spend in their new ultralight, asymmetrical tunnel tent. It was cramped and narrow, barely wide enough for two, and felt more like being in a coffin than resting in the most expensive micro-shelter in the Cruickshank and Spears catalogue. No doubt it was perfect for a lightweight trek across the Arctic, or a solo expedition into the Andes. But in the heavy rain and high humidity of the storm system that swept across the hills the night they arrived in Sarlat-la-Canéda, she felt as if she'd been buried alive and was sharing the rapidly diminishing air supply with an organism she was increasingly wary of.

The first rule of tenting in the rain, item one on the camping catechism she had learned from Nick in Brittany, was to keep away from the fabric of the outer shell. But she now had an even higher priority: avoiding physical contact with a man she couldn't trust herself to be near. Caught between these irreconcilable objectives, she reluctantly edged towards the middle of the tent. A close-quarters game of tag followed and they bumped shoulders, elbows and finally legs. Eventually he turned on his side and his breathing deepened as he drifted asleep.

Hyper-alert to every movement of his body, she listened to the rise and fall of his chest and thought about what the constant proximity was doing to her mind. For two days she had been unable to take her eyes off him, noting new layers of detail about his ways and habits. But the close observation had done nothing to clarify what was eating at her the most: the way he had seemed to squeeze her hand as they lay together on that Sunday morning in les-Eyzies. Was it just the auto-reflex of a man who was mostly asleep? Was he remembering girlfriends past? Or, after the rebuff she had given him on the Loire, was he too sending a deniable, no-fault signal? She just couldn't tell, and the fear of being wrong, of bursting the exhilarating but exhausting bubble she was now living in, held her in check.

The worst of the storm passed and she managed to sleep a little, but when she woke around seven she was, for the third time in as many days, curled close into his back. Turning her head she looked around the weird space she now called home and decided it was the only reasonable way for two people to share it. Anxious that he didn't wake while they were so close, she eased herself up and crawled out into the fresh morning air.

It was their first full rest day since leaving Saint-Émilion and they had agreed to spend it exploring Sarlat-la-Canéda. After an extended stay under the shower she dressed in her only off-tandem clothes: a knee-length travel skirt in a mid-plum colour that the C&S marketing team was calling aloe, and a 'crease-resistant' cotton blouse that failed completely to live up to its unique selling proposition.

Looking at herself in the mirror she saw a woman who had obviously just crawled out of a sleeping bag and stepped into clothes that had been crushed at the bottom of a pannier. Her hair completed the disaster. The short, heavily graduated bob had only ever worked within easy reach of a blow-dryer. Left for more than a month to fend for itself, it now looked like something a street urchin would disown. She teased at it with her fingers then turned away from the mirror, hoping that a quarter of an hour in the morning breeze would perform some sort of miracle.

Steve was idling in front of the tent when she returned, watching a small curl of steam rise from the spout of the kettle. He looked up at her and smiled. 'You look especially pretty this morning.'

She turned through a full circle then gave a little curtsy. 'It's just something I found at the bottom of my pannier. Literally at the bottom.' She ran her fingers through her mostly-dry hair and added, 'I wish just this once I could choose from a full wardrobe of crisply pressed clothes. And be pampered by a master stylist with an industrial-strength blow-dryer.'

'You're perfect just as you are,' he replied, delivering exactly the line that was expected of him. 'But you're on a day off from cycling. You could throw away your rule book. Shop till you drop. Treat yourself to something frivolous.'

She shook her head. 'You know the deal. Everything I wear on this trip has to come out of the Cruickshank and Spears catalogue.'

'Rules are for breaking, aren't they? Anyway, who's here to notice a minor infringement every now and then?'

I will, she thought as he passed her a mug of tea. *And eventually I'll find myself confessing it in print.*

As she jiggled the teabag she realised that she couldn't bear to go through another day like the one that had just passed. Sending out constant subtly-crafted signals and raking through his reactions for non-existent clues was exhausting. She needed a break and that meant being on her own for a while.

Half-looking at him, she said, 'I think we both need to take some time out from all this today.'

'That's a good idea,' he replied, without looking up from his tea. 'We could just wander a little in the centre of town, nourish the urban side of our souls.'

She wondered if he was being deliberately slow. 'Actually, I meant apart. Alone.'

'Oh.'

He lifted his head now and stared at her. She thought he looked disappointed, but couldn't be sure. 'Steve, I just have to. You know what it's like on the tandem. It feels like I'm chained to someone the whole time.'

'Do you remember that old movie – *The Defiant Ones*. Sidney Poitier and Tony Curtis played convicts who escape from a work gang, chained together. They couldn't stand each other, couldn't wait to separate. It's not that bad I hope.'

'I didn't say it was bad,' she snapped, instantly hating herself for showing so much emotion.

'The thing is,' he continued, 'they ended up liking each other in the end. Got the shackles off, went their separate ways for a while. But they realised they couldn't survive apart.'

'Listen. I just want to spend a couple of hours on my own. Don't go reading anything more into it than that. Okay?'

He held up his hands in surrender. 'Maybe you're right. A day apart will do us good, give us both a little breathing space.'

They walked together into Sarlat and parted near its central square. Watching him disappear into a side street, Catherine was both relieved to see him go and annoyed that he had sauntered away from her with such a carefree swagger.

Alone, she wandered aimlessly for the rest of the morning. It was the largest town they had been in since Brittany and she was soon window-shopping for clothes, even though there was no room on the tandem for so much as an extra handkerchief. In a shoe shop she frittered away half an hour trying on everything in her size with at least a four-inch heel. It was a complete self-indulgence. She almost bought a pair purely as an act of rebellion but knew that after twenty-four hours they would be a burden she would have to discard. She left the shop empty-handed.

Her shopping genes, repressed for more than a month, had been reactivated with a viral intensity, and their quest for a luxury item, something frivolous that had no place on a tandem tour, quickly became unstoppable. It took a while to satisfy but eventually she emerged from a small boutique wearing an insanely expensive white linen blouse. Five minutes in a pannier would reduce it to a crumpled ball but for the rest of the afternoon she was going to feel good about wearing it.

A little further along the street she stopped outside a unisex hairdresser's and tried to talk herself into walking in. It was all wall-to-wall glass and mirror, bare floors and bleached surfaces. The lookalike staff were dressed in white lab coats, wore too much make-up and had brutal, blunt fringes. The whole atmosphere set alarm bells ringing – it looked like a carbon copy of the salon in Kensington where a year earlier she'd had her worst ever haircut.

It had been Liz's idea. A rival tabloid had just run a story on the reappearance of '80s-style mullet haircuts on models at a Paris fashion show. Liz wanted to go one better and had somehow convinced Catherine that a mullet cut make-over at an exclusive salon was a perfect angle on a great story. The result was predictable: amusing for about twenty-four hours, with a pang of regret longer than the wispy mullet tail that dangled limply down her neck.

The memory reminded her just how much she missed Liz, her co-conspirator on the most extreme, and frankly ridiculous, story ideas she had worked on. She tried calling but went straight through to voicemail. Instead, she sent a tweet that said:

She kept walking and found the beginning of a signposted tourist trail through Sarlat's medieval core. At the Lanterne des Morts, a cylindrical tower next to the cathedral, she found a seat and drafted a post on the importance of occasionally not cycling on a cycle tour.

As she wrote, Liz surprised her with a call. 'I hope it's me you were referring to in that tweet about missing your best friend. I'm going to assume it is, but I'd begun to wonder after your calls dried up.'

'Who else would I be talking about? You'd better book a very long lunch for the first week I'm back. I have so much to tell you.'

'Sounds intriguing. But if it's that good it should be in the blog. And why have you stopped tweeting about all that juicy tension between you and Nick? Has peace broken out at last?'

The truth, Catherine knew, would make Liz quiver with excitement. Instead she replied, 'Nick and I haven't had an argument in days. Sorry if that disappoints you. I'll try harder from now on if you really want me to.'

'Kate, pretend I didn't say it. This job has me flipping personalities more often than Jekyll and Hyde. My evil side lives for the daily dose of juicy copy people like you are sending her. But the other Liz – the real one, I hope, but who knows any more – would love it if you've found a way to be happy.'

'God I've missed you,' Catherine replied. 'A tandem can be a surprisingly lonely place, even when you like the person sitting in front of you.'

'Well you know where both of me are. Try calling us more often.'

A rattling keyboard announced that Liz was crossing back to her dark side. Catherine ended the call and turned back to the draft of her latest blog post, quickly reviewing and publishing it. With work out of the way her thoughts turned to Steve again. Perversely, having made a point of wanting to be alone all day, she now felt lonely and was beginning to wish they were together. She tried texting him on the off-chance he was missing her too.

He replied almost immediately, suggesting they meet for lunch. In seconds she was up and walking away from the Lanterne des Morts, a haste that she realised was telling.

She found her way to the Place du Peyrou and saw him sitting at an outdoor restaurant. When they had ordered, he touched the sleeve of her new blouse and smiled. 'I see you went shopping after all.'

'You were right about breaking the rules. But I don't know how I'll squeeze this into a pannier.'

'Well here's a radical idea. It's called clutter clearing. When something new comes along that you really think is worth having, try letting go of something old. I've always found that works pretty well.'

'Doesn't that mean you're always throwing things away, never sticking with anything?'

He shrugged. 'What's so great about sticking to things? It's pretty hard for a fly to argue that it's getting anything positive out of being attached to a length of flypaper.'

She wondered exactly what this meant but there was no chance to ask. He held up a plastic carrier bag and added, 'I'm glad you've relaxed your strict rules a little. It means you can't refuse the little gift I got you.'

She peeled the bag open and saw that he had bought her a sun hat. She tried it on, playing with the wide, floppy brim. 'How do I look?'

'Perfect. It's made from a natural fibre that's guaranteed not to lose its shape even after it's been squeezed, scrunched, or stuffed into a bag. That seemed to me to have cycle touring written all over it.'

'Squeezed, scrunched, and stuffed into a bag. I know exactly how that feels.'

She wanted to use the gift as an excuse to lean over and kiss him, just a casual friend-on-friend peck on the cheek. But the waiter was hovering with their entrées and she was forced to continue toying with the hat. 'Thanks Steve. It's a perfect gift.'

'I thought a present might go some way towards making whatever is wrong seem a little better.'

'I'm fine. Really.'

He looked at her sceptically. Then he dug into his bag again and pulled out a pair of ultra-dark sunglasses.

'I bought myself something too.' Putting them on, he added, 'Now we're even. I can't see what you're thinking, and you can't see what I'm thinking. That should work out well, don't you think?'

She looked down, avoiding his eyes. 'Don't make fun of me.'

'Then help me out. Explain why the last few days have been so strange.'

She shifted uncomfortably but remained silent. Frustrated, he took out his iPhone and opened the blog post she had just published. 'Maybe there's a clue among all these endless words you keep churning out. Let's see if this clarifies anything.'

He cleared his throat and read aloud:

> If Oscar Wilde had been a cycle tourist, I'm sure he would at some point have observed: 'There is only one thing better than cycling, and that is not cycling.'
>
> Rest days matter. Physically they make the difference between grinding to a halt and keeping your edge. Mentally they matter even more. Long-

distance, self-propelled travel is a quirky business. Some days you just wake up and know it's never going to work, no matter how hard you drive yourself. You may as well stay in bed.

Taking a rest day before you get to that point smooths out the bumps in a journey. It means you get to keep a little control over when and where you will run out of puff.

Which is why we're on foot today in Sarlat-la-Canéda, a medieval town whose core is rich in golden limestone buildings. The fifteenth-century streets and squares are beautiful, rightly chosen as the setting for a dozen romantic films.

I'm in love with Sarlat. And it's the kind of place where I would want to fall in love. If I was a character in a romance, that is. But I'm not. I'm on a tandem tour. And just taking a much-needed day off.

He looked up. 'Not much help, is it. There's something you're trying to say here, but I can't quite figure it out. If only you'd thought to write it in plain English for once. No code, no diversions. Let me know if you ever feel like doing that.'

She turned away and looked across the square, wondering if this was the right moment. When she looked at him again he was still staring at her. He'd forgotten to detach the manufacturer's label from his sunglasses and it dangled absurdly in front of his nose. She tried not to laugh but couldn't help it.

'All right,' she said, her pulse quickening, 'I'll tell you. But it's something that might force us off the tandem and bring all of this to an end.'

'If it's that serious then take your sunglasses off. I want to see your eyes while you say it.'

'You first.'

'Together.'

With their glasses off she felt raw, under observation. It wasn't just Steve. The couple at the next table had stopped eating and were taking a keen interest in their talkative English neighbours. They were almost certainly French. Catherine hoped they were also monolingual.

She drained a glass of water in a single swallow, and began. 'I love the time we spend together. It's the best thing that's happened to me in a long time. I can't explain why we're such a good fit, but I think you know it too. We just are.'

He nodded. 'It's true. But I don't see why that's a problem.'

'Because things aren't the same as they were before.' She looked down at her half-eaten entrée and pushed it away. 'I didn't mean for it to happen but I let something change between us.'

She raised her eyes and risked a glance. He had lifted a forkful of salad from his plate but it was frozen halfway to his mouth. He looked ridiculous and she wished she could make fun of him and change the subject. But she had to press on. 'I haven't been able to get you out of my mind for days. Sitting inches behind you on the tandem is driving me crazy. I can't sleep next to you in that stupid little tent any longer. I think I've completely fallen for you.'

For a moment he was blank, frozen in place while he digested her words. Then his eyes lit up and his face relaxed into a wide smile. He reached across the table and took her hand. 'How long have you been carrying that around inside you?'

'Openly since Sunday. But I'm beginning to think it's been there all along. Does that shock you?'

'Shock me? How could it?'

'How could it not?'

'Because it first struck me the moment I met you in the rain that day in Brittany. And I knew for sure when we had coffee together the next morning. But I couldn't say anything. How could I?'

She raised her eyebrows and leaned back in her seat. 'You might have given me an occasional hint.'

'I did. Again and again. Have you forgotten that night on the banks of the Loire? But after you turned away from that kiss, and said what you did about us just being friends, I knew I would have to let you make the next move.'

'Is that why you've stayed with this crazy cavalcade all this time?'

'Anyone else would have run away screaming after the first week. But I had to hold on to the idea that there would be a moment like this.' He rolled his eyes at her. 'God knows, Kate, it's taken you long enough. There were times when I've wanted to pick you up and shake it out of you.'

She laughed, not quite believing that her fears had been so completely unfounded. 'For days I've been afraid that you'd just shrug me off or, worse still, laugh in my face. I wanted to be completely sure before I said anything. Then it finally dawned on me that you can never be sure, not until it's out there and sitting right between you.'

'How we got here doesn't matter any more. It's out at last and we can enjoy every moment of being truly together.'

She couldn't stand being at the table any longer. The last month of tandeming had turned her into someone who could only think on the move. 'Do you mind if we leave now? I just can't sit here like this.'

From the square they turned into a network of narrow lanes that worked their way between the stone buildings of Sarlat's medieval core. In a parallel world they would already have been arm in arm, perhaps kissing in the pale amber glow of the wrought-iron gas lights. But the circumstances and backstory seemed too much to overcome and she suddenly wanted to be free of the place.

Already there was a new awkwardness between them, an awareness that they were moving irretrievably beyond the safety of their old friendship. Sensing that they needed the familiarity of their old routine, she said, 'I know it's a rest day but we still have the whole afternoon ahead of us. Could you stand to get on the tandem, maybe even make it to Rocamadour?'

'I thought you'd never ask.' Slipping his arm around her, he added, 'Right now, we need to be doing something that comes as second nature. And just let everything else unfold on its own.'

She stopped and faced him. 'There's just one thing I need to know. The other morning in the tent, back in les-Eyzies-de-Tayac. Were you awake? Did you feel my arm around you and deliberately squeeze my hand?'

He looked at the sky and drew in his breath. 'Why does it matter if I was asleep or not?'

'I don't know. It just does.'

He paused, as if deciding what to say. 'If I was awake, then I must have known you were looking for a sign and I gave it to you. If I was asleep then how can I know what was going on in my mind?'

The answer was a fudge but she could see that it was all she would get. She decided to let it go. What mattered was that they were together now.

She leaned close to him and they put their arms around each other and kissed.

16

After hours of traffic-free cycling along the valley of the Alzou, the tandem was flung into a snarl of tour buses, cars and camper vans at the base of Rocamadour's cliffs. The traffic jam and the crowd of pedestrians milling around the car parks were enough for Catherine to suggest delaying their own visit until the next morning. Instead of turning into the village they ground slowly to the top of the cliffs and followed the signs to the nearest campsite.

All afternoon they had struggled to make sense of the new dimension in their relationship. The effort of cycling had allowed them to push it into the background, but once the chores of setting up camp were out of the way, Catherine felt the uncertainty bearing down on her again. It made her dress formally in the off-tandem clothes she'd worn in Sarlat. Steve's response, she saw when he returned from his own shower, was to do the same.

He sat opposite her and watched as she stirred the contents of a large gourmet tin of cassoulet. She had already poured two glasses of wine, and she passed one to him.

'So,' he said, raising his glass.

'So,' she replied, touching hers to his.

From his bar bag he produced a pair of stubby white candles. He pushed them into the ground next to the picnic plates, then struggled to make them catch alight in the breeze. When they were both flickering, he said, 'I thought we should make a little extra effort tonight.'

'It's sweet. You haven't been carrying them around since day one have you, just on the off-chance?'

He pretended to be shocked. 'I found them in the *épicerie* we shopped in on the way out of Sarlat.'

'So you do plan ahead, even if it's only by a few hours. I thought that was totally against your principles.'

'You've somehow developed a completely distorted view of my outlook on life. I do make plans but only enough to ensure that things are moving in the right direction. Which is what the candles are for. There's nothing wrong with adding a hint of romance to a tandem tour.'

'I like the sound of that. It's what I thought the whole bicycle-built-for-two thing was supposed to be about.'

He nodded. 'A candle-lit dinner in a world-renowned tourist location. Fine wine. Tinned cassoulet. I don't see how it could get much better.'

'You are a true romantic after all, Steven Munro.'

She didn't know where the dinner was leading, or whether it was wise to let it go anywhere at all. But she was determined to try letting things unfold, to stop herself from worrying about consequences. The turning point came near the end of the meal, when he put his plate down a little clumsily and knocked one of the candles sideways. They both put a hand out to steady it. He got there first and her hand closed around his. She left it there for just a moment then lifted his hand and kissed the flat of the palm. They drew apart and finished their meal, both aware that it wouldn't end there.

When they crawled into the coffin tent a little later the tiny space seemed almost normal for the first time. They undressed slowly and lay side by side. Then they hesitated, aware that they were on the edge of an irrevocable change. In the shadowy half-light from the moon he looked unusually serious. Catherine felt the same but made herself smile as she ran a finger along the outline of his jaw. He returned the smile then leaned forward to kiss her. The caution left them and they held each other close, losing themselves in the moment.

Afterwards they lay with their heads just inside the open flap of the tent. Catherine felt relaxed and completely at ease as she looked up at the night sky through the partly open fly. Her mind was pleasantly empty and she lay happily in his arms until she drifted asleep.

In the morning they sat with hot drinks in front of the tent. On the ground between them, lying askew in the dewy grass, was one of the candles from dinner. Catherine picked it up and wiped it dry.

'We should keep that,' she said, passing it to him. 'A souvenir from Rocamadour. And we might need it again.'

'I'm sure we will.'

In the next *emplacement* an elderly couple opened the door of their caravan and began to set up a table and chairs a few metres away. They waved and called out their *bonjour*s. Steve returned the greeting. Then, in an aside to Catherine, he said, 'It looks like the neighbours are still talking to us. We must have managed to keep things relatively quiet last night.'

She laughed and reached across to take his hand, weaving her fingers into his. 'It's funny,' she said. 'The tent didn't seem as cramped last night as it did before.'

'I don't suppose that endorsement will find its way into next summer's Cruickshank and Spears catalogue.'

'Hardly. I thought we'd keep this just between you and me for a while.'

'I'm not so sure. I've modified my views on privacy since Brittany. This morning I feel like shouting it from the rooftops.'

'It's a lucky thing then that we don't have a rooftop handy.'

He looked at her with a mischievous grin. 'You're not the only one with a Twitter account, even if mine is practically dormant. It might be fun to see how long it takes to cross the six degrees of e-separation between us. I might even help it on its way with a juicy hashtag. Something like #iloveyoucatherinepringle should do the trick nicely.'

'Not yet, Steve. Please.'

'All right. I'll give you just a little while to catch me up. But not if you're going to waste time worrying about what you've set in motion.'

'I'm just trying to make sure that nobody gets hurt.'

'Nobody?' He pursed his lips and whistled quietly. 'That's a pretty tall order, Kate.'

'Maybe. But that's how I want it to be.'

After breakfast they cycled back to Rocamadour, gliding down the cliff-side road and through the Porte du Figuier into the village.

Inside the gates the crush of tourists made cycling impossible. They dismounted and pushed the tandem along the cobblestones to the Place de la Carreta where they locked it to a lamp post. From there the route into the ecclesiastical sanctuary lay up the hundreds of stone steps of the Grand Escalier. About halfway up, when they had stopped for a photograph, Catherine heard her phone buzz and couldn't resist checking it. There were more than a dozen new messages since her last check in Sarlat, including one from Nick.

'Look at this,' she said, passing the phone to Steve.

He read the message aloud: '*Hi, hope things are going well. Call me as soon as you can. We need to talk.*'

'Not the text, dummy. Look at the time.'

'Last night at 21:55. Maybe we did make the earth move after all.'

She play-punched him on the arm. 'This is serious. Not a word since Saint-Émilion and he suddenly sends a message at exactly the moment we were … you know …'

'You're worrying for nothing. He just happened to call you last night. Not surprising since he hasn't spoken to you for days. Why don't you call him back right now.'

'I don't think I can.'

'Just do it. And try to act natural. You've done nothing to feel guilty about.'

'Guilty? Of course I feel guilty.'

She walked away to give herself a little privacy and pressed Nick's speed-dial entry. She expected to go through to voicemail, and was rehearsing a message when she heard him say, 'Hello, Kate. Where are you?'

'Rocamadour. On the Grand Escalier, going up.'

'Give my regards to the Black Madonna when you get to the top.'

'I'll say hello for you. How about you? Where are you today?'

'About two miles from the ruin of the castle at Montségur. Werner's gone on ahead. I just can't do the climb.'

She paused while she decided how to go on. 'You rang last night.'

'I thought I'd catch you when you weren't busy.'

'Well, you didn't.' She winced at the edge in her voice and tried to soften it. 'What was it you wanted to tell me?'

'Are you still planning to pass through Albi?'

'Yes.'

'Werner and I will be there too. We're meeting a couple of Cathar experts at the cathedral on Monday morning. Stay in touch and we'll meet up with you.'

The news shocked her. She wasn't ready to see him again, not this soon, and her first thought was of doing all that she could to avoid it. 'It's still a few days away. I can't be sure we'll be there if there's bad weather or we have trouble on the tandem.'

'Wherever you are on Sunday night we'll come to you. It doesn't have to be Albi, so long as it's within driving distance.'

Knowing she was beaten, she replied, 'Okay.'

'How is it going?' he asked. 'Just the two of you together the whole time.'

'We're a good team on the tandem. You know that.'

'I know. But this isn't what we planned, is it?'

'No,' she said, feeling more guilty than she wanted to. At the same time she wondered why it took a separation of more than a hundred kilometres for him to talk to her like a human being.

After a pause, Nick said, 'I've been a bit of a shit in the last month, haven't I?'

'I hope you're not expecting me to deny that.' She knew she should say more, that the right thing was to tell him they were both at fault. But she didn't feel ready to concede this. 'And it's more like six months, actually. Maybe longer.'

'I know. And I'm sorry. But that's all going to change. I've been seeing a counsellor for the last week. A German. You might know him.'

The thought of Werner rummaging around inside Nick's mind alarmed her. But she no longer felt she had a right to object. If Nick thought it was doing some good, then she was determined not to say anything against it. Knowing that he was waiting for her to respond, she managed to force a little laughter into her voice as she replied, 'I hope both of you are up to the task.'

She saw Steve pointing at his watch and decided to end the call. 'Look, I've got to go. Let's talk about this in Albi. Take care, Nick.'

She looked ahead of her, up the time-worn stone steps of the Grand Escalier. Minutes before the call she had read that penitents once made the journey up the hundreds of steps on their knees. She wondered for a moment if there was something she should be making amends for. Deciding that there wasn't, she put her foot firmly on the first step and began the climb.

The call with Nick, and the news that they would soon be reunited, brought an edge of guilt to her second night with Steve. It was still good, something she wanted to do. But it came with an awareness that there were consequences, even if she didn't know yet what they were.

The next morning the mood had somehow changed. A sourness lurked around them at breakfast and began in earnest as they meandered along the endless loops of the Lot valley. Catherine couldn't remember what the first niggle was about. It might have been the rain, which appeared without warning after four days of perfect cycling weather. Or perhaps it was the constant, energy-sapping rises and falls in the road as it hugged the river's southern bank. Whatever the reason, they were soon arguing with a passion and she had to live with the suspicion that she had started it.

The sniping intensified after the sharp climb to the plateau of the Causses du Quercy. The rain had evaporated, giving way to an abnormally steamy heat that brought a loud chorus of cicadas out into the roadside fields.

'I hate this,' Steve said, after Catherine had snapped a particularly caustic remark at him. 'We're squabbling like an old married couple.'

'I don't know what the matter is.'

He glanced over his shoulder at her in disbelief. 'You really don't know?'

'I'd say if I did.'

'It's obvious. One phone call from the world's greatest living explorer and everything is turned upside down. You're panicking about seeing him in Albi.'

She started to deny it but knew he was right. It made her even more angry that he could say it so clearly, when she was unable to. 'I know what you're trying to do,' she said. 'Force me into an argument, make me jump into your camp or his. Well, I'm just not going to.'

'Maybe I should do the talking for you then. You're afraid of not taking a chance, of ending up right back where you started. Back on that little strip of flypaper he caught you up in. I have news for you, Catherine. You've worked your way free. It would be really stupid to reattach yourself.'

She leaned back in her seat and let out a long, silent scream. 'Look, I don't regret anything that's happened in the last few days. But I don't know yet what it means. It's all very well for you to say there's no going back. But surely you can see it might look different from my perspective.'

As soon as she had said this, she wanted to take it back. The possibility of going back to Nick hadn't entered her head. She had meant only that the change between her and Steve was so quick that she needed time to absorb it. Finding a new way of saying this without making things worse was beyond her and they fell into an angry silence that lasted until Limogne-en-Quercy.

As they passed its red-bordered road sign, she tapped him on the shoulder and tried to undo some of the morning's spite. 'Let's stop for a while in Limogne. Maybe get some coffee and figure out how to make a fresh start.'

'A fresh start to the ride?' he asked, not ready yet to give up the argument. 'Or were you thinking about something bigger.'

'Just take things at face value. Don't make it any more complicated than it has to be.'

Laughing at this, he replied, 'You're a fine one to say a thing like that.'

The road dropped suddenly into a sweeping curve that brought them to the five-way intersection in the centre of Limogne. Facing them was a row of shops, a mini-supermarket flanked by an *épicerie* and a *pharmacie*. To the right were two cafés, their tables spilling together beneath a pair of pollarded plane trees.

They freewheeled over to a shaded boules area next to the *pharmacie* and leaned the tandem against a low retaining wall. Catherine peeled off her cycling gloves, turned them inside out, and slotted them onto the ends of her handlebars to dry in the sun. Then she unclipped her helmet and eased it off.

Their arrival had attracted the usual attention. Soaked in perspiration, and feeling more than usually vulnerable to the casual stares from passers-by, she turned her back and tried to tease a little life into her sweat-damped hair. The result didn't feel like an improvement and she turned to Steve for help.

'I wish I was anywhere else but on this tandem tour,' she said. 'I'm sick of feeling like a freak every time we reach civilisation. Once, just once, I'd like to waft elegantly into town in a cool summer dress, with flawless hair and perfect make-up.'

She wanted reassurance and a little affection from him, but the running spat had gone too far for that. 'Maybe you should learn to adapt to your circumstances,' he replied, 'instead of hoping for something you just can't have.'

He saw this time that he'd gone too far and tried half-heartedly to make amends. Reaching across, he brushed aside a strand of her hair that had kinked onto the wrong side of its part. It fell forward again over her eye and he struggled not to laugh.

Finally, he said, 'Leave it. I like it like that, anyway.'

'Like what, exactly?'

'I don't know … unforced … free to do whatever it wants.'

She dug into her bar bag for her sunglasses and thrust them on. Then she walked a few paces across the pavement. 'I don't give a damn what you like. I've just about had all I can take of this arrangement.'

'You're not the only one.'

She turned and crossed the road to put some distance between them. She badly wanted to continue the fight, to puncture the smug self-assurance he sometimes couldn't keep to himself. Even more she wanted to convince him, and more importantly herself, of her willingness to change.

She stopped on the opposite corner, aware suddenly that the village's two cafés were on the same side of the road as the tandem. She smacked the palm of her hand against the top of a free-standing sign, irritated that she would have to retrace her steps and probably make herself apologise. Her hand stung where it had landed on the sharp edge of the metal, and she looked angrily at the sign. Shaped like a pair of scissors, it was rotating in the breeze, each puff presenting the word *Masculin* on one side and *Féminin* on the other.

An idea flashed in her head. She turned and shouted, 'You're wrong, you know. I'm perfectly capable of change, of taking all the risks I need to.'

'If you were a risk-taker we wouldn't be having this argument.'

This was the final spur she needed. She turned and walked along a narrow side street until she found a tiny paint-peeled shopfront labelled *A Carnot. Coiffure – Masculin – Féminin.* Standing outside she glanced back at Steve. His arms were folded across his chest and he was watching her closely. Even from a distance the body language was obvious. Flashing like neon, it said: *I know you're bluffing. And so do you.*

Waving to him with exaggerated nonchalance, she forced herself to open the door.

Inside, the tiny space was like a museum. A pair of battered barber's chairs, a fusion of ancient chrome and worn red leather, dominated the shop. They faced a tired mirror that ran the length of one wall, its silver backing blotched and speckled with age. Below this a marble-topped counter was strewn with a jumble of combed and bladed paraphernalia.

An ancient barber was sitting in the chair closest to the window. He was pencil-thin and wearing a crisply starched white jacket buttoned high on his neck. Catherine half-expected the faded newspaper in his hands to be announcing the Normandy Landings or the Liberation of Paris. He rose and, in a sleepy voice, greeted her with, '*Bonjour Madame.*'

Her own voice, when she returned the greeting, was wafer-thin. She suddenly had cold feet, was certain this would end badly. But the thought of Steve sitting outside, expecting her to come straight back out again, made her say, '*Je ... je voudrais ... une coupe, s'il vous plaît.*'

The old man blinked as he decoded her French. '*D'accord.*'

He gestured to the chair he had just vacated and stepped sideways, shepherding her away from the safety of the door. Thinking to herself that she must be mad, she sank into the soft red leather seat and watched as he tossed a striped cape over her. He clipped it around her neck, then took a comb from his breast pocket and tugged it through her hair, combing it forward and searching among the tangles for its elusive part.

Seeing herself in the mirror, her wayward fringe hanging in her eyes, her first thought was to play it safe. Then it struck her. There was nothing remotely decisive about a light trim. She was there to make a statement, to prove she could be bold. And she needed something that would shock Steve into eating his words. With a surprisingly steady voice she assembled a few words of basic French and said, '*Plus court, Monsieur … le tout plus court, s'il vous plaît.*'

She held her nerve through the string of follow-up questions. It helped that she had no idea what the old man was asking. Regular shrugs and repetitions of *plus court* eventually brought the discussion to an end. By then she had convinced herself she was enjoying the experience and was memorising the details for her next blog post.

She watched with a mixture of excitement and dread as he untangled his electric clippers from the clutter of antique equipment on the bench-top. They screamed to life and he made a series of short rapid strokes up the back of her head. In minutes he had cropped both sides as well, exposing her ears for the first time ever. Then he switched to scissors and comb and began a cutting frenzy across the crown of her head. It climaxed with an elaborate multiple-flourish of the scissors that whisked away most of her fringe.

When it was over she saw in the mirror a pale-faced, crop-headed stranger who was biting her lip and staring coldly out into the room. Intense and accusing, it was the gaze of a victim looking for someone to blame. Right at the start, before the first stroke of the clippers, she had briefly imagined something French-chic, a gamine crop with maybe a hint of Jean Seberg in *À bout de souffle*. But the truth was more brutal, a real-world short back and sides that seemed to expose every nerve end. Catherine mouthed an apology to herself and tried to like what she saw. It was shocking but it suited her mood exactly.

She nailed a smile onto her face and kept it there long enough to pay and *merci monsieur* her way to the door. Outside she turned right and walked quickly along the lane away from the centre of the village. Turning into the first street she came to, she stopped and felt the downy softness at the back of her head. There was almost nothing there and she felt tears well in her eyes.

She forced them away and continued around the block, doubling back towards the tandem by another route. Steve was where she had left him, still facing towards the street corner with the rotating scissors. When she was a dozen paces away he did a classic double take, glancing first without a hint of recognition, then turning away and suddenly back as his brain processed the new-look Catherine Pringle. His mouth came open and his eyes widened. The shock on his face was immensely enjoyable, almost worth what she had just put herself through.

By the time she reached him he had struggled to his feet. His mouth was still open and she reached out and pushed his jaw up.

'Don't say anything,' she said, putting her arms around him. 'Not a word. And don't ever accuse me again of being timid, or holding on to things I should let go of.'

He squeezed her and she buried her head in his chest. Then he put his hand on top of her head and felt the softness of the crop. 'I can't believe you did this.'

'Doing it was the easy part. Getting over it is going to be a lot harder. Do you think you can get used to me?'

'You look wonderful,' he replied. 'But it was just a silly argument. You didn't have to do it.'

'I wanted to. There was something I just had to prove to myself. And it's a perfect solution to all that worrying about helmet hair. I just wish I had a week to get myself used to it before we have to meet Nick and Werner. I don't think I can face anyone other than you right now.'

'I wouldn't worry if I were you. They're so focused on the Cathars that neither of them will even notice.'

'You are kidding, aren't you? They'd have to be blind not to spot something as radical as this.'

'I'm serious,' he insisted. 'Five pounds says they don't notice at all. A tenner says Werner mentions it long before Nick.'

She laughed. 'That's almost a certainty. But I have just a little faith left in Nick's powers of observation. Particularly where I'm concerned. You're on.'

17

Albi's cathedral glowed red in the evening sun as Catherine and Steve strolled across the Place Sainte-Cécile towards it. They paused below its sheer brick walls, trying to take in the enormous scale of the building's exterior. Stark but beautiful, it dominated the old core of the city and seemed the perfect landmark for a rendezvous. Until, that is, Catherine turned and looked around her. Almost everything, she realised, could arguably be described as 'just outside the cathedral'. It took a phone call with Nick to pinpoint him and Werner to a bar across the square.

As they approached the outdoor table she turned to Steve and said, 'I've decided I'm going to tell him everything.'

He raised his eyebrows in surprise. 'Are you absolutely sure that's a good idea?'

'Of course not. But I can't face him if I don't. I'm just going to start and see where the conversation goes. How's that for letting things unfold?'

'I'm impressed. Do you want me to be there too?'

She shook her head. 'I need to be alone with him.'

'Then give me a nod when you're ready and I'll think of an

excuse to take Werner away from the table. But not before we settle our little bet about your new haircut.'

He tried to pull her sun hat off but she dodged sideways and walked on ahead, reaching the bar a few strides ahead of him. She encountered Werner first and double-kissed him. After a slight hesitation she did the same with Nick. Waving a hand at the empty beer bottles in front of them, she said, 'So this is what the process of location scouting actually looks like.'

'You should have seen us an hour ago hard at work in the cathedral,' Werner said. 'And yesterday at Quéribus. Tonight we're celebrating ten days of solid effort. What about you? It's going well too?'

Catherine glanced at Steve who had taken the seat opposite her. Turning back to Werner, she replied, 'Steve and I have achieved a surprising amount together. For one thing, more than five hundred kilometres since we last saw you. Compared to before we really are on fire.'

Werner reached across and offered her a high five. 'Five hundred. That's really something. Right Nick?'

Nick had been quietly nursing his beer bottle. 'Not bad,' he agreed. 'It just goes to show you what two sets of good legs can achieve.'

It obviously hurt that his legs were no longer part of the team. But he had a consolation prize and she turned the conversation to that. 'How is your quest for the Cathars going?'

'Perfect,' he replied. 'We've found some excellent locations ...'

'As I knew we would,' Werner broke in. 'This is what brings us to Albi. And, of course, we wanted to see you, dear Käthe.'

Pointing across the square to the cathedral, which even from a distance dominated the open space, he continued, 'We're never out of the shadows of the Cathars. Sainte-Cécile has the beauty, scale and impact of all the great medieval cathedrals. But it's like a fortress too, a daily reminder of the brute force the church could bring against those who sought to resist it.'

Nick leaned forward and said, 'That power is one of the themes we will explore in the series …'

Werner took over again: 'And there is no better example of it than the cathedral in front of us.'

Catherine stifled a laugh. After a week exclusively in each other's company they had almost fused into a single organism. She bit on her bottom lip to keep herself focused but was soon lost in the endless detail they seemed determined to share. Her own social skills had been blunted by ten days of cycling. Behind the cover of her sunglasses she glanced across at Steve and saw that he too was struggling to keep up.

Only half listening, she almost missed the news that had driven Nick and Werner to meet them. Werner was taking his turn with the talking token, and she caught only the end of what he said: '… so Avignon was the obvious place for the conference. We set the dates for the 4th and 5th of August.'

'Conference?' she asked.

'That's what we're calling it,' Nick replied. 'But so long as there are representatives from Balchoffer, Cruickshank and Spears, and the two television production companies, then we'll be happy.'

'What exactly are you talking about?'

'The key people we need. Brendan is confident Aidan Cruickshank will be there. And Karina is almost certainly free.'

'But why would they be coming to a conference?'

'Because we want their money, of course. And we need to convince them to part with it.'

Catherine was still lost. 'You'll have to start again. But keep it simple. We've been in a sort of social bubble for the last week. It's hard to concentrate.'

Nick drew in his breath. He opened his mouth to speak, then leaned forward and stared at her. It was as if he had just seen something different and was trying to decide exactly what it was. He turned suddenly and looked at Steve too, then back at her again, his head cocked sideways, chin lifted, as he tried to sniff out an answer.

'It's really very simple,' he said, eventually. 'Werner has kicked off discussions with a couple of media production companies. They're interested and are willing to come on board. But only if we can show that we've got the funding package in place.'

'Which is where my darling Karina comes in,' Werner added. 'And of course Aidan Cruickshank. We've proposed an investment partnership, a fifty-fifty split between them. They're going to meet us in Avignon to talk it through. If we get lucky they'll sign on the dotted line straight away.'

'I suggested the location,' Nick said. 'It's perfect from a tandem tour point of view. Just thirty kilometres from Pernes-les-Fontaines.'

'From where?' Steve asked.

'My cousin Richard and his wife Lucy run a gîte business at Pernes-les-Fontaines. We can all stay there during the Avignon meeting. And when it's over I'll be free to rejoin the tandem.'

'Rejoin the tandem?' Steve looked darkly at Catherine, clearly expecting her to respond. When she didn't, he added, 'One of us must have made a wrong assumption about that.'

Nick smiled cryptically at him. Then, gliding over the difference of opinion, he turned back to Catherine and asked, 'Can you be there by the 2nd of August?'

She shrugged, still trying to catch up. The conversation had taken a very different turn from the one she had imagined. 'We're nothing to do with the Cathar thing. Why do you need us?'

'Aidan still thinks I'm on the tandem. Brendan warned me it isn't a good idea to let him in on the secret just yet. He's got to believe in us totally if he's going to commit funds to the Cathar project. We don't want to give him the impression I'm not a reliable investment.'

'And are you?'

'Reliable? I've always thought so. Why? Do you think I'm not?'

'I'm not sure any more. I was hoping you might say something definitive that would help me make up my mind.'

Werner stood and stretched. 'If you two are going to have one of your spats, I might take the opportunity to go indoors and powder my nose. Then I think it's time we found somewhere for dinner.'

'I'll join you,' Steve said, also rising and looking pleased to make his escape.

'Let's leave these two lovebirds to get themselves reacquainted. No?'

Catherine dreaded what was coming. She sipped on the last of her beer, delaying the beginning of her confession for as long as she could. The hesitation was fatal. Nick leaned forward in his seat, clearly spoiling for an argument. Choosing what she thought was safer ground, she said, 'You and Werner are closer than ever. I'm finding it pretty hard telling you apart.'

'In case you've forgotten, I'm the one you came to France with.' He stared at her for a moment and she wondered if he was going to say something about her and Steve. But his expression softened and he added, 'Coming on the back of the accident and last year's trouble in South America, it's just such a relief to have something go right for a change.'

'Do you think you can get this documentary off the ground?'

'Werner knows what he's doing. He's done it all before for German-speaking audiences. Last night he even sounded me out about co-presenting the English language version with him. Of course, we'll need a third person, a woman to balance the on-air team. I'm leaving that to him to sort out.'

She imagined what it would be like for the stranger who would complete this on-air threesome and was glad it wasn't her. 'I'm happy for you Nick. I really hope it comes off.'

He picked at the foil around the neck of his beer bottle. 'How about you? You didn't really say much on the phone the other day.'

She shrugged. 'It was awkward. I was in a crush of tourists.'

'Werner's going home after Avignon. I'll be completely free again.'

The implication was obvious and they both let it hang between them. Eventually, she managed, 'And you still want to come back onto the tandem?'

'There's no reason not to. My leg is stronger now. I want to do the ride north.'

'It's not about what you want any more. I told you that back in Bergerac.'

He leaned forward and put his hand on hers. 'Kate, the two of us can make it work again. We could reset the clock, begin again as though it was two years ago and we were meeting for the first time.'

This was so completely unexpected that she found herself abandoning any thoughts of a confession. She nodded non-committally and was relieved when she saw Werner and Steve emerging from the bar.

They set off through Albi's pedestrianised zone in search of a restaurant. Werner drew Nick ahead early on to point out the architectural features on a succession of medieval buildings along their route. Catherine and Steve lagged a little behind. When they were out of earshot he asked, 'Is everything sorted between the two of you?'

She shook her head, being careful to avoid his eyes. 'I just couldn't do it. The whole thing suddenly seemed like a bad idea.'

'What whole thing? You and me being together? Or you

telling him about it?'

'Don't you start on me too.'

'I'm just looking for a little reassurance. I wasn't bothered either way about you telling him tonight. But now that you're hesitating, it's starting to seem important.'

She stopped and faced him. 'Steve, nothing has changed. Nothing. Please believe me.'

'I want to, I really do. But I'm beginning to get a little nervous. When, for instance, were you going to tell me that Nick might go north with you on the tandem?'

'It was the only way I could get him to keep paying your expenses from his travel budget. And I didn't mention it because I really didn't think it would come up again as a possibility.'

He looked hard into her eyes. 'Maybe you're just not ready to burn your bridges with him. If that's the case, I'd rather know it now than find out later.'

Catherine stepped back, shocked at the thought. Then her chest tightened as she began to wonder if there might be some truth in this. 'It isn't like that at all. At least I hope not. But letting someone you've cared for go, even when you know you have to, isn't easy. Especially when they unexpectedly pop up again as soon as you think they're out of the way.'

'Look,' he said, his face softening, 'this is the wrong time to talk about any of this. All we need to do is get through tonight and be on our way. We can figure this out when we're alone again.'

She nodded, and put her arm through his, hoping that the gesture would reassure both of them. 'And I say nothing about us to Nick?'

He squeezed her hand. 'Just keep your lips sealed. And remember the old saying: Careless lips kill tandem trips.' Smiling, he added, 'Besides, I've still got a five-pound bet with you and I want to see how it turns out.'

'No.' She touched the brim of her hat for comfort.

'Come on. It's almost dark. Even two men with their heads trapped in the history books will soon wonder why you've still got a particularly wide-brimmed sun hat screwed to the top of your head.'

He reached up and whisked it off. They wrestled over it for a moment until she realised that her security blanket was gone for good. She gave up and walked on ahead of him.

Werner and Nick heard the commotion and turned together. It was impossible to tell who noticed her hair first, but Werner was the first to react. His face widened into a grin and he walked back to her. 'Käthe! It's fantastic. What a little fox you are hiding it from us like that.'

He put his hand on top of her head and stroked it. 'That's really cool. And it suits you too. Right, Nick?'

This was the moment when she clearly saw the difference between the two men. Werner was unfailingly generous and had set out to make her feel good, regardless of his real opinion. Nick lagged well behind. He couldn't bring himself to come closer. Instead he stood back for a more objective, and disapproving, appraisal.

When the silence became noticeable he glanced at Steve. It was an accusing look, as though he was sure that Steve was somehow responsible. Then he turned back to Catherine and asked, 'What made you do it? And when?'

'Yesterday. It was just one of those spur-of-the-moment things. I wanted to make a statement, to do something recklessly bold, something that said things are different now. Do you think you can come to like it?'

'Of course he does,' Werner cut in, anticipating the void. Putting his arm out to escort her, he added, 'He'd be crazy not to. Come on. Let's find that restaurant. And on the way, you can tell me how the whole thing happened.'

After dinner, as they returned to the campsite, Werner insisted that all four of them sleep in the Balchoffer tent. Catherine was only too happy with the arrangement. Her official reason was that she could for once sleep on a proper mattress. But it also avoided having to make an overt choice of sleeping partner, something that had been worrying at her since Nick's call in Rocamadour. In the end they all slept together in separate corners of the Balchoffer tent's main living space.

Catherine woke early, shortly after Werner and Nick, who crept from the tent around seven. She waited a few minutes until she was sure they had gone, then followed and made her way to the toilet block. As she returned she encountered them in a vacant section of the campsite. They were midway through a set of callisthenic exercises and she watched as they performed a mesmerising rhythmic routine with Indian clubs.

When it was over, Werner left Nick to continue with his knee exercises and jogged over to greet her. 'Käthe, I was wondering if you'd like to walk with me over to the *boulangerie*. We can have a little talk on the way.'

Intrigued, she agreed. He ran back for a shopping bag, then rejoined her and they made their way out of the campsite.

'I love this time of the morning,' he said, after a few minutes. 'I can see that you do too.'

'In the beginning it was the only time of the day I could have to myself. Now it feels completely natural. So much has changed in the last six weeks. I don't know if I can go back to the person I was before.'

'Don't ever go back to anything. That's not what life is for. I think of myself as being like a kayaker descending through the rapids on a river. Going back upstream is never an option. Not if you want to stay dry and upright, that is.'

She stopped and looked at him, wondering what, if anything,

he was trying to tell her. But he had his aviator sunglasses on and his deadpan face gave nothing away.

Suddenly, he asked, 'What exactly is going on with you and Steve? If you don't mind telling me.'

Stunned, she struggled for a response. Seeing this, he continued, 'You're not denying it, at least. I'm pretty sharp at seeing this sort of thing. But with you it doesn't take much of a gift. It's obvious a mile off.'

'Does Nick know, do you think?'

'It may look like we've got our heads full of Cathars, but we're not stupid. Although, in his case, he seems a little less gifted emotionally than yours truly. But anyhow, it's as plain as the noses on our faces.'

She burst out laughing at the unintended clumsiness. Werner smiled. 'Laugh all you want, Käthe. It doesn't change the facts already.'

'I thought six weeks ago that Nick and I just had to spend more time together and all our problems would go away. Instead we seem to have gone our separate ways completely. Maybe we just have to admit that we are happier apart.'

'Being in a relationship isn't all plain sailing. I've given up a lot – and I'm not just talking about my name here. But I know Karina and I are always there to support each other when it counts. I wish it could be like that for you and Nick. If you try to stick it out with him, there's a chance of that happening. But if it isn't to be, the two of you have got to think about moving on.'

'I wonder if it isn't too late already. Maybe it was all along, before we even came to France.'

'All these maybes make it sound like you still have some thinking to do. Take my advice, Käthe. Use your journey along the Tarn like a trip into the wilderness. Get deeply in touch with what you really want. And make sure you make a firm choice and then stick to it. Nobody should waste time being unhappy. Not you, and not Nick.'

She waited outside the *boulangerie* while he bought the bread and croissants. She needed time to reflect on what he had just said. But she was also afraid that he might try to continue the therapy session while queueing for bread.

As they began the return journey, she said, 'It may not seem like it, but the last thing I want is to hurt Nick. He's had a pretty rough time in the last year.'

'I know. But working with me is good for him. He's changed even in the few weeks we've been together. If the two of you are going to part, then I'll be there for him.'

'Has Nick talked to you about any of this in the last week?'

Turning to her, he replied, 'That's between him and me. Just as this conversation will stay between the two of us. If you want to know what's inside his mind then the easiest way is to ask him yourself.'

Left on her own she might have avoided doing so but, shortly after breakfast, Werner manufactured an opportunity by asking Steve for help to repack the vast quantity of equipment in the trailer attached to his car.

Alone with Nick, Catherine opened out a map and showed him her planned route through the Gorges du Tarn and along the Corniche des Cévennes. He listened with close attention and offered a little information about places of interest on the way. As she noted them down she felt his eyes on her. She looked up and caught him staring at the top of her head.

Suddenly it mattered that in the twelve hours they'd been together he hadn't managed a single comment about her hair. Determined that he say something, even if it was bad, she stared directly at him and said, 'You still haven't told me if you like my new look.'

'I thought we told you last night.'

'No, that was Werner. You were very careful not to say anything at all. Here's your chance now.'

When he hesitated, she jumped in. 'I'll help you get started, shall I? Saying that you like it is obviously too much of an ask, so how about we stick to something more your style. Try getting this out: Catherine, that's the most practical and efficient haircut you've ever had. Think of the time it will save every morning. We can get earlier starts. Cover more distance. Well done, you.'

'Stop it, Kate. I'm sorry. I should have said more last night. I was lost for words. I still am.'

'Then just say the first thing that comes into your head. I won't complain, so long as it's the truth.'

'All right. It's amazing. How's that?'

'Thank you. Anything else?'

He thought for a moment, then added, 'You look so different. It gave me a shock. And it made me wonder what else has changed. But it doesn't have to be permanent, nothing that's happened in France is. There's another five or six weeks left before you're back home. You could be halfway to looking like your old self again.'

To stop herself from biting back she looked down at the map. She folded it angrily and thrust it into the bar bag. Then she turned and began to push anything within reach into a pannier. When she felt she could speak, she said, 'I was wrong about you and Werner being alike. For one thing, he understands that I'm never going to be my old self again. And he wouldn't have it in him to say it the way you just did. Not without coating it in chocolate first.'

'Well, you and I don't do chocolate coating. We never have.'

'Do you know, I'm beginning to wish we did. No-holds-barred darling this and my sweetest that. Maybe, just maybe, if you were a little more like that, I could stand to get on the tandem with you again.'

'We could try. Both of us. Equal partners, just like we agreed on that first day in Brittany. All the choc coating you want too.'

'Nick, no offence, but how could I even be sure you'd stick with me all the way to the end?'

He bristled. She knew that questioning his commitment was striking at his core. He rubbed the thigh of his injured leg and was about to snap a reply at her, but she held up her hand. 'I'm not talking about your commitment to travel or rising to a challenge. It's your commitment to me I'm wondering about. I think you'd be more inclined to want to finish the ride if I wasn't on it too.'

He looked away and she knew she was right.

When he turned back, he said, 'I never quite adjusted to travelling with you. I didn't get a chance. From day two there's always been someone else around. And I haven't really been all that sure you wanted me. It began to look like you were happier in the company of my stand-in.'

It was her turn to look away. She was ashamed, not of the things she had done with Steve, but of her inability to be completely honest. In minutes she had turned an opportunity to be straight with him into another argument. She hated herself for it but couldn't seem to stop. 'I don't know exactly when things started to go downhill between us,' she replied, 'but it was long before we came to France. And probably before your Amazon trip too.'

'Then we should both make one last effort. From Avignon it's maybe three days' ride north to Lyon. We could stop there for a few days, just the two of us. Treat it as a fresh start, get to know each other again, then go home together. What do you say?'

His eyes were imploring her to agree, and she realised there was still something about him that she found hard to dismiss. But the realist in her needed more than half-promises. 'Tell me you're not just saying this because you want Aidan Cruickshank to see you riding north from Pernes-les-Fontaines on the tandem.'

'That's part of it, I can't lie about that. But I do want us to try again. I really do. Being apart for the last ten days, it's given me a chance to reflect a little. To see things from outside my normal perspective. Werner's good for helping with that.'

She laughed. 'I don't have any trouble believing that.'

'I feel like I'm slowly coming alive again for the first time in a year. And I want us to have a shot at things being the way they were before. You don't have to say yes now. Just tell me you'll think about it. You owe me that, after everything we've been through together.'

'All right,' she replied, conscious that she was taking the easy way out again. 'But don't ask me for an answer right now. We'll talk about it in Pernes.'

She turned and saw that Steve was standing just a few metres away. He was staring directly at her and it was obvious that he had heard a good deal of the discussion. She looked helplessly at him, tried to transmit an apology, to tell him that he shouldn't believe what she had just said to Nick. But in a crushing gesture, one that she realised she probably deserved, he shook his head sadly at her before turning and walking away across the campsite.

18

East of Albi, along the valley of the Tarn, Catherine felt for the first time a cumulative exhaustion from constant travel. With more than six weeks of cycling behind her she had developed the strength and stamina for a challenging ride, but her reserves were being more easily drained. It was partly the landscape: still beautiful, but stark and imposing, a barren valley squeezed between towering limestone cliffs. The weather was harsher too, with temperatures reaching thirty degrees on most days.

The hardest demand was on her mind. The easy nature of riding with Steve was still there. They were still a good team, always knowing instinctively how the other felt. But after Albi the talking seemed to dry up. For hours they rode in an unspeaking companionship – the sparkle was gone, at least in part, evaporated by the heat.

The void was filled by the voice in her head, and this was interested solely in the choice she would soon have to make. For the two days of the journey through the gorge she replayed the conversations with Werner and Nick, and tried to unpick the emotional knot she had tied herself into.

Werner's talk about always flowing in a new direction seemed to counter any thoughts of staying with Nick. It felt that he was saying she had to move on. But the discussion with Nick and his talk of making a new start together had completely surprised her. She wanted to believe he was capable of such a change. The ideal Nick, the man she used to think he was, certainly would be. The reality of him was more complicated. He was cast in a certain mould, one that worked for him and the solitary life he liked to live on the road.

In the deepest and starkest section of the gorge, just downstream from Sainte-Enimie, she let all of her worries go and returned once again to the simplicity of being on the tandem with Steve. It wasn't perfect – there was an air of uncertainty now that hadn't existed before, but she tried not to let it intrude. If the journey around France had taught her anything, it was that living in the present mattered more than fretting about the past or worrying about the future. She realised that, whatever happened, her approach to life would always be different now.

She finished the ride drained but certain that she had emerged tougher and stronger. She had also reached a decision about the journey home and turned to Brendan for the help she needed to make it happen.

'I'm going north on the tandem with Steve,' she told him in an early evening call from Florac.

'Steve? I don't see how that's possible.'

'It's possible all right. And it's going to happen.'

After a short silence, he asked, 'Have you told Nick?'

'Not yet. Not in so many words. But he agreed in Bergerac it was my decision who rides the tandem home.'

'I don't know how you got that idea into your heads. This is a Cruickshank and Spears sponsored ride, not some jolly that you can stop and start whenever you want. Nick had no right to let you think it was your decision.'

'Bren, I kept this trip going when he was ready to quit. Are you telling me that counts for nothing?'

'That's exactly what I'm saying. One day, maybe, we'll tell everyone all about it. And they'll pat you on the back and say how grateful they are. But, right now, nobody at C&S knows a thing about it. Believe me, you don't want them to. Are you forgetting the contract you signed?'

'That was just a formality for insurance cover.'

'Don't pretend you're that naive, Kate. They'll sue the lycra pants off you if you do anything to disrupt the tour.' Softening his tone, he added, 'I know this is hard for you but Nick has to get back on the tandem. His job depends on it. The Cathar thing has complicated everything. Aidan won't commit funds to it unless he's convinced Nick is someone who will see things through.'

Catherine played her only remaining card. 'If he stays, then I go.'

'Think about what you're saying. For a start it really would mean Nick losing his job. And probably the Cathar opportunity too. Then there's your own job to think about. Liz might be a friend but she'll still chew you up and spit you out when she finds out everything you've kept from her over the summer. Do you really want all of that to happen?'

'I'm just tired of the whole deceit. It's so complex, it's become three-dimensional. I want it to stop.'

'It will. And soon. But what you're proposing isn't the right way. Look, it's only a couple of days till Avignon. Just put your head down, grit your teeth and grind it out till then. Let me see what options I can pull together for you in the meantime.'

From the Cévennes they detoured south to the marshlands of the Camargue and Aigues-Mortes.

With daily temperatures now in the mid-thirties it might

have seemed like madness to extend the ride by another hundred kilometres. But Catherine had succumbed to the temptation of seeing the Mediterranean. When Steve suggested it she had agreed immediately. She wanted to be alone with him just a little longer, to indulge in the illusion that they might go on as they were forever. It was also an excuse for delaying the arrival in Pernes-les-Fontaines, a thought too attractive to ignore.

During one of the post-lunch siestas they'd taken to having on long riding days Catherine checked her phone and saw that she had several new messages from Liz. They had been out of touch for days, mainly because of a reluctance on Catherine's part. She was losing interest in delivering the kind of personal detail in her blog posts that Liz wanted from her and had grown tired of filtering the content down to material that gave nothing away. The flurry of texts felt like a warning sign that reality was about to catch up with her.

Knowing she would soon have other things to occupy her, she decided she had to tackle the problem head on. She took a breath and made the call.

'What a surprise,' Liz said acidly, when Catherine finally got through. 'I was beginning to think you'd met with an accident. Something that prevented you from pressing the speed dial on your phone.'

'Nothing like that. Just incredibly focused on the job. And I can't always get a signal.'

'Be honest, Kate. You're avoiding me. And that has me wondering if there's a reason.'

There was just a hint of a suspicion that Liz knew something, but Catherine stuck to her story. 'The last week has just been extremely demanding. That's all.'

'For both of you, I expect.'

'That's right. For both of us.'

'You used to call every few days. Then, after Sarlat, nothing.'

'I know how busy you are.'

'People read a lot into the spaces, the words others choose to leave out. One of our readers – one of yours actually – happened to point that out in an online comment yesterday. I don't suppose you've seen it since you can't get a signal. She analyses text and has put together some interesting charts and graphs from the content of your daily blog.'

'Like what?' Catherine knew exactly what was coming, had read every word of the comment.

'Little things she says add up to a pattern. Some of it is trivial, but still revealing. For instance she sent me some interesting data on word frequency. Words like *we* and *Nick* have fallen through the floor in the last two weeks. The analysis gets a lot more complicated than that. In fact, she thinks there are factual inconsistencies too. It's all nonsense, I suppose.'

'Absolutely. Like I said, I'm just tired. Both of us are.'

'Maybe I can say a quick hello to Nick now. Ask him how he's holding up after six solid weeks on a tandem with you.'

'He's just gone into a *supermarché*. His turn to buy the supplies. He should be back out in ten minutes if you want to hang on.'

It was a calculated risk but one that paid off. 'I'm about to go into a meeting. Maybe next time.' After a pause, Liz added, 'Kate, forget for a minute that I'm your editor. I'm concerned for you as a friend. If you need to talk to someone, I want to know that you feel you can call me.'

'Of course. You know I would.'

'Well, I'm asking now. Is there anything you want to tell me?'

'Nothing.'

'You're sure?'

'Completely.'

In the silence that followed, Catherine felt utterly ashamed. She knew that Liz could sense there was something unsaid, and that she was on the point of demanding to know everything.

'All right,' Liz said, eventually. 'There's one other thing, and this is with my editor's hat on. Just a bit of a heads-up. The editorial team is worried about the quality of your Saturday column. It's been a little pedestrian since Saint-Émilion, like you've distanced yourself from it. We need a lot more pizzazz if we're going to keep running it. I'm sorry, but the next one is make or break.'

'Just give me a few more days. Once we get to Pernes-les-Fontaines, and I have a few days off the tandem, I'll get my head properly back together. I might even concoct one or two juicy confessions for you, if that's what you really want.'

'That's more like it. I knew you wouldn't let me down. Give my love to what's-his-name.'

'I think the name you're searching for is Nick.'

'Oh yes. It was on the tip of my tongue. You should mention him in your blog more often, so I don't forget.'

The struggle across the sun-baked marshlands of the Camargue was worth it. At Saintes-Maries-de-la-Mer they saw for the first time the pale blue waters of the Mediterranean, washing ashore on a sandy beach below the town. Catherine knew in an instant that she wanted a photograph of the tandem at the water's edge. It was a cliché but an irresistible record of the outward journey's end.

Forcing the fully loaded cycle across the soft sand was hard work but soon they were only a few metres from the sea. Their route took them past an elderly couple who were sitting on the last ridge of dry sand. Steve *bonjour*ed and made a camera gesture with his iPhone and passed it to the old man.

They turned the tandem broadside on and triumphantly faced the lens. When the photographs had been inspected and approved, they left the tandem lying on the beach under the watchful eye of the couple's poodle. Then, still in their cycling clothes, they raced into the water.

Catherine plunged under the surface, then came up and floated on her back. After a while, Steve surfaced beside her. 'Thanks for suggesting this,' she said, 'It's beautiful.'

'And worth the last two thousand kilometres?'

'God, yes.' She thought about the last six weeks in France, and about the time she had spent with him on the tandem. It meant everything to her and she felt tears welling in her eyes. Wiping them away as best she could with wet fingers, she said, 'I'm so proud of what we've achieved together.'

'It's a wonderful feeling. A sense that together we could tackle anything and succeed.'

She rested a hand on his shoulder and kissed him. Then they floated on their backs and looked out to sea. After a while, Catherine felt the wave of satisfaction ebb a little and a seeping return to reality. 'Today's the last day in July.'

'Is it? I'd completely lost count.'

'It's also the turning point, the furthest we'll ever be from home. Every kilometre from now on takes us back.'

In a mock German accent he replied, 'I told you already, Käthe, you should never go back. Always go forward.'

'Be serious for a moment. Listen to me. I've made my decision. It's over between me and Nick.'

'So this isn't the end of the ride. We're going north together after all.'

'I didn't say that. I'm splitting with Nick but I still have to finish the trip with him. I have to.'

He ducked his head under the surface and was gone for a while. When he resurfaced he was a few metres away and had to swim back to her. 'You've got a funny way of breaking up with people. What do you expect me to do in the meantime?'

'You might start by showing a little understanding.'

He stared at her, then slowly shook his head. 'Sometimes I think you're way too complicated for me. And for your own good. Liz knew exactly what she was doing when she picked you for the summer column. You're guaranteed to create a fresh dilemma every day of the week.'

'Leave her and the paper out of this. I'm just trying to make things work for everyone.'

'Well I wish you'd stop.' He let his head sink underwater again. When he resurfaced, he said, 'Kate, I don't want to do this. Not here. Not tonight. We have two more days together before Avignon. If that's all we're going to have together, I don't want to waste a moment of it arguing.'

She let out a gasp of frustration and swept a handful of water into his face. 'Is that how it would always be with you? Just drifting through life, making sure to avoid anything that's difficult.' Turning away, she began to breaststroke towards the shore. Over her shoulder she added, 'Enjoy the rest of your swim. Stay in as long as you like. But don't come out until you're ready to talk it through.'

She waited for him on the soft sand beside the tandem. When he joined her, the poodle rose from its resting place next to the front wheel. It snarled at him and looked about to sink its teeth into his ankle until its owner hurried over and dragged it away.

When they were sitting side by side, facing the sea, Steve said, 'Kate, the last couple of weeks have been fantastic. I don't want it to stop. But, frankly, I'm not sure we can escape from all the baggage that's stuffed into the panniers of this journey.'

'Do you wish we could?'

'Of course. I want to go on with you to the end.'

'And after that?'

'I don't see a difference between now and what comes after.'

'You might not, but I do. A tandem tour isn't real life, it's just a time away from it.'

He shook his head. 'Nothing is more real than what we're experiencing now. We're more alive, more full of feeling and emotion, than we could ever be in London.' He reached across and rested his hand on hers. 'But we need to stay together until we're sure we can make it last.'

She pulled her hand free and ran it through her hair, tugging at it until it hurt. 'I can't let Nick lose his job, or the chance to do the documentary. I don't want that on my conscience.'

He looked intently at her. 'And if I asked you not to get back on the tandem with him?'

'It's something I have to do.'

'Then let me make it really clear. A nice, simple choice for you to chew on while we finish the ride to Pernes. I don't think we'd survive if you spent another month with him. So, if you go north with Nick, then I'm moving on. I won't be around when you get back.'

She turned to face him, expecting him to break into a smile and tell her he hadn't meant it. But his face had an edge that only occasionally revealed itself. He was deadly serious and wasn't going to change his mind. 'What are you saying, Steve? Is it that you don't trust me to stick to my word?'

He looked out to sea and stared implacably into the distance. 'Catherine, I don't want to lose you. I really don't. But if you're not willing to choose me and let go of everything else, I don't see what there is to talk about.'

'So. No pressure, then.'

'No. No pressure at all. Him or me.'

She took his hand. 'I'd rather make you happy than anyone else, but forcing me into such a black and white choice is the wrong answer. I won't stop looking for a practical solution that works for all of us. Until I find it, you'll have to be happy with the thought that you're my tandem captain of choice.'

He smiled back at her, then turned to watch the waves run gently ashore. Catherine thought there was just a hint of sadness in his eyes, as though he wanted to believe it was going to work between them, but was sensibly reserving judgement. She let the thought go, and turned towards the sea too, reassuring herself that she could somehow make it work.

My Tandem Tour de France
By Catherine Pringle

Day 45, Monday 01 August
Arles

I realised somewhere deep in the valley of the Tarn that life really is just like a cycle tour.

It sounds almost Forrest-Gump-like in its simplicity, but the plain fact is, it's true. What works on a tandem works in real life too. Which means that my Golden Rule of Cycle Touring applies off the bicycle as well as on.

The Golden Rule? Never miss a chance that comes your way.

I learned that weeks ago in the middle of a long, hot cycling day, when we encountered a possible detour to a château that I really wanted to see. An extra hour of cycling when we still had a long way to go seemed too much, and we both said no. I've regretted the decision ever since. I thought it didn't matter, that we might be back another day, but let's be honest, that was never going to happen. I should have insisted, and I won't make that mistake again.

It matters in relationships too. And everything to do with relationships is magnified on a journey like this. When it's going particularly well a tandem makes it seem even better. You feel so close, so perfectly synchronised, that you wonder why you would ever want to do anything on your own again.

When it's not working – and believe me, there are days when even the closest couple might end up killing each other – that's a day when the Golden Rule definitely applies. Miss your chance, put it off when you need to get to the source of the problem fast, and you're going to regret it for a long time to come.

I say this, because there's something worrying away at me that I should have dealt with back in Albi. That's five hundred kilometres of regret, more than enough to spin it into a tight little knot that's sitting deep in my gut. I won't do it again – my opportunity is coming in Pernes-les-Fontaines, and this time I swear I'll grasp it with both cycling mitts.

Saint-Émilion to Pernes-les-Fontaines

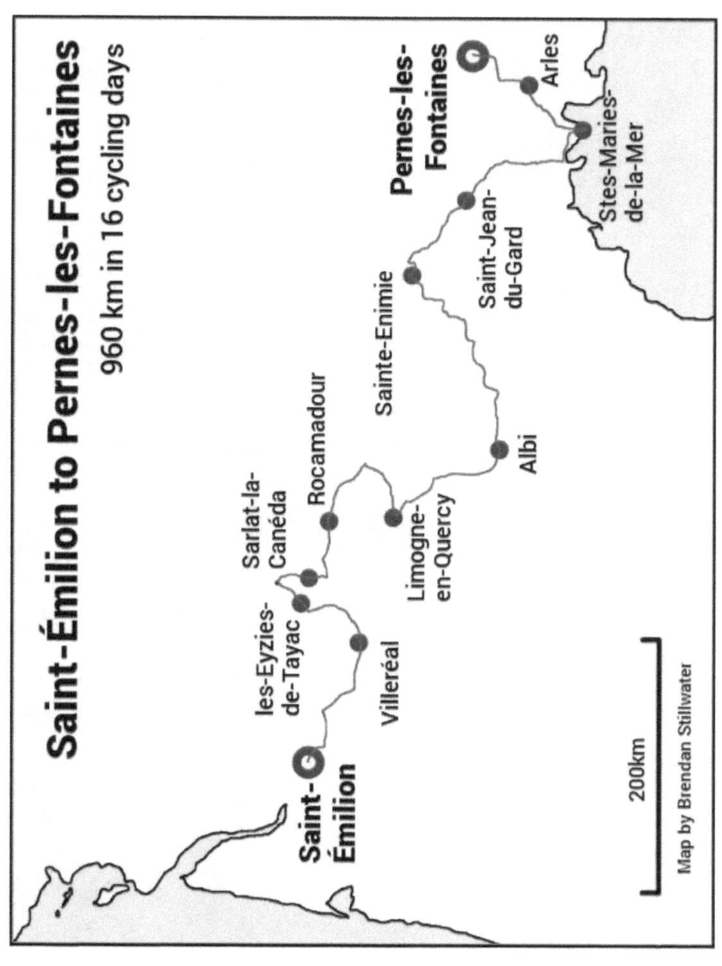

Whatever it takes

19

The Maison de la Vieille Vigne ranged along the western slope of a short ridge about a kilometre south of Pernes-les-Fontaines. It lay well away from the main road along an unsealed track that cut through a field of sunflowers and a small vineyard. After the last row of vines the track squeezed between a pair of tall stone gateposts and opened into a small courtyard that was bordered on three sides by the main farmhouse and its adjoining outbuildings.

Steve guided the tandem towards a shallow fountain that stood in the centre of the courtyard. He and Catherine rested it against the pool's retaining wall, peeled off their helmets, and looked at each other, aware that things between them would never be quite the same again. She took his hand but, before she could speak, Lucy Farne appeared at the open front door of the farmhouse. Wearing a light summer dress, and with her dark hair bouncing on her shoulders, she crunched in sandals across the gravel towards them.

She stopped suddenly when she saw Catherine. Her eyes widened and her mouth fell open. 'My God. Is that really you,

Kate?'

Flushing, Catherine ran a hand across the top of her head. After ten days the übercrop showed no sign of softening. On the road it hadn't mattered but among friends again the extra attention was something she would have to endure.

They hugged, then Lucy put her hand up and felt Catherine's hair. 'I had no idea France would change you so much.'

'It's nothing compared to what's going on under the surface. I'm almost a different person.'

'It feels amazing. I read your blog post about it but I didn't really believe it could be as short as you said.'

Catherine pretended to be hurt. 'I'm beginning to get a little paranoid. You're the second person in as many days to question the accuracy of my blog.'

'You have been known to exaggerate things just a little. I thought that's why people read your stuff.'

Lucy turned to shake hands with Steve. Smiling, she said, 'And this is the man who saved the whole tour.'

'Now you've caught the exaggerating bug,' he replied. 'The truth is, I just helped out a little from time to time.'

'That's not how Nick tells it. He makes it sound like you're the perfect stand-in.'

'He's not perfect by any stretch,' Catherine cut in. 'The more you get to know him the more trouble he turns out to be. Is everyone else here already?'

'Almost everyone. Nick and Werner got in around this time yesterday. Brendan this morning. And Karina is due tomorrow just before the conference starts.'

'It's like Grand Central Station.'

'I know. Luckily we're in the gîte business. I wish it wasn't true in midsummer but we have tons of room this week.' Looping her arm through Catherine's, she added, 'Come on. Let's get out of the sun. We'll find Rich and he can show you where you're sleeping. I should warn you. Uncle George is here.'

Catherine stopped and faced her.

Lowering her voice, Lucy continued, 'He came down in June and shows no sign of wanting to go home.'

'How are you coping?'

'Oh, you know. It's always good to have at least one loose cannon rolling about the place, isn't it?'

'He's your Uncle George?' Steve asked.

'Oh my God, no. He's Nick and Richard's great-uncle. The only one left from that generation of the family. Unfortunately he loves France and we have so much room. So he manages to get himself down here most summers. He's having his afternoon nap right now so you should be in the clear until pre-dinner drinks. Plenty of time to get your stories cross-referenced and fact-checked before then.'

'Stories?'

Lucy grinned. 'Just a figure of speech, Steve. He might be in his nineties and half-blind but he can sniff out a vulnerability in seconds. You'll see. The great thing about having so many extra people around the place is that Rich and I can have a few days out of the spotlight to rebuild our shattered psyches.'

Being in a group again was like stepping into an alien world. After three weeks alone on the tandem with Steve, Catherine's grasp on the rules of social interaction had been seriously impaired. She made it through the next few hours mostly by just listening, or agreeing completely with whoever was doing the talking. But the tactic began to wear thin. It was a great relief when, on the dot of seven, George Farne's approach to the farmhouse's main reception room was telegraphed by a series of banging doors, creaking metal, and the squeaking of rubber on bare floorboards. Catherine, who knew exactly what was coming, glanced across the room at Steve. He looked completely baffled and she had to turn away to stop herself laughing.

The door flew open, revealing an ancient, spare-framed man sitting stiff-backed in an antique wheelchair. His hair and moustache were blizzard-white, a complete contrast to the mottled flush of his cheeks. Despite the heat he had dressed in shirt, tie and navy blazer. His lower half was draped in a tartan travelling rug that somehow managed to draw attention to, rather than conceal, the space where his left leg should have been.

'Well, get on with it,' he snapped at the room. 'Haven't you seen an old fool in a wheelchair before?'

Nick, who was nearest the door, limped across to hold it open. 'Had a good rest, did you, Uncle George?'

'I'm completely rejuvenated, you'll all be delighted to know.'

Nick stepped aside as the wheelchair bore down on his shins.

'Shut the door behind you,' George ordered as he rolled past. 'There's always a tremendous draft swirling about this bloody place.'

Watching Nick, who still relied on a walking stick, shuffle back across the room, George slapped the side of his chair and added, 'Anyway, what's the matter with you? You look like you need one of these things.'

'My accident, remember. We talked about it last night.'

'There's nothing in the official log about an injury.' He looked sharply at Catherine. 'I've been through everything she's written from Brittany to the Loire. Nothing. Therefore it can't have happened.'

Catherine managed a smile. 'I didn't realise you were following my column so closely.'

'I wasn't. I don't normally read the papers and I wouldn't touch the rag you work for. I just wanted the facts, but it seems I'll have to root them out on my own. Now come and kiss me.'

Catherine kissed the side of his cheek, catching with her lips a patch of bristles that had escaped his razor. 'How are you, Uncle George?'

'I'm fine,' he said, smiling for the first time since entering the room. 'Don't fuss about me. I'll outlive you all. Stand back so I can take a look at you.'

She straightened and waited while his milky eyes swept over her. 'What have you done to yourself, girl? You're completely different.'

She rubbed the back of her neck, conscious that he was about to be brutally honest about her hair.

'I don't mean that,' he added. 'Perfectly functional. I just hope you didn't give the perpetrator too much of a tip. No, there's something else.'

'Probably just all the exercise I've been getting. And living the outdoor life.'

He chuckled, and jerked a finger at Nick. 'The outdoor life doesn't seem to be doing him much good. He leaves England hale and hearty, steps ashore in France, and next thing you know he's walking like a bloody cripple. Still, can't hold that against him. Much the same thing happened to me, only it was Normandy in my case and not Brittany.'

He wheeled his chair around until it was facing Steve. 'And who are you?'

'Steven Munro, sir.'

Catherine stifled another laugh. It hadn't crossed her mind that Steve would ever address anyone as sir. Uncle George had his back to her and she took the opportunity to come stiffly to attention and mock-salute Steve, who quickly lowered his eyes.

'Pleased to meet you, Steven Munro,' George continued. 'Now get out of the way. You're standing in my spot.'

Steve looked dumbly down at the floor as though it might actually reveal a marker. 'I'm sorry,' he said, making way for the old man, who swung around and reversed into position with his back to the wall.

Catherine watched as Richard Farne handed George a large whisky. The two men were so alike that they might have been father and son. They had the same piercing eyes, prominent cheekbones and solid jawline. There was also a strong family resemblance to Nick, who was a slightly smaller and much lighter-framed version of the other two.

'Thanks Rich,' George said, after taking a large swig of the whisky. 'I see Nick's German friend is still here too. *Guten Abend, Herr Balchoffer.*'

Werner snapped his heels together and inclined his head. Then, after a carefully snatched glance at Catherine, he responded in a theatrically German accent. 'Nick's uncle and I are already old friends. This is so, yes, Herr Farne?'

'I suppose we are, Werner,' George replied. 'I don't as a rule like Germans much. But with you I can't seem to help myself.'

Wheeling around to Steve, George added, 'I suppose I can understand what the German's doing here. But why an Australian? Come over here Steven Munro and tell me your story.'

Relieved that she had dropped under the radar, Catherine turned away and joined Lucy. They grinned at each other, then Lucy rolled her eyeballs. 'He's been reading every word you've written since the day he got here. I have to open it up on the iPad for him every morning. A typical Farne. Thinks that being blunt with both barrels is an acceptable substitute for honesty.'

'If I'm even partly responsible for him learning how to use an iPad, I'll consider the last couple of months a complete success.'

'Rich will make sure Werner sits next to him during dinner. That should give everyone some breathing space. If you feel like escaping come and give me and Rich a hand in the kitchen.'

At the dinner table Catherine found herself separated from Steve by a buffer of Farne children. She lapsed into an uncomfortable silence, struggling still for topics of conversation that didn't involve being on a tandem or at a campsite. When one of the boys asked a technical question about brakes and gears she was grateful for the chance to talk about something that easily came into her mind. She was well aware of the irony: two months earlier she would have been hard-pressed not to yawn if someone else had droned on about it for longer than a few seconds.

At the far end of the table George continued to tease anyone who crossed his sights. Mostly it was Werner but occasionally, just for added entertainment, it was Brendan or Steve. The latter continued to come under scrutiny solely for his presence. 'What I don't understand is why they need you on a tandem tour at all. There's already the two of them. What exactly is the point of you?'

Steve laughed as he aligned his fork and knife on the empty plate. 'I'm beginning to wonder that myself. In the beginning, after Nick's leg injury, they needed me to help carry their gear.'

'Leg injury! Leg injury! You can't be serious.' Whacking his hand against the rug on his lap, George added, 'This is a leg injury. Nick doesn't know what he's talking about. And neither do you.'

Catherine glanced across the table at Nick. They burst out laughing together and for a moment there was a hint of the way they used to be, before France, before the Amazon. Still laughing, she looked down at her wine glass and wondered at the lost year they had gone through together.

As Lucy and Richard cleared the entrée plates Brendan walked across the dining room and leaned down to whisper in Nick's ear. Feeling excluded, Catherine said, 'You two look conspiratorial.'

'What the hell are you talking about up there?' George cut in, sensing that something was afoot. 'Can't stand whispering.

Speak up.'

Brendan sighed. With a deliberately raised voice, he said, 'Aidan Cruickshank just called me. He's arrived at his hotel in Avignon and wondered if he might drop by to meet everyone tonight. We were just discussing what to do. Can't really say no, can we?'

He looked at Richard, who smiled and replied, 'He's welcome to join us for coffee. The more the merrier.'

Brendan opened a door and went out onto the terrace to make the call. As he did so, George Farne shouted after him, 'Don't suppose I get any say. If that little runt Cruickshank is coming, then I'm clearing off to bed early. I'd advise the rest of you to do the same.'

For a man whose family fortune depended on the great outdoors, Aidan Cruickshank managed to look completely ill at ease in it.

Watching him across the terrace, deep in conversation with Nick and Steve, Catherine could see in his every gesture just how uncomfortable he was. It was partly his build, a spare, hollowed out, almost desiccated look that gave the impression he had been stored in a cupboard well past his use-by date. Even the gentle moonlight filtering through the vine leaves above them seemed too harsh for his complexion. His clothes accentuated the problem. He had chosen from the C&S summer catalogue a coral pink sleeveless T-shirt and matched it with a pair of lime-green cargo trousers that zipped off at the knee. It was a look, Catherine thought, that no man in his late sixties should attempt to carry off.

From the far side of the terrace, where she sat with her back against the stone wall of the barn, she watched the three men lean closer and share a whispered joke. As they laughed at the punchline, Brendan appeared on the terrace. Nick shuffled over to speak to him, leaving Steve and Aidan to carry on a short, intense conversation. Catherine watched it unfold on Steve's face, seeing the tiny tells that she now knew so well – the arching of his right eyebrow, a lifting of the chin. He was interested but trying not to show it. When Cruickshank finished talking, Steve gave a half-shrug, then he beamed and nodded. Whatever the question was, he was saying yes.

Catherine sensed suddenly that she was under observation. She turned and saw that Nick was watching her in the same way that she had been looking at Steve. Embarrassed, she rose and strolled out into the shadows where the terrace ended and the garden began. She found a dark corner and sat on the top of a low retaining wall. The moon had waned since the Cévennes and she stared intensely at it, longing to be back at the campsite in Florac, lying in front of the tent and listening to Steve read from Stevenson's travel memoirs.

She heard footsteps on the gravel and looked up, expecting Nick. Instead it was Aidan Cruickshank.

'It's Catherine, isn't it?' he said, as he lowered himself onto a flagstone next to her.

'That's right, Aidan,' she replied, wondering why he seemed to be having trouble placing her. 'It's quite a different setting from the last time we met.'

'What's that? Yes ... I suppose so.'

'The C&S Christmas party. Last year.'

'Oh, of course.'

Realising that Cruickshank was still completely lost, she gave up and sipped on her coffee, waiting for him to take the initiative.

'I'm very impressed with the work you're doing on this tour,' he said, eventually.

'Thank you. But it's not that special. We're not exactly crossing oceans or hacking our way through impenetrable jungle.'

'Never understate a personal achievement. In my experience there are always plenty of other people willing to do that for you. When you get all the way around France you'll be in reasonably exclusive company. It's a feat that requires effort … tenacity …'

He ran out of praise. Catherine smiled at him vaguely and wondered where the conversation was going.

'I'm told,' he continued, 'that it can be pretty hard to settle back into normal life again. When a thing like this is all over.'

'It's funny you should say that. I was just having the same thought a few minutes ago. I don't think I want to go back to what I was doing before.'

'Which is?'

'I write for a newspaper. I used to call it journalism, maybe it once was, but I've realised recently that it's mostly just content. Padding for an already over-bloated internet.' More seriously than intended, she added, 'If I stopped doing it tomorrow, I don't think anyone would notice.'

'Then what would you like to do? If you were given the chance.'

'Anything else.' After a moment, she shook her head. 'No, that isn't true. I want to make a difference, find more serious issues to write about. Just about anything would tick that box. Perhaps the environment, or climate change. Or something about the life journeys people make. You know, the search for meaning.'

This seemed more than Aidan wanted to know. Resurrecting his own theme, he said, 'I just wanted to let you know that I appreciate your efforts. And to say that Cruickshank and Spears is always looking for ways to nurture talent such as yours.'

She looked at him for clues to his meaning but his face remained pale and impassive. 'I'll bear that in mind, Aidan.'

'I'm serious, Catherine. I want us to find a way to bring you into the orbit of Cruickshank and Spears. Just as soon as you and

Nick are back. Which is when?'

'The end of August.'

'Good. Then come and see me at the beginning of September.'

Bewildered, she watched him make his way across the terrace to Brendan and Werner. Having shown absolutely no memory of meeting her before, he had suddenly segued into a job offer. It was too confusing and she stared up at the moon again, wondering if it wasn't full after all.

She was still smiling at the heavens when she sensed someone else at her side. It was Fi, Aidan's personal assistant. In her mid-twenties, with an easy confidence in any situation, she had a well-deserved reputation for sweeping up in Aidan's wake. Catherine had met her several times but they had somehow never quite clicked.

'Private joke?' Fi asked, as the smile faded from Catherine's face.

'Afraid so, Fi.'

'Pity. I could use a laugh after the day I've had. For a man who runs an expedition and adventure business he really doesn't travel at all well.'

'Then sit down and take a load off your feet.'

Fi sat beside Catherine and they looked awkwardly at each other. 'It's great to see you again, Kate. Love that tan by the way, and the hair of course. So incredibly brave. I don't think I could ever put myself through a thing like that.'

It was nearly an hour since Catherine had felt awkward about her hair. She watched Fi flick and preen her own expensively sculpted and probably extension-rich locks, and wished she'd shown a fraction more caution in the barber's chair at Limogne. Cooling even more towards the young woman next to her, she replied, 'Please, let's talk about something else. I'm just liable to start weeping if we don't.'

'Actually there is something we need to talk about. It's a little delicate, I'm afraid.'

'Fire away Fi. Give it to me straight. No need to hold back.'

'I saw you talking with Aidan a moment ago and I was wondering if you wouldn't mind telling me what he said.'

'Oh, you know. It was mostly just two travellers exchanging stories about being on the road. He was telling me how much everyone at C&S thinks of me.'

'And we do. We do. I was wondering if he might actually have mentioned the possibility of you coming to work for us.'

'He might have.'

'The thing is, Kate, Aidan being Aidan and all that, he's not really up to speed with the constraints of our current business position. We're not actually hiring at the moment – if anything, it's a bit the other way. Sorry. I hope he hasn't offended you. He'd be mortified if he thought he had.'

Catherine put her drink down and rubbed the back of her neck. 'Thanks for telling me, Fi.'

'I'm so sorry.'

'How did you know?'

'Aidan is a serial hirer, always trying to expand what he calls his talent pool. He's like a vast creative engine that's been hooked up to a tender with hardly any coal in it. He doesn't realise the delicate state we're in. Take this Cathar thing with Nick. There really isn't any money for it. I can't see how Aidan will persuade the rest of the board to invest. Not unless Nick proves he's capable of delivering. Which, to be honest, isn't the first thing people associate with him after that little episode in the Amazon.'

'I don't really see how the two are related.'

'Aidan was less than thrilled when he found out tonight that Nick has been carrying a serious injury since day two. To him it's a loyalty thing. He doesn't mind what people get up to so long as they don't keep things from him.'

'You're saying that Aidan won't commit the money to the documentary unless Nick finishes the tour?'

Fi shrugged. 'He can be frustratingly hard to pin down, a complete mass of contradictions. But I think he will turn it down unless Nick gets back on the tandem and rides all the way to a Channel port. I just wanted you to know how important that is.'

The conversation was straying into territory that Catherine wanted to avoid. She looked across the terrace at Nick and Brendan, who were deep in conversation again. Brendan had his arm around Nick's shoulder and was gesturing with his fingerless hand as he talked. As he spoke, he glanced at Catherine but quickly turned away when he saw that she was watching.

Smiling innocently at Fi, Catherine asked, 'Did anyone ask you to tell me this?'

'Kate, I don't know what you're talking about. Looking after Aidan is more than a full-time occupation. I haven't got the spare energy for anyone else's little schemes.'

'My mistake, Fi. Thanks for clarifying the situation.'

Rising, Fi smiled and said, 'No problem. Good luck with the rest of your journey. I'm following it eagerly on your blog.'

'You might read about this then.'

'I hope not. That would be even more problematic for Nick. I'm not the only one at C&S who reads your every word. Now I must go. It's way past Aidan's bedtime.'

Fi walked back across the terrace and rejoined Aidan. She leaned close to him and whispered in his ear. Seconds later he detached himself from Nick, Brendan and Werner. Gesturing at his watch, he made his excuses and left.

With its bare walls and floors and its cavernous barn-like spaces, the farmhouse at night was like a giant echo chamber, full of woody creaks and groans. Even the rubberised scuffling of

George Farne, wheeling himself along the wooden corridor on his regular visits to the toilet, reverberated through every corner of the guest wing.

Unable to sleep indoors after a month in a tent, Catherine dozed fitfully. In the periods when she was awake she listened to Nick's light snoring and wondered how she had come to be sleeping in a bed with him again. It seemed wrong, just as it would also have been wrong to sleep at the farm with Steve. She had planned to find a corner of her own, but on arrival, when Richard had shown her into Nick's room, she hadn't been able to make the announcement without telling Nick first. With so many other people in the farmhouse there had been no time alone with him and the situation had been impossible to correct.

Lying next to him, she tried for a while to match his breathing, thinking it might relax her into a slumber. But the more she tried, the more the knot of frustration grew. After hours of not sleeping, when the first light of the new day began to play through the uncurtained window, she rolled out of the bed and crept from the room. She went slowly downstairs, taking care to make as little sound as possible, and walked carefully along the hall to the kitchen.

Opening the door she was surprised to find the room already occupied. Uncle George was wheeling himself towards the cooking range. He had a small tray with a teapot on his lap.

'Come in, come in,' he barked, only just keeping his voice low enough to stay inside the room. 'And shut the bloody door or you'll wake the whole house.'

She did as she was told and crossed to the sink where she poured herself a glass of water.

'Looks like we're the only ones up,' George said. 'Us and that boyfriend of yours.'

She shook her head. 'Nick's still asleep.'

'Not him. The other one.'

'You mean my cycling partner, Steve?'

'Call it whatever you like, my dear,' he said, pouring water into the teapot. 'I'm not one to make judgements. It's none of my business what you do together, is it?'

'Then why did you say what you just did?'

'Decades of sitting in this bloody chair with nothing better to do than watch people. You get to know how to read them. And the signs with you two are like a beacon. I even gave him the chance to state it to the world last night at dinner.'

'When you asked what the point of him was?'

He nodded. 'He had his chance and he blew it. The question is why.'

'Left to himself he would have said it without hesitation. I'm surprised he didn't. I think he was protecting me.'

'And your excuse is?'

'I don't have one. Maybe I'm just stupid. What I want seems to have gotten all caught up in my obligations to others.'

'Well, both of you should learn to say what you mean. Then get on and live life like there's no tomorrow. At the end of the day that's what counts the most.'

The door opened and Steve slipped into the room. Surprised to see Catherine, he smiled as he walked over to the range.

'It's going to be a beautiful day,' he said, checking the kettle. Satisfied there was enough water in it, he set it back on the hotplate.

'I wouldn't know,' George replied waspishly. 'I can't exactly get all that far into it.'

'I'm sure you could find a way if you really wanted to. I'm available for the next couple of days to take you anywhere you feel like going.'

George ignored him and continued to stare at Catherine. She wondered if he would try to say anything to Nick about her and Steve. Behind the bluster the old man had a sensitive side and cared about his extended family, particularly Nick and Richard.

Realising she was unlikely to guess his intentions, she turned to Steve and said, 'I guess Nick is going to be pretty busy for the next few days with the conference in Avignon. I don't suppose you'd like to do a short tandem ride each morning, just so I don't forget how to make it work.'

'Missing it already?'

'More than I can put into words.' She noticed that George was still watching them and wished that she and Steve were alone.

Reading her mind, the old man said, 'Just pretend I'm not here. Talk about whatever you want.'

He held up the teapot and shook it. She nodded and crossed to the cupboard for the mugs. As he poured the tea, he added, 'I suppose you're going down to Avignon with Nick for the presentation.'

'He hasn't asked me to. The Cathar proposal is very much his thing – him and Werner.'

'Oh, I'm sure he'd want you there.'

'Do you really think so?'

George shrugged. 'Just a feeling I've got. He told me yesterday how he felt he'd let you down in the last few weeks. He's not much of a talker any more, never had my sort of people skills, but I got the impression he'd really like your support.'

She looked at George and wondered why he was telling her this. It seemed impossible that Nick had asked him to, and George wasn't the type to take direction from anyone. She concluded that his words were genuine. 'I really hadn't planned on going anywhere near the Cathar meeting. But maybe you're right.'

Steve joined them at the table, a mug of coffee in his hand. He said, 'You'll never guess what happened to me last night. I've been offered a job.'

'Aidan Cruickshank?'

'Yes.'

'Me too. Shame it all came to nothing.'

'What do you mean?'

'You know – Fi trailing around in his wake retracting the offer.'

'That's the funny thing. She did exactly that. Had a quick chat with me, told me what's what. Then a few minutes later, Aidan came back over and said to ignore what Fi had just told me. The offer still stands.'

'It does?'

'He wants me to meet him next week.'

'He's staying on in France?'

Steve shook his head. 'He meant back in the UK. He wants me to go and see him at the Cruickshank and Spears head office next Monday.'

'I see,' Catherine said. She felt a sinking in her stomach. 'And you're going to go?'

'So far, it's the only firm offer I've got for next week. I can't afford to say no.'

20

From her seat at the side of the hotel's conference room the Cathar pitch looked to Catherine like an extremely low-budget episode of *Dragons' Den*. Aidan Cruickshank, with his imaginary pile of family wealth, and Karina, with her stash of chocolate money, were the key players in the room. They sat side by side at the top end of the conference table with their respective acolytes arranged to each side. The remaining seats were allocated to representatives of the two television production companies, one English and the other German.

Werner opened the conference, deploying all of his charm to welcome the group. He came quickly to the point, telling Aidan and Karina directly that he and Nick wanted their money, and plenty of it. Watching him work the room with the same ease he had shown when they were travelling together, Catherine decided he was just the kind of talent she would want to take a risk on. If she had her own pile of cash, which she didn't. And if she really was a taker of risks. Which, given the way things were working out, it seemed she wasn't.

Nick took over after the opening statement. He started

quietly and a little hesitantly, and it looked for a while as though he would suffer in comparison to Werner. Gradually he found his pace and began to talk with a growing passion about the project. Soon he was making well-timed jokes, mostly at Werner's expense, and the audience began to warm to him.

Catherine wondered as the morning progressed why she saw so little of this side of him. Then it dawned on her. He only came to life when presented with an all-consuming challenge. Long-distance tandem travel in France, a major effort for her, was a mere trifle for him. Then there was her presence on the tour, a constant reminder of his relegation to the lower leagues of adventure travel. It was obvious now that he couldn't be happy unless he was thousands of miles away, climbing a personal mountain on his own.

At noon the meeting reconfigured for a working lunch. Catching up with Nick, she congratulated him on his performance. He was still flushed with the success of the morning and thanked her warmly. Then he insisted that she take the afternoon off, telling her there was nothing coming that she hadn't heard already. They engaged in a quick serve and volley of refusal and insistence, a game she made sure to lose graciously.

As he walked her to the door, he said, 'Thanks for coming, Kate. You didn't have to but I really appreciate it.'

'I'm glad I did. I got to see you full of enthusiasm again. You're quite impressive when you get going like that.'

'I feel as if things are beginning to come good again. Like I've suddenly got hold of something I was afraid I'd lost forever. The ride north will be so different. I'm sure of it.'

She kissed him on both cheeks and left him at the door of the hotel. Another opportunity to announce that it was over between them was gone, but the timing would have been cruel.

Unexpectedly alone, she strolled down to the Rhône and walked a few spans out onto the Pont Saint-Bénezet. Watching the fast-flowing river beyond the last broken arch, she thought about her overdue blog post and tried to find a topic that would be both neutral and interesting enough to keep Liz's superiors at arm's length. A tour group with an English-speaking guide arrived on the bridge and she decided to attach herself to it. She followed them as far as the Rocher des Doms gardens, then peeled off and sat at a bench in the shade.

As she worked on a draft of a post about travelling in a group, a message came in from Lucy. She was in Avignon shopping and about to leave for Pernes-les-Fontaines. On impulse Catherine texted back to ask for a lift.

Stepping onto the terrace at Pernes, Catherine saw Steve lying in the shade on a recliner. She crossed to him and pulled a chair close to his. They said nothing at first, each content to enjoy the other's company. After a while Catherine reached out and took his hand, weaving her fingers into his. 'It all feels so unreal, like I have one foot in two very different worlds.'

'You just picked the wrong thing to do with your day, that's all. I spent a very normal and pleasant morning with Uncle George down at the lake. It turns out he's a bit of a dark horse. He might only have one flipper but he can swim like a fish. I had a hard time keeping up.'

'What kind of an Aussie are you? Letting a one-legged old man best you in the water.'

'It was almost enough to make me experiment with performance-enhancing drugs. Still, after I let him win, we had a really good chat. He told me why he's going to be giving the two of us a pretty hard time if we don't do what he thinks we should.'

'We meaning me, I suppose.'

He grinned sheepishly at her. 'Well, we did more or less agree that you were the main problem.'

'It wouldn't take a genius to work out what he wants. He is Nick's uncle, after all.'

'That's where you're wrong.'

'What then?'

'I'm not about to tell you for free. You've got to earn it.'

Catherine frowned at him. 'Come on Steve. I've already had a hard day. First I sat through another round of Cathar history. Then on the drive home with Lucy I suddenly burst into tears. It was so bad she had to stop the car and let me out. I ended up standing waist-deep in a field of sunflowers weeping more water than an agricultural sprinkler system.'

He laughed. 'I can't say I'm totally surprised. I hope you found it cleansing in some way.'

'I think so. Maybe not as much as I need, but it was a good start.'

He put his arm around her shoulder and pulled her a little closer. 'Will you miss me next week?'

'Of course I will. The thought of it is making me miserable.'

'We always said it was just about living in the now and not thinking about later. I suppose we just reached the end of now sooner than I expected.'

She lifted her head and looked at him. 'It's not like that at all. Do you think I want you to go?'

'But you don't want me to stay either.'

'I have obligations I can't ignore.'

'I know all of that. That's why I'm clearing out, to let you get on with it.'

When she didn't object, he said, 'A little bit of me was hoping you'd make a scene. Maybe fall to the ground and wrap your arms around my leg.'

'If you think it will help, I'll gladly do it.'

He shook his head. 'It's best that you don't. Apart from anything else, Uncle George and Lucy are watching from opposite wings of the farmhouse. Between them, they won't miss a moment of the action.'

Absorbing this, she leaned across and kissed him. It was short and sharp, full of emotion, and it took him completely by surprise. Pleased with the effect, she said, 'That should get our audience thinking.'

'It's got me thinking too. But, I'm still leaving.'

'Will you do something for me before you go?'

'Of course. Anything.'

'Come with me on one last ride together. Tomorrow.'

He glanced at the window on the far end of the terrace. Then he nodded, and quietly said, 'Uncle George really will approve.'

'He will?'

'He thinks we should do anything to stay together. But that we're too stubborn to agree on how to make it happen. Behind the harsh exterior, it turns out that George Farne has a very soft centre.'

'That almost makes me want to go north with him instead.'

Steve turned and looked into her eyes. 'As if a choice of two partners isn't complicated enough for you.'

On the tandem the ease of being together was stronger than ever. The ride north through Châteauneuf to Orange felt like the best of their cycling. They spent hours in Orange, longer than they should have, abandoning the tandem and strolling around the town to explore its Roman sites. At lunch Catherine almost gave in, was on the verge of asking him to stay on. But there didn't seem to be a solution that would make it work.

On the return journey they stopped on the edge of town at the Roman arch. Steve stopped a passer-by and asked him to take a picture of them astride the tandem with the monument in the background.

'I'll email it to you if you like,' Steve said to Catherine, when he had selected the best shot.

'I'd like that, thanks.'

This short exchange marked the beginning of a sudden formality, as if they were on the way to being mere acquaintances again. The professional distance remained with them for the whole of the ride back to Pernes, a confirmation that they were leaving something behind in Orange. It was almost a relief when the farm and its buildings came into view. They rolled into the courtyard, dismounted and wheeled the tandem into the barn.

'Thanks Steve,' Catherine said, as they walked out of the barn. 'I'll never forget a single day of our time in France.'

He turned and stared at her. It looked like he was going to reopen the discussion about the ride north, so she pulled him into an embrace. They were still together like this when the Balchoffers' car crunched into the courtyard. It slid aggressively to a halt, leaving two long furrows of gravel between the fountain and the farmhouse. When the driver's door opened it was Karina, not Werner, behind the wheel. She waved and hurried over to join them, followed at a distance by Aidan Cruickshank.

'Hey there, you two,' she said, greeting them with more passion than usual. 'Having a good day, I hope.'

'We're just back from a ride up to Orange,' Catherine replied.

'Lucky you. I almost wish I'd come.'

'Tough day at the office, Karina?'

Karina only had time to roll her eyes before Aidan caught up with them.

'Aidan,' Catherine said a little coldly, the puzzle of the retracted job offer still in her mind.

'Catherine.' He looked pleased that he had remembered her name. 'Still cycling, even on your day off?'

'I could go on doing it forever. Given the right sort of company.'

'And Steve. Getting yourself ready for the return journey, I imagine.'

Steve shrugged. 'I haven't really thought about it yet. Too busy enjoying the last of my time in France.'

'Well, don't forget,' Aidan added, as he turned towards the house. 'I'm expecting to see you on Monday.'

When he was gone, Karina said, 'What a bore he is. Completely self-centred. He spent the entire journey in the car putting me and my company down. He's got the idea, somehow, that Balchoffer is new money because we were founded as late as the mid 1800s. His ramshackle lot has its origins only forty years earlier. Honestly, I tell you, I'm almost ready to turn the car around and leave.'

She realised that Catherine and Steve were staring at her, and began to laugh. 'Listen to me. Competing on how old our stuffy family companies are. I need you to stop me, when I get so utterly ridiculous.'

'It's just a reaction to another two days of Cathar proposals,' Catherine replied. 'I think I might have gone over the edge if I'd sat through the whole thing again.'

'My beloved is depending on my money, so I had to stay. Otherwise ... ' She shrugged her shoulders.

'Have you and Aidan come to an agreement on the funding?'

'That's the reason we were in the car together. The decision will be announced tonight.' She turned as Brendan's Land Rover crunched into the courtyard. 'But first, I think I need to lock myself away for a while. Get me some much-needed Karina time.'

The participants from the two-day conference assembled on the terrace at Pernes-les-Fontaines for drinks and a buffet dinner. Despite the setting's informality there was a tangible air of tension, heightened by Werner and Nick who started to drink heavily as soon as they arrived.

The need to indulge seduced Catherine too, although for her own very different reasons. Wine glass in hand, she circulated freely. She even had a reasonably light-hearted conversation with Aidan, during which she teased him about the retracted job offer. He was adamant that there had been some kind of misunderstanding but the ever-attentive Fi rescued him before the issue could be resolved.

Shortly after, Catherine was joined by Brendan. She was aware that he had been avoiding her for days, the result, she thought, of his failure to come up with an option that would mean she could go north with Steve. Not that she blamed him. There just wasn't an answer that would work.

'So, Kate,' he said, tentatively. 'This Cathar sideshow will be over tonight. One way or another you can put it all behind you.'

'I hope it's that easy. Nick and Werner have been together every day since Augmont. Five full weeks. The day after tomorrow will be cold turkey for both of them. Imagine what it's going to be like for me and Karina having to nurse a recently separated twin.'

'You'll have some adjusting to do, too. You've changed in eight weeks. Which is only natural. That's what this sort of travel does.'

She smiled at him. 'The wisdom of a man who has walked from Cape Town to Cairo.'

'Alexandria actually. But the marketing people thought Cairo sounded better. They wanted me to stop there, but after three years on the road, I wasn't about to let anyone else tell me what I could and couldn't do.'

'I didn't realise,' she replied.

'Cape Town to the Med. That was the plan. It mattered to me that I stuck to it.'

Catherine emptied her glass. 'You're telling me I need to stick to the plan too. Pull myself into line, get back on the tandem with Nick and finish the job.'

'I'm not *telling* you anything. I'm hoping you will want to do it. But it has to be your choice.'

'My choice!' She realised she was shouting, but didn't care. 'I don't really remember having any serious choice since we landed in that ditch in Brittany. Every step since then has been a consequence of that. Okay, maybe there was one thing I chose all by myself. But that doesn't seem to have worked out quite the way I wanted it to.'

She was interrupted by the rumbling of a muffled gong at the far end of the terrace. They turned to see Aidan Cruickshank banging tentatively at a large brass disc with a felt-covered hammer. He was standing beside Karina, who looked as though she wanted to rip the instrument from his hand and do the job properly.

'Gather round please,' Aidan said, gesturing with his hands for silence. 'Karina and I would like to make an announcement.'

When he had everyone's attention, he continued, 'We've listened with great interest to the proposals put to us over the last two days, and are pleased to announce that the Balchoffer AG and Cruickshank and Spears Ltd have taken the decision to jointly fund a series of six programmes on walking in the Cathar country. Congratulations Werner and Nick.'

After a round of applause, Lucy and Richard emerged from the kitchen carrying trays of champagne. When everyone had a glass in their hand, Karina lifted hers and said, 'Please join us in a toast to *Walking the Cathar Country*.'

After the toast Aidan called for silence again. 'I would also like to draw attention to the other work that Nick is doing on behalf of Cruickshank and Spears.

'For the last seven weeks he has been travelling in France with his partner Catherine Pringle. As we are now aware, they suffered a serious setback in Brittany when Nick injured his knee. Despite this they have stuck admirably to their task and are just about to begin the return journey. I'd like to propose a second toast to the completion of this venture, and to single out Nick, who has struggled on despite his injury and somehow kept the journey on track.

'So, a toast to the successful completion of the tandem journey and to the professionalism of Nicholas Farne. The tandem journey and Nick!'

As glasses were raised, Catherine's simmering anger reached boiling point. She opened her mouth to object, but stopped when she felt Brendan's hand on her shoulder.

'Kate,' he said, his voice low against the buzz of conversation. 'Please. Don't make a fuss right now.'

'Why shouldn't I?'

She drained her champagne glass and tried to take a fresh one from Richard who was passing with a tray. It was just out of reach and she steeled herself to face Brendan with nothing more than an empty glass in her hand.

'Without you,' he said, 'this tour would have come to an end long ago. We all know that. Even Aidan. What he was really saying is that the funding for the documentary is there so long as Nick finishes the tandem tour.'

'I don't have a problem with that. I'm happy for Nick. It will take a load off his mind to know he's still a major catch in Aidan's talent pool. I just can't stomach the inaccuracy of it. Listening to him, you'd think Nick carried the weight of the whole trip on one leg. The truth is, he was more interested in Werner and his project than making the tandem ride work. Steve and I kept it going.'

'And we all appreciate it. But Aidan can hardly say it in public, can he? Behind the scenes he's making sure Steve is looked after.'

'You mean the job offer?'

He nodded. 'And I think there might eventually be something

for you too. If that was what you wanted.'

'A job?' She gave a snort of contempt. 'You must be kidding. Why would I want to work for an oddball outfit like Cruickshank and Spears?'

'Maybe eccentric is a better choice of word, something we can all coalesce around. Anyway, who said anything about a job? That was never on the cards.'

'But we talked about it last night. And Fi made sure it was retracted.'

Brendan chuckled as he realised how the misunderstanding had arisen. 'I think Aidan has something entirely different in mind. He's on the board of a mid-sized publishing company, one that has an imprint specialising in travel. This is going to be the deal: they'll offer you a tempting advance for a tell-all book about the tandem tour. If you complete the ride with Nick.'

It was clearly a bribe, one that Catherine couldn't help being interested in. Lucy passed with another tray of champagne. Brendan took two glasses and handed one to Catherine. Her head was already spinning and she struggled for a response to the book offer. 'So, you think I should just smile sweetly, climb onto the back of the tandem, and ride quietly north.'

Brendan sipped at his champagne. 'How do you feel about doing exactly that?'

'I don't feel like it at all. But I'd already decided I wasn't going to let Nick down. So the bribe is unnecessary.'

'There you go picking confrontational words again. It's not a bribe. Think of it as a bonus for completion. You won't turn that down, surely. Now drink up and we'll go and talk to Steve.'

Catherine lost Brendan on the journey across the terrace. She found Steve in the crush around the buffet table. He had an arm around Fi's shoulder and their heads were conspiratorially close as she laughed exuberantly at something he was saying.

Instantly jealous, Catherine stopped in her tracks. She tried to logically process what she was seeing, but her mind, addled by champagne, flooded with the darkest thoughts about Fi.

Before she was ready Steve turned and caught her lurking behind him. 'Enjoying your favourite view of me?'

'You with your arm draped around another woman? I don't think so.'

'I meant all of that sitting behind me on the tandem, staring longingly at the back of my head.'

She saw now that he had been drinking heavily, and hoped he was only using Fi as a physical means of support. But the smile on his face was a little too knowing, and she realised he might deliberately be trying to make her jealous. Deliberate or not, it was working.

Sizing up the situation, Fi lifted Steve's arm from around her neck and eased herself away. 'I should check in with Aidan. Make sure he hasn't cut himself on anything sharp.'

As she turned to go Steve reached out and caught her arm. 'Wait, Fi. Would you mind taking a picture of me and Kate?'

He passed his iPhone to her then leaned close to Catherine, who couldn't help being pleased when he put his arm around her waist. While they studied the results, Fi slipped away. Steve didn't give her so much as a parting glance, and Catherine decided that she had probably been uncharitable towards both of them after all. Picking safer ground, she said, 'I'm sorry about the way they treated you earlier.'

'Earlier?' His speech was beginning to slur. 'I can't remember much before my last mouthful of champagne.'

'Aidan's toast. He didn't mention you. It wasn't fair.'

Steve shrugged. 'You know, I don't give much of a stuff about what he says.'

'You should, if you're really going to work for Cruickshank and Spears.'

He laughed at the thought of this. 'I suppose you're right. I guess I'll learn to toe the line before Monday.'

'You will send me the picture Fi took of us, won't you?'

'I don't know. Maybe staying in touch would be the wrong thing for both of us.'

There was an awkward silence. She wanted to plead with him, but it was clear he was telling her she had made her choice. Instead, she asked, 'What time are you going?'

'Early-ish. I'd rather we said goodbye tonight. I don't think I can bear to go through it all again in the morning.'

She put down her drink and wrapped her arms around him. When she lifted her head she was aware that it was noticeably quieter on the terrace. Their embrace had somehow become the centre of attention. In the sudden silence she felt like making a final statement. She leaned in and kissed him hard, then turned and walked into the house.

When she heard the first sounds of movement downstairs, Catherine eased herself off the bed and crept out of the bedroom. At the foot of the stairs she almost bumped into George who was wheeling himself with exaggerated care along the hall. She followed him into the kitchen and shut the door before risking conversation.

'Couldn't sleep,' she explained.

'Hardly a surprise after the amount you put away last night.' She began to bristle but he held up a hand and smiled. 'Baiting you is too easy. I promise to give it up altogether. If you're staying on much longer, that is.'

'We're leaving tomorrow morning.'

'Unlike your erstwhile partner.'

'Have you seen him yet?'

'He's outside at the car but he'll be here in a minute. I'm just making him some tea.'

'Let me do it.'

The kettle was just coming to the boil when Steve slipped into the room. He looked at Catherine, who was standing by the stove, and then at George. 'Looks like everyone is fighting to take care of me this morning.'

'Don't get too cocky, Steven Munro,' George said. 'There are only two of us, and we're both gasping for a cuppa ourselves.'

'Still, it's nice to be loved. Even if no one is willing to actually say it.'

He stood beside Catherine and watched as she poured water into the teapot. 'I told you last night I wanted to slip away without anyone noticing.'

'But I didn't say I would let you, did I?'

'I don't remember too much of anything that was said last night.'

This was too much for George to resist. 'Well, I heard just about everything. Saw everything too. As did everyone else.'

Catherine turned her head away to hide a smile, but not fast enough to escape the old man's notice. 'Just pour my tea,' he said, 'and I'll leave the two of you alone.'

'Actually I'd rather you stayed,' she replied. 'It might sound strange, but I kind of like there being someone else around to see how we are together.'

She poured three mugs and passed them out, then went back and stood next to Steve. 'What time are you leaving?'

'In a few minutes. I want to be gone before everyone else is up.'

'Remember back in Rocamadour when I said that I didn't want anyone to get hurt?'

'Kate, don't say any more. Last night I wanted to argue with you. But not today. The decision's made. There's nothing else to say.'

They stared at each other for a moment, then he added, 'I'd

better finish my tea in the barn. I've still got to kick the tyres, check the oil, initiate the launch routine.'

She put her hand in his and there was a moment when they might have kissed. But he backed away before it could happen and started for the door. She closed it behind him and leaned her back against it, determined that she wasn't going to cry.

George was watching her closely, obviously disappointed. 'Very touching, Catherine,' he said. 'But I really don't understand what you're doing here inside the room with an old fart like me. He's the one you should be with.'

'It's too late. I've pushed him away.'

'Just open the bloody door and go after him. Say goodbye like you mean it. Tell him you'll be back in London soon and he'd better be waiting for you when you get there.'

She leaned over and kissed his cheek. Then she walked out of the kitchen and down the hallway to the front door.

By the time she had reached the barn Steve was already in the car. Seeing her, he turned and searched through the overnight bag on the back seat. Finding what he was looking for, he passed a small plastic bag to her through the open window.

'Something to remember me by,' he said. 'I'm down to my last few, but I'd like you to have one of them.'

She opened the bag and took out a T-shirt, one of his cache of *Aestivation Zone* sleepwear. She smiled a thank you, but he was already reversing out of the barn.

She watched the car until it had disappeared into the vineyard. Then she turned to walk back to the front door of the farmhouse. As she crossed the courtyard she saw movement at an upstairs window. Nick was staring down at her through the half-open curtains. His face was frozen, without emotion.

They held each other's gaze for a moment, then she turned away and walked glumly into the house.

21

It was more than three weeks since Catherine had been on the tandem with Nick. She realised with a shock that they had lost completely the knack of spending entire days together. Rediscovering it would mean that they first had to wipe clean the memory of their seven weeks in France. Neither of them was able or willing to do this. Instead, everything that had happened during the summer sat between them from the moment they cycled away from the farmhouse.

At first the ride north followed the route she had taken with Steve two days earlier. In Orange, where they stopped for a late lunch, she felt a flash of déjà vu when Nick suggested they eat at the same brasserie Steve had chosen. After that, it hardly came as a surprise when he also decided to stop on the way out of town at the Roman arch. Channelling the thoughts of his one-time stand-in, he too wanted a picture in front of it astride the tandem.

When they looked around for a suitable photographer Catherine was stunned to see the same man who had taken the picture of her and Steve. She got to him first, anxious that Nick's greater command of French might lead to a conversation she didn't want them to have. It was apparent when she passed the smartphone to the old man that he remembered both her and the tandem. The recreation of the scene from two days earlier, with one of the participants so clearly substituted, was obviously a puzzle for him. He stared at Catherine inviting her to explain, but she just shrugged and smiled, trying with some success to appear completely mystified herself.

A pattern of basic communication entrenched itself during the three-day ride to Lyon. When they spoke, it was mostly about the practicalities of cycling: stops and starts, braking and gear changes, eating and planning the next day. This was the common ground they now seemed to share. In her more objective moments Catherine could see that they were both grieving for a lost soulmate. And they were dealing with the loss by taking it out on each other. She suspected that Nick knew this too. But there was no way to openly discuss it.

Even on the rest day in Lyon, nothing changed. Nick's leg had made less progress towards recovery than he wanted everyone to believe. Three long riding days on a fully loaded tandem had pushed it too far and he decided he needed to stay in their hotel room to rest.

Catherine was only too happy to escape on her own into the city. She wandered aimlessly through a succession of shops, buying nothing, wanting to buy nothing. It was a miserable experience, a reminder of the morning she had spent alone in Sarlat, but without the sense of hope she had felt that day. It made her long for contact with Steve, the only person likely to understand what she was going through. She tried to put him out of her mind, but couldn't, and eventually allowed herself to compose and send a short text message. It began as a simple hello but somehow expanded to include a guarded admission that she missed him. He didn't reply and by the end of the day she had begun to realise that she would have to find her own way through the trials of the journey home.

She joined Nick for the evening meal at a restaurant in the city's Presqu'île district. After struggling through the entrée in silence she looked up from her smartphone and saw that he was texting away too. Two months earlier his phone had rarely been switched on. This was another change that Werner had wrought in him.

'Do you remember what you said in Albi?' she asked.

He looked up and stared at her, his mind returning from somewhere very far away.

After a few seconds she tried again. 'You said that on the ride north we'd stop in Lyon, just the two of us. It was going to be a new beginning.'

'I haven't forgotten anything.'

'Well if this is it, I don't think I can stand much more of it.'

He stared coldly at her. 'Correct me if I'm wrong, but it seems to me that things have moved on somewhat since Albi. Maybe my thinking was already out of date by that point.'

Almost a week had passed since the night of the party at Pernes and Catherine still had no way of knowing if Nick had seen her kiss Steve. She assumed from the way he sometimes spoke to her that he had. But there was a world of difference between assumption and fact. A dozen times on the tandem she had formulated a direct question, but she had always stopped short of asking it.

Staring back at him across the table, she decided again that it was better to leave the question unasked. She said, 'Then is there some way we can come to an arrangement? You know, to make this work on a practical level.'

'Maybe. But it's going to take time before things are back on an even keel. Meanwhile, we have an obligation to get this trip over with. Plus, I've got to think about the next one too. That's number one and number two priority for me right now.'

'That's it? That's what the next thousand kilometres are going to be like?'

'Kate, I don't know about you, but that's about all I can handle right now. Don't push it any further.'

She looked down at her smartphone and began to laugh. In the parallel world of her blog she had just finished drafting a post on the importance of working together. She had even added the photograph of them under the triumphal arch in Orange to illustrate the point. The draft was ready, just waiting for a final read-through back at the hotel. Running her eye down the text, she decided that the moment was perfect to upload the post. She pressed the publish button.

After Lyon, Catherine had little hope that anything would change. Neither of them seemed able to make a move that would relieve the tension and she was grateful that sitting behind him on the tandem excused the need for anything more than limited conversation. When they were off the bike she fulfilled her need for human interaction by texting or emailing. From the little that she could see, Nick seemed to be doing the same.

The stalemate reached a monastic silence on the morning of their visit to the abbey at Cluny. They wandered separately among the ruins, insulated by their own thoughts. She watched him for a while across the cloister and felt a tension grow deep in her gut. The inevitable confrontation was coming, and soon, but she felt incapable of driving it into the open on her own.

The catalyst came shortly after lunch when they had ridden about a dozen kilometres north-east towards the Saône valley. At Catherine's request they stopped for a few minutes on the edge of a forest to use the cover of the woods for a post-lunch toilet break.

As she returned to the tandem Nick was shouting into her phone. He turned when he heard her coming and said, 'Why did you do it, Kate? Why?' When she didn't respond, he added, 'Don't pretend you're innocent. You set this up days ago. Then you coldly sat behind me on the tandem and waited for the shit to hit the fan.'

'Nick. I don't know what you're talking about.'

He thrust the phone into her hand and stumped away along the side of the road. Bewildered, she put the phone tentatively to her ear and said, 'Hello?'

It was Liz. 'Kate, thank God it's you. I couldn't get any sense out of him.'

'What's this all about? I don't understand.'

'*You* don't! How do you think it is for me? I ring with a simple question about the photo you uploaded, and Nick goes ballistic.'

'What photo?'

'The one with you and the handsome stranger on the tandem in front of the Roman arch at Orange.'

'Orange? That was Nick.'

'Think again, Kate. It looks nothing like him.'

Catherine closed her eyes as she began to realise what had happened. The two visits to Orange, both recorded by the same photographer, one picture mistaken for the other in her haste to publish the post. She ran her fingers through her hair as she struggled for a story that would explain the mix-up.

Then, tired of the lies, she gave up. Taking a breath, she said, 'Liz, he isn't a stranger. His name is Steve Munro. We met him in Brittany and he rode on the tandem with me most of the way to Avignon. Somewhere along the way I fell in love with him. And I wish he was here right now ...'

When the call was over she walked slowly along the road to join Nick, who was sitting on a tree stump a dozen metres beyond the tandem, tracing a pattern on the ground with a stick.

'Nick,' she said, 'I'm sorry ...'

'You don't have to hold anything back. I heard just about everything you said to her.'

'The picture was an accident. I don't know how they got mixed up.'

He nodded. 'I know that now. So you were there with him too?'

'It was the second day of the Cathar pitch. I asked him to go for a last ride with me.'

'I can't believe you let me stop at that exact spot for another picture. And didn't say a word.'

'I'm sorry. I just didn't know where to start. It's been hard enough, us being on the tandem again, without all of that being between us.'

He rubbed his face with his hands. Then he looked at her again. 'When did all this start, you and him?'

'In the Dordogne. After you went off with Werner.'

A look of understanding came into his face. 'I saw in Albi there was something different. When the two of you sat down at our table you both looked like cats that had got the cream. I stupidly thought it was something to do with us all being together again.'

'It's my fault, not Steve's. We were alone together for all that time. I just let it happen.'

'You don't just let things like that happen, Kate. Not unless you want them to.'

'You're right.' She looked at the ground, avoiding his eyes. 'I did want it. And it lasted right through until we reached the Med.'

Having started the confession she wanted to tell him every detail of it. But she knew he wouldn't sit still long enough to hear it. Already he was on his feet, pacing backwards and forwards.

After a while he stopped and turned to her. 'Is it true what you just said to Liz? Do you wish he was here instead of me?'

'I'm sorry. The answer is yes.'

'So, why did you start north with me?'

She looked at him and wondered what to say. She had been asking herself the same question every day since Pernes-les-Fontaines. But there really was only one answer. 'I thought it was the only thing I could do. It seemed like your job depended on finishing the trip. Everyone was saying that.'

'There wasn't even a tiny part of you that thought we might get back together?'

'If there was it didn't last beyond the first day.'

'You know, I actually feel relieved to hear that. It's like a burden has been lifted from me. I feel exactly the same about it as you do. I think I've known it for a while, but I got too focused on seeing the ride through to the end. And being around Werner and Karina, it made me want a little of what they had. It wasn't until we started north that I realised how wrong it was.'

He turned suddenly and walked a little way into the forest. She let him go then stood and paced along the road. It was a relief that it was finally out in the open, even though there was nothing she'd told him that he hadn't already suspected. And it felt good that there was no way back from it.

When he returned he was adjusting his cycling shorts and it was obvious that he'd only gone into the forest to relieve himself. He stopped a few metres from her, still deep in thought.

When she couldn't bear it any longer, she asked, 'So, what do we do now?'

'Well, it seems that there's nothing else left but to get back on the tandem. We're still twenty-five kilometres from Tournus. It's not going to get any closer if we just sit here all afternoon feeling sorry for ourselves.'

She laughed. It was high-pitched, almost hysterical, like

steam venting through a safety valve. At first she wondered how he could make such a clinical suggestion. But when she thought about it, it was no more absurd than anything else they had done together in France. 'Sure,' she replied. 'I'm ready if you are.'

'Let's get going then. I can't think of anything I want more than a cold beer.'

As they passed the red-bordered road sign that marked the beginning of Tournus, Nick half-turned and said, 'I think we should go to a hotel tonight, if you don't object.'

'Of course.'

They rode along the Rue Jean Jaurès into the centre of the town and stopped opposite the Hôtel-Restaurant les Quatre Saisons, a terracotta-pink four-storey building a few hundred metres from the eastern bank of the Saône. Catherine waited across the road with the tandem while Nick asked about vacancies.

When he returned a few minutes later, he said, 'We're in luck. They were down to their last few rooms.'

They locked the tandem in a garage opposite the hotel and carried their panniers into the foyer. At the top of the stairs on the third floor he turned and held out a key. 'Your room is on the next floor up.'

'My room?'

'This seems the best arrangement from now on. Don't you think?'

'Yes, I think you're right.' She took her key and checked the number. 'I'll see you in the restaurant later.'

'If it's all the same to you I'd rather we just met for breakfast. I need to do some thinking and I'd rather do it alone.'

'I'll see you in the morning then,' she said, and turned quickly to climb the stairs.

Her first instinct was to hide away in her room, but after

showering she remembered Fi's words about the team at C&S monitoring the blog. It was only a matter of time, she realised, before Aidan's marketing people saw the photograph. She decided she had to go downstairs and warn Nick.

She knocked on his door but there was no response. At reception she found that he had left the building a quarter of an hour after they'd arrived. The manager also told her that Nick wouldn't be eating in the hotel's restaurant that night. She declined too and walked back along the Rue Jean Jaurès hoping that she might somehow pick up his trail.

At the first corner she realised it was hopeless. She tried phoning but went through to voicemail, where she left a message asking him to call. With nothing more to do except wait, she wandered into the Place de l'Hôtel de Ville and found a bar. She sat with a glass of white wine at an outside table and tried to decide what to do about a text message that had just arrived from Liz.

The call in the forest had been awful. Liz had barely said a word, a first that in other circumstances she might have been proud of. Instead Catherine had been desperate to end the call and get back to Nick. Gulping down her wine, she made herself open Liz's message, which read:

> *I'm furious. FURIOUS! How could you keep this from me? Don't even try calling back, because I've blocked your phone number. Permanently!*

A follow-up message arrived as she was reading the original. This said:

> *I'm also impressed. Can't decide whether to fire you or give you a bonus. I want to know more, all of it. Better still, I want to read all of it in your next article. That's the only way we can patch this up. So, get writing.*

The thought of a full-blown confession made Catherine

queasy. She couldn't allow it to happen, would die of shame if everything was made public. She pushed the phone across the table, sat back, and hoped for a sighting of Nick among the growing stream of homeward-bound shoppers crossing the square.

A little later her phone rang and she picked it up straight away, thinking it might be him.

It was Brendan. 'Kate, I've been trying to call Nick but his phone's turned off. Can you put him on the line.'

'He's … gone off for a while … on his own.'

'He left a strange message on my phone. Something about the ride being over. And that you're coming home.'

'Home?' The possibility of this hadn't occurred to her. Despite everything, she wasn't ready for that to happen.

'He wants me to collect you both from Dijon in a couple of days. What's going on Kate?'

She hesitated, trying to decide on the size and scale of the disclosure. 'We had a fight about something. It's pretty serious but I didn't think it would make him just disappear like this.'

'That's the effect you seem to be having on the men you travel with.'

'What do you mean by that?'

'Steve's gone too. Failed to show for the meeting with Aidan on Monday. A shame, but maybe he decided on a clean break from everything that happened over the summer.'

The news stunned her. She had been certain that Steve would accept Aidan's offer. His failure to reply to her texts and now his disappearance seemed to confirm everything Brendan was saying, that he had permanently cut himself off. Catherine put her phone on the table and buried her head in her hands. She felt numb, couldn't believe that he was gone, that he wouldn't be waiting when she returned to London. For the first time in months she felt utterly alone.

Eventually, she heard Brendan shouting into the phone. She picked it up and asked, 'Are you sure about Steve? Have you tried calling him?'

'Yes. And I keep leaving messages. Fi's been trying too. But he doesn't answer.'

'Don't give up, Bren. And keep Fi on it too. Please.'

'Will do.' He paused, then added, 'Look, I should get off the line in case Nick calls back. I'll check in with you later.'

She found a shorter route from the square back to the hotel. Nick's room key was still hanging on its hook at reception. She asked the manager to let Nick know, if he returned, that she would be in the restaurant.

She also asked, somewhat hopefully, for a table for two, then sat with a kir and pretended to study the menu. The waiter made regular visits to her over the next half hour. She followed the kir with a white wine, and finally, realising that it was futile to wait, ordered an entrée and a main course. Even in a crisis she couldn't stop herself from wanting, needing, a full meal after a day on the tandem.

She had just finished the entrée, a *tarte à l'oignon*, when her phone rang. It was Brendan again. 'Kate. Nick just rang.'

'Did he say where he was?'

'In a bar somewhere. He said you shouldn't go looking for him. He doesn't want to talk right now, not to you.'

'What else did he tell you?'

'Pretty much what I said earlier. That you're both coming home early. We talked about the practicalities of me collecting you.'

After a moment, she said, 'Did you ask him why?'

'He said that it's over between you. And that he wants to come home and start the preparations for the Africa trip. He says he's going to fly out there early.'

'He can't go home yet, can he? Aidan won't let him. Not if he wants the funding for the Cathar thing.'

The waiter arrived with her main course and put it in front of her, clearly upset that she was making a phone call during the meal. She shrugged, and smiled an apology while she waited for Brendan to reply.

'Bren,' she asked, eventually, 'what's the matter?'

'I had another call a few minutes ago. From Aidan this time.'

'And?'

'Nick spoke to him before calling me. Told him everything, all about you and Steve. Aidan was so shocked – that's how he put it anyway – that he told Nick to drop you and come home straight away. To look after himself before anything else. Africa, the Cathar series, they're still all right for Nick. I don't know exactly what Nick told him, but Aidan got the impression that what you've done might be enough to tip him over the edge.'

'I don't believe it,' she said, struggling to understand the implications of Aidan's intervention. 'So, if I'd just told Aidan everything back in Pernes-les-Fontaines, I could have come north with Steve?'

'To be honest, I doubt it. Aidan was still angry then about being left in the dark. I think if you'd told him then, he would have just turned around and gone home. By doing what you did you secured the Cathar funding and the Africa trip.'

'Well I hope someone tells Werner to put my name in a very large font at the bottom of the credits.'

'I'm amazed you can make jokes at a time like this.'

'It's the only way I can keep myself from crying into my *rôti d'agneau*. I've already upset the waiter by taking this call. I think, from the way he's looking at me, I might be asked to leave if I showed any further disrespect for the meal.'

After a pause, Brendan added, 'I'm so sorry, Kate. I feel partly responsible for it all. Throwing the two of you together on a tandem for three months maybe wasn't the best thing to do.'

'Actually it feels good to face it at last. If you hadn't done that we might have gone on as we were, growing slowly apart. We would certainly have arrived at the same place eventually.'

'Tell me if there's anything you need. I'd like to think that I'm still Base Camp for both of you, equally.'

She thought for a moment then realised there was something. 'Nick's dead wrong about one thing. It might be over between us and he might be going home early. But there's no way I'm doing that.'

'But you can't ride a tandem alone.'

'Who said anything about a tandem? I'm thinking of that solo touring bike you bought for Nick at the start of the tour.'

Brendan chuckled. 'I'm impressed, Kate. Do you want me to bring it over with me?'

'Dijon will only be two thirds of the way around France. There will still be a thousand kilometres to go. It seems more important than ever to finish what I started.'

22

Catherine went down to breakfast early, prepared to stay in the dining room all morning if necessary. She had only just selected a table when Nick walked in. They sat facing each other, unexpectedly relaxed, neither showing the least emotion.

'I've just spoken to Brendan,' he said, eventually. 'He says you're going on alone.'

She nodded. 'I've slept on it and it still seems the best thing to do.'

'You didn't forget about the solo bike, then,' he said, smiling ruefully.

'It just stuck in my mind from the moment you mentioned it. I didn't know why until now.'

'I'm glad you thought of it. Staying in France is the right thing for you.'

'I think you've made the right decision too.'

The waiter came with coffee and a basket of bread and croissants. As they ate, Nick casually said, 'I'll be in Africa by the time you get back.'

Catherine nodded. She knew he was confirming that it was

finally over between them. It should have hurt but she felt nothing at all. 'I hope it goes well for you, Nick.'

'I've got a good feeling about this next trip. I'm due for a change in my luck.'

He stopped eating and looked at her. 'I said some pretty terrible things about you to Aidan. I had to, to make him think I might be cracking up a little. You've got every right to be angry with me.'

'Last night I was. But now I've had a chance to cool down, I'm actually quite impressed. You handled him brilliantly, got him to think it was his idea for you to go home.'

He smiled. 'I somehow thought you'd understand.'

'Anyway,' she added, 'I hardly have the right to claim the moral high ground, do I?'

'Kate, I don't blame you for any of this. I just feel a kind of peace today that I haven't had in ages. I was making myself unhappy, making both of us unhappy, without being able to stop. We both were.'

She reached over and squeezed his hand, then they continued with breakfast as though it was just another day on the tour. He pulled a map from his pocket and they talked about the ride north to Dijon. But when they left the hotel, and settled onto the tandem for their second last day together, she realised they were now riding on separate agendas: he was counting down the kilometres to the end of his time in France, while every kilometre for her was a transition to her time as a solo cyclist.

After the rural peace among the vineyards of the Côte d'Or, the ride into the centre of Dijon was a shock. It took over an hour to make their way through car-crammed streets to the rendezvous with Brendan. They found him in the open space of the Place de la Libération at an outdoor café directly opposite the Palais des Ducs.

'It's good to see you both,' he said, reaching his arms around them before they'd had a chance to dismount. It was an excessive amount of bonhomie but he was automatically compensating for the air of professional distance that hung over the tandem. 'Come on. You need a beer and a rest. Then we can talk.'

Catherine excused herself while he ordered the drinks and went inside to find a toilet. The end, now that it was coming, was suddenly eating at her nerves and she wanted it to be over as soon as possible. She hadn't discussed with Nick what they would do that night but the thought of sitting through a meal together while Brendan forced the conversation was too much. On the way back outside she was determined to find an alternative.

Brendan and Nick were deep in conversation when she returned. She sat opposite them, drank some of her beer, and let her eyes roam across the square towards the ducal palace. After the nightmare ride into the city they were in a traffic-free haven, an attractive and fitting place to end the tour.

After a few minutes she tuned in to the conversation, and heard Brendan say, 'You must have made good time today from Beaune.'

'It was a good ride,' Nick replied. 'Vineyards almost all day long.'

'How's your leg holding up?' Brendan asked.

'Not so well. We went too far too fast on the first three days out of Pernes-les-Fontaines. My fault entirely. I was trying to prove that everything was all right again, exactly as it was before the accident. I couldn't have been more wrong.'

'How about you, Kate?'

'Physically, I've never felt better,' she replied. 'But I could use a day's rest and it looks like Dijon has plenty of non-cycling diversions.'

Nick finished his beer and limped inside to the toilet. When he had gone, Brendan asked, 'Are you sure about this? There's plenty of room in the Land Rover if you want to come home too.'

She shook her head. 'I've never been more certain about anything. I've started this trip and I'm going to finish it.'

When Brendan smiled at her, she asked, 'What are you thinking?'

'Don't be offended. But you sound exactly like Nick when you say things like that.'

'I'm not offended. I've come to understand that part of him better than ever. It's the rest of him I seem to have lost touch with.'

'We don't have much time before he's back. I just wanted to know if there's anything I can do.'

'About the two of us?'

He nodded, and she replied, 'Nothing. Really. It's best left the way it is.'

'He wants to start back tonight. Do you mind?'

This was such a relief that she felt tears welling in her eyes. She pushed them away then rubbed the top of her head in a gesture that had become a comforting habit. Leaning back in her seat, she replied, 'That's fine with me. I really just feel like being alone.'

'Then let's find you a hotel. We'll get your gear sorted, then leave you to it.'

He stretched out his hand and squeezed hers with his remaining fingers. Then he looked sadly at her. 'You know, Kate, I'm still Base Camp for the rest of this trip. Anything you need, anything, just let me know.'

'Maybe there is something. You can help me try to understand what's happened here. I started this journey thinking I knew exactly what I wanted, both in my private and my working lives. A couple of months later I've lost hold of all of that. Is that what travel is supposed to do to you?'

Brendan scratched at his beard with his free hand while he considered his answer. 'Long-distance travel has been accused of doing many things to people. But in my experience there are only a few lessons you're guaranteed to learn from it. First, and this is by no means a trivial matter, it teaches you not to be afraid of getting wet.'

Catherine laughed. 'Well, I think I can safely say that this trip has accomplished that.'

'Second, it lets you see that there are always alternative paths to take. That's what happened to you: you saw alternatives that you had to explore. But there's something else too, a compression in time that means living in the now with no thought for what comes later. It makes you reach for things that back home you might have left alone.'

'Might have, or should have?'

'That's a judgement only you can make. But for me, I could never criticise anyone who wants to strive and reach for something they think is better.'

'So what do I do now?'

'What you're already doing. Keep going until the end. Wherever that is.'

They saw Nick come out of the restaurant. Brendan withdrew his hand, adding, 'If anyone asks how you are, what should I tell them?'

'Have you heard from him?'

'No. But if I do ...'

'Tell him I miss him. I thought in Pernes that this was the right thing to do. But it has only made things worse for everyone.'

The final parting was a low-key reversal of the night before departure at Base Camp. Brendan's Land Rover became a makeshift substitute for the Map Room. The contents of their panniers were emptied into the back, and the three of them, led by Brendan, made a decision about each item she would carry on her solo journey. Their objectives were very different: Brendan and Nick couldn't help wanting to go through every item and make an objective decision on its value; Catherine wanted it to be over as soon as possible.

The chaos in the back of the Land Rover eventually resolved itself. Everything she intended to take with her was packed into four new panniers. There was nothing left to do but say goodbye.

She hugged Brendan first. Then she turned to Nick. They looked at each other for a moment, then she double-kissed him before putting her arms around him one last time.

'I hope the solo ride goes well for you,' he said, as he eased himself into the car.

'Look after yourself in Africa.'

She watched the Land Rover until it turned at the far end of the street. Suddenly, two months to the day after the wobble on the road to Base Camp, she was alone in France with a thousand kilometres of cycling ahead of her. Tired and hungry, but looking forward to the next phase of her adventure, she picked up her new panniers and carried them into the hotel.

Solo cycle touring took more than a little getting used to. Catherine no longer had a partner right under her nose, acting as a windbreak and blocking most of the view. And she now had sole charge of route planning, gear selection and brakes. Every decision was hers alone: she could go where she liked, stop when she wanted, was completely free from interference. But with this freedom came a sense of loss, an awareness that everything now would be driven by her alone. She reacted by retreating into herself and looking for her own sense of purpose.

Her only interactions for the first few days were basic

conversations about eating, camping and sightseeing. At the end of each day she had her blog posts to work on and a regular number of messages on her phone to work through. Brendan stayed in daily contact and made it clear that he expected regular updates from her. This began as an extra chore but she quickly realised the regular text exchanges with him were an invaluable anchor.

By the end of the week she was in Troyes, celebrating the completion of her first solo stage with a two-night stay at a hotel. She had been avoiding contact with everyone except Brendan for days, but the time had come for a return to the world, even if it was just the virtual one.

Over a pre-dinner drink in the pedestrianised core of the town she worked through her messages and made ruthless choices about who she was going to respond to. Among them was Karina, who had sent a message to say that she knew through Werner that the tandem ride was over. It was a message of support, and Catherine settled down to answer it in a way that revealed as little detail as possible.

After ordering her meal she sent Brendan his daily update, including the announcement that her new cycle computer had already recorded three hundred solo kilometres. In minutes he had responded with a message that read:

Well done, Kate. Knew you could do it alone.

She smiled at the message, and responded:

I don't feel alone while I've still got a Base Camp.

He replied straight away:

You've got more than just Base Camp supporting you. I took a chance that you wouldn't mind hearing from one of your new friends. Hope you'll forgive me.

She was wondering exactly what he meant when a new message that seemed to solve the mystery arrived. It was from

Karina, and it read:

> *Just heard you are taking a rest day. A Balchoffer-*
> *sponsored support pack is being organised now and*
> *will be with you soon. Enjoy.*

When Catherine went down to breakfast the following morning a small package, which had been couriered overnight from Germany, was waiting for her at reception.

Deep within the bubble-wrapped outer layers was a white cardboard box about fifteen centimetres square. Its lid was stamped with the Balchoffer logo. When she lifted this, she saw that the box contained a pair of chocolate figures, one made from milk chocolate, the other from dark, both sitting on a delicately crafted white chocolate tandem. The milk chocolate figure on the rear seat of the tandem was, she thought, clearly recognisable as herself. The dark figure at the front was male, and generic. She wondered if Karina had issued deliberately vague instructions to its creator.

There was also a hand-written note from Karina. She opened it and read:

> Dearest Kate,
>
> I hope you like the enclosed, which is just something I was inspired to have my team create in your honour. It shows, I think, that Balchoffer craftsmanship is next to none.
>
> I feel more than a little guilty that my darling husband and I have somehow contributed to your recent troubles. So I am determined, through Brendan, to keep an eye on your progress on the journey home. If there is anything I can do to help, please let me know.
>
> By the way, the gift is for eating straight away – that is the Balchoffer rule where chocolate gifts

are concerned.

Karina

Catherine bit into the dark chocolate cyclist, removing the head and shoulders. Then she wrote a quick message to Karina thanking her for the gift. She finished breakfast and was drinking the last of her coffee when her phone vibrated. She checked the inbox, expecting a reply from Karina, and was surprised to see that it was from Steve.

It took her more than an hour to decide that she was ready to read it. She found a seat in a small square, took out her phone and opened the message. It read:

Kate,

I've tried to stop myself communicating with you, but don't think I can any longer. It seemed the best thing to do while you were on the tandem with Nick.

I'm sorry if you thought I had abandoned you completely. I know now that the tandem ride has come to an end and that you are continuing solo. Good on you for finally taking the advice of that guru you met on the road to Saint-Émilion!

I miss you and would like to be in touch again, but will understand if you'd rather not. Please let me know.

Steve

She read and reread his message carefully. And for the rest of the morning she tried to decide how to respond. It was a relief that he had finally broken his silence and explained his reasons for being out of touch. After lunch she started on a reply:

I thought maybe you'd decided to cut yourself off permanently. Thank God you didn't. Please stay in touch. I do want you to.

She had walked barely a few hundred metres when he replied:
    Where are you now?
CP: *Walking through the centre of Troyes.*
SM: *Not cycling today?*
CP: *Allowing myself a day off. How about you?*
SM: *I'm busy planning my next travel project. Leaving London later today. Not sure how long for. Maybe this is the one where I'll finally find my Shangri-La.*
CP: *I'm glad we're in touch again.*
SM: *Me too. I'll leave you alone now, but not for long. I intend to be in regular contact.*
CP: *Good. Till later.*

The next day, as she rode north towards Épernay, she felt almost as if the solo part of her ride was over, that she was with people again, even if the contact was virtual. The sense was so strong that she began to feel there was actually someone on the road with her. A half-dozen times on the hundred-kilometre ride, she turned and looked behind her, not sure exactly what it was that she was expecting to see. Invariably there was no one there, just empty road stretching away to the south. Despite the sense of being observed, her spirits were high and she managed a good pace as she rode past the vineyards and wheat fields of Champagne.

It felt good to be camping again. At the end of the day she lay in front of her tent with a half-bottle of champagne and composed a blog post about the five essential elements of Champagne cycle touring. She began with the necessity of choosing the best possible route. Then she touched on the need for physical and mental preparation, before moving on to talk about the importance of equipment.

It was easy writing. But the final element brought her to a dead halt. Even after two glasses of champagne, she didn't know what to say exactly about the topic of solo versus tandem cycling. A part of her wanted to let go, to confess to the world that she was now on her own. But the logical extension of that was also admitting that she had been a fool to let her perfect partner go. She hesitated to write anything at all, but the more she thought about it, the more she realised that cycling was best when you had someone to share it with.

She finished the post:

> You can always ride alone, and for many people I'm sure this is the ideal. A bicycle, and the feeling of moving at your own pace through an interesting and challenging landscape, are perfect companions for a solo traveller. The sense of movement, the rhythm and cadence of the turning cranks, the little mechanical sounds from the cycle – all of these wrap you in a comfortable, pleasant bubble.
>
> And that could well be enough for most of us. But for some, and I count myself among them, the missing dimension is a cycling partner to share it with. It's risky riding with someone else – it could be a joyful experience or an utter trial. Sometimes the same partner might bring both emotions with them.
>
> But I've been lucky enough to know a cycling partner who was ideal for me. We could talk as much as we wanted and not find it irritating. Or ride silently together for hours, happy with just our own thoughts and the knowledge that we had a companion within touching distance. A complete team, a match in fitness, emotion and style. I'm grateful for the opportunity I've had to know this feeling and will never forget it.
>
> Champagne cycling, for me, has to mean being

in a peloton of two.

She scanned and corrected the post, then published it as she drank the last of her champagne.

The post soon drew comments from readers of her blog and they were split evenly between those who thought there was no ideal partner and those who considered her immensely lucky to have found one. They all assumed she was talking about Nick and she wasn't inclined to correct the error.

The few people who knew she was now on her own responded to the post by making direct contact. The first was Liz, who congratulated her for starting to come clean in print at last, and urged her to make a clean breast of it to the paper's readers. Her text ended:

> *Kate, I'm not joking. You have to put the lie to bed before you cross the Channel. This is Liz Jekyll, your best friend telling you this. Don't wait until the other Liz makes you do it. That way lies regret.*

Worn down by the daily pleas, and hoping that the truth might also bring something like a sense of redemption with it, Catherine replied:

> *All right. But only because I want to. Get ready to stop the presses for a five-hundred word confession from Catherine Pringle.*

The post also brought a reaction from Catherine's mother, who wrote in a text:

> *Kate, dearest. I might have my head too much in the history books for your liking, but I do live sufficiently in the real world to know this: all those words you've written about the ideal partner can't possibly be referring to Nicholas Farne. Does this mean there's someone else?*

Catherine replied:

There was someone. And, even though I haven't got any right to think this, I haven't entirely given up hope that there might be again one day.

Eleanor Pringle:

Well I'll be very happy for you if that happens. And your father and I want you to know something else too: we both are proud of you and everything you've done. Someone took us to task recently for not making that clear enough to you. I thought it a little cheeky of them at the time, their being a complete stranger, but on reflection I've realised that we really should tell you more often that we love you.

Reading this, Catherine laughed at the thought of anyone telling her mother how to think. Then as she reflected on it, she began to wonder if her blog might have been responsible. She texted her mother:

This someone. Had they been reading my blog, do you think? I hope I haven't been too mean to you in it.

Eleanor Pringle:

Don't worry on our account. We're made of sterner stuff than that. He was an unusual character. Quite forward in an engaging sort of way. And he came out with the strangest things. He wanted me to know that he has a strong and clearly argued position on the contribution of the Carolingian Renaissance to Western civilisation.

Suspicious now, Catherine asked:

When did all of this happen?

EP: *Just a few days ago. He had a quick chat with your father too.*

CP: *Let me guess. About Jane Austen?*

EP: *It was, actually. But enough of him. My message was supposed to be about you. We'll be following your journey home with interest.*

The following day she regularly checked for new messages, but it was evening before the one she wanted most arrived. Steve's message read:

Where are you tonight?

She replied straight away:

In the centre of Reims. Eating outdoors at a restaurant in the shadow of the cathedral. What are you doing?

SM: *I'm in a restaurant too. Wish I was at yours.*

CP: *Me too.*

SM: *Where to tomorrow?*

CP: *Northern leg finished. Going east tomorrow through Saint-Quentin towards Compiègne. Steve, did you by any chance visit my parents recently?*

SM: *If I was with you right now, I'd be shaking my head and saying: That is so Catherine Pringle. She thinks that the world revolves exclusively around her. What makes you think a crazy thing like that, anyway?*

CP: *Oh, nothing really. (And I've noted that you're not denying it!) Just that they had an encounter with a stranger who waffled on about Charlemagne and Jane Austen.*

SM: *Astonishing! But I can't see why you'd think it was me. Could have been anyone who has read a little too much of your blog this summer. Anyway, what motive could I possibly have had for that?*

CP: *I really don't know. But I'm curious to find out.*

When he didn't reply she finished her dessert and asked for

the bill. As she left the restaurant, she texted him again:
> *Can I call you? I really want to hear your voice again.*

SM: *Can't tonight. I'm not alone. But I promise we'll talk tomorrow. And the next day. And the one after that if you like. Deal?*

CP: *Deal.*

My Tandem Tour de France
By Catherine Pringle

Day 66, Monday 22 August
Reims

My name is Catherine Pringle and I am a persistent liar.

For the last two months, since the second day in France, my columns and articles have deliberately deceived you. They lied by omission, concealing events very different from those I reported.

Like every addiction, the lying started innocently enough. At first I was doing nothing more than stretching the truth a little. An occasional embellishment, a slight exaggeration, makes for more entertaining reading. From there I fell into a spiral of deception that took me further and further from reality.

There are countless tiny moments I allowed you to think happened in a different way. Every one of them matters, but they pale in comparison to what I think of as The Big Lie. This was a whopper, a tangled pattern of evasions and deceptions that weighed down our panniers for most of the tour.

I'm deeply ashamed of my part in it and wish I could go back to Brittany to wipe it clean. Instead I have to go forward and that means setting the record straight. So here it comes – the truth, and nothing but the truth:

> Nick injured his knee on our second day in France and was unable to cycle for large stretches of the tour.

> His place on the tandem was taken by Steve, a man we met in Brittany. (I promised never to write about him in this blog, not without his

permission. Please forgive me Steve, but the truth – the truth about what you mean to me – is more important than breaking my promise to you.)

Steve cycled more than two thirds of the tour with me on the tandem. Somewhere along the way – it might even have been the moment we met – I fell in love with him. I still love him and wish he was here with me now.

Nick and I are no longer together. Since Dijon I've been on my own, cycling the final quarter of the journey on a solo touring bicycle.

There's more, much more still to tell. But that will have to wait for another day. If you're still willing to listen, that is.

After all of that, you must be wondering if there's anything I can say that you will believe. Statistics don't lie, so here's something I am still proud of: the total distance ridden in France is 3,000 kilometres in 49 cycling days. Since Dijon, I have ridden 430 kilometres of that alone in 6 cycling days.

Catherine Pringle has been clean, free from the lies, for one whole day now. To be honest it doesn't feel a whole lot better yet. But she hopes with each day that passes – given your help and encouragement – a day will become a week, a week will become a month. Gradually it will loosen its grip and she will be free of The Big Lie.

Pernes-les-Fontaines to Reims

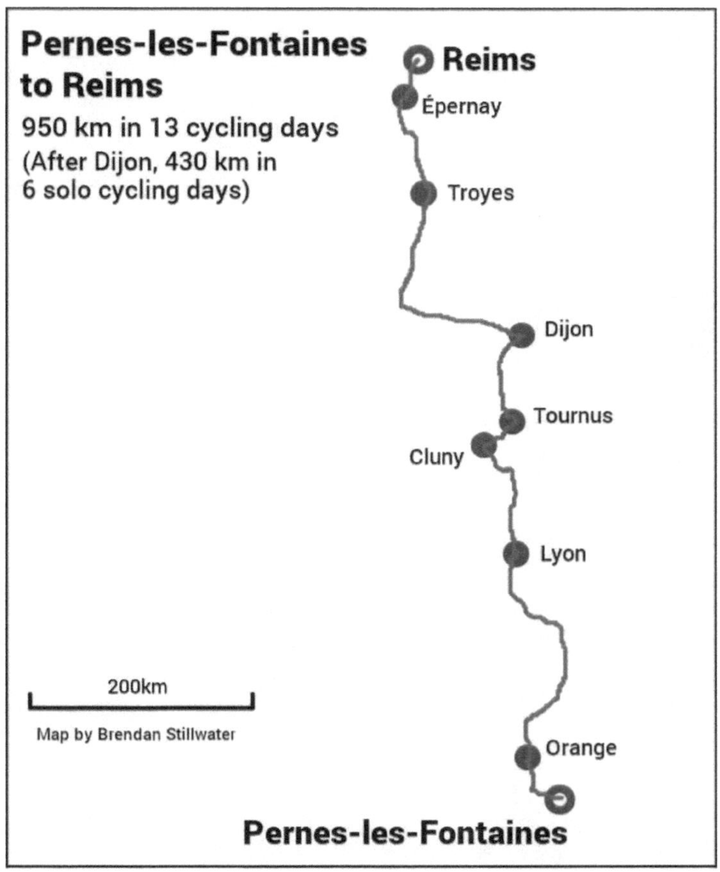

Peloton of two

23

The ride east from Reims was like a new beginning. The contact with Steve and the prospect of speaking to him soon gave Catherine a sense that the worst was over. She had her phone set to its highest volume and waited less than two hours before it announced the arrival of a new message.

She stopped at the side of the road and confirmed that it was from him. It read: *Where are you today?*

She replied: *Almost at Lagery. You said you'd call me this morning.*

    SM*: I promise we can talk at lunchtime. And all afternoon*
       if you like. Let me know when you're likely to stop
       and I'll make sure I'm free.
    CP: *Will stop for lunch in Fère-en-Tardenois. Maybe*
       around one.
    SM: *I promise we'll talk then.*

At Fère-en-Tardenois she found a small restaurant and ate a two-course *menu du jour*, her smartphone resting on the table beside her plate. When she finished the meal there was still nothing from him and her mood began to drop. She tried calling but went straight to voicemail, where she left a message asking him to call her back.

She was outside and about to get back on her cycle when Steve responded with a text message telling her to make sure to stop for a look at Fère's ancient grain hall before leaving the village. It was a curious request. Suddenly he was location-specific, an expert on a village she had chosen randomly as a lunch stop. Suspicious, she tried calling again, but he still didn't answer.

She found a sign that pointed to *L'ancienne halle aux grains* and freewheeled towards it along a narrow street that soon opened into a small, triangular marketplace. The grain hall was an open-sided building, constructed of squat stone pillars that supported a steeply pitched, tiled roof. Catherine rolled around to the front and was pleased to see that another cycle tourist had already left a bicycle against one of the pillars. As with every touring bike she encountered, she played the game of guessing the cyclist's nationality. She noted as she leaned her own bike next to it that the brand on the frame was European, possibly Dutch or German. She unclipped her helmet and walked into the shaded interior, hoping for a quick exchange with a fellow long-distance traveller.

The interior of the market hall was empty, and she decided to wait in the shade and give Steve another ten minutes to get in touch. Her phone rang as soon as she sat down, and she answered it with a haste that surprised her.

'Steve,' she said, realising she sounded like an anxious teenager. 'I was beginning to think you were going to string me along like this for days.'

'There were just some things I had to organise before we could talk.'

'It's so good to hear your voice.'

'Yours too. It's been too long.'

'Eighteen days,' she said, 'since Pernes-les-Fontaines. I counted them last night.'

'That sounds a little bit like you missed me.'

'You could see it that way, I suppose. It might appear a little self-centred if you did, though.'

He laughed. 'I don't mind how it looks.'

'I did miss you. More than I want to admit.'

'Thank you. It really helps to know. So how is the trip going?'

'I passed the 3,000-kilometre mark the day I arrived in Reims.'

'You're more than three quarters done.' After a short pause, he added, 'How do you feel about what lies ahead?'

He could have been talking about the cycling, or anything else. She decided to take his words at face value. 'I've come this far. I'm not going to stop now.'

'No, I don't believe you will.'

'I wish you were here right now. There's so much I want to tell you.'

'Do you really wish that?'

'I also wish I could undo the past couple of weeks. Right back to Pernes-les-Fontaines.'

'God, no,' he said, sounding pained. 'That would mean having to go through all of it again. I'd settle for a fresh start.'

'Me too.'

'Do you mean that Kate? I have to be sure.'

'Of course.'

'Then, will you do something for me? Without asking why.'

'The last time someone asked me that, I ended up quite literally with egg on my face.'

He laughed. 'I hope that doesn't happen to either of us this time. When I tell you to, I want you to hang up. No questions. Do it now. Just hang up and wait for a minute.'

She ended the call but kept the phone in her hand, expecting him to send another message or a photograph. There were footsteps now at the far end of the grain hall and she turned, annoyed that a newcomer was breaking the spell of whatever Steve was going to do. The figure, a cyclist, entered the periphery of her vision and her eyes moved automatically, focusing on him as he emerged from the shadows.

She froze when she realised it was Steve. Her mind slowly engaged and she managed to say, 'But how?'

'The how was easy,' he said, coming towards her. He stopped just out of reach, his smile unable to hide an uncertainty about how she would react. 'I was more worried about this being the right thing to do. I still am.'

She stepped towards him, still trying to react. But as they neared each other the tension melted and she threw her arms around him. When they finally separated she put a hand up and touched his cheek. He smiled, his relief obvious.

'When did you dream this up?' she asked after a while.

'I only heard you were on your own a few days ago. I decided I just had to come.'

'All this way just on the off-chance that you'd get a hug out of it.'

'I'm reasonably confident there might be more to it than that.'

He took her hand and led her out of the grain hall. They stopped by the touring cycle that stood next to hers. Resting his hand on the handlebars, he said, 'I was thinking you might enjoy a little company for the rest of the ride. Separate bicycles this time. You'd still be more or less independent.'

Her mind was racing, trying to catch up with the fact that she could choose not to be alone. When she didn't answer straight away, he asked, 'Is it such a hard thing to decide?'

'Of course not. I'm just struggling to think of words that would tell you how sorry I am for sending you away.'

'You don't have to. We were both stupid. But it's over now

and we can begin again.'

'Brendan was part of this, wasn't he?'

'Not until last night. It was Karina, mostly. She called me after she found out that you and Nick had parted. She thought we should be together.'

'When she said there was a Balchoffer package on the way, it wasn't just the chocolate. It was you.'

He nodded. 'She said to tell you that chocolate is all very well for the times you can't get the real thing.'

Catherine laughed. She turned and walked back into the shade of the grain hall. Steve followed her, staying a few paces behind. Turning to him again, she said, 'Can you really forgive me for sending you away? Is it that easy?'

He looked serious now for the first time since his arrival. 'At first, when I got back to London, I didn't think so. I tried to move on, I really did.' He smiled again. 'But I just couldn't. For one thing, behaving like that would have proved you right about me being someone who never makes a commitment. So I decided to test myself a little, to imagine what it would be like if we really were together. And that led me on a strange little quest, a kind of *Everything there is to know about Catherine Pringle* tour.'

'Wow,' she replied. 'And after all that you're still here.'

'It wasn't so bad. I had some fun along the way.'

The pieces of the puzzle were now falling into place for her. 'I'm guessing that the fun somehow included a short meeting with my parents.'

He nodded. 'I don't know what they made of the whole thing, but I enjoyed meeting them.'

'I think they found it mostly positive. From memory, I think my mother found you quite forward in an engaging sort of way.'

Steve threw back his head and laughed. 'By then I was a little distracted. Karina had just been in touch to tell me that you were travelling on your own. I knew right away what I had to do. She supported it and helped with the practicalities.'

Pointing back at his cycle, he said, 'Do you recognise the bike, by the way?'

She turned and stared at it. 'It's Werner's, isn't it?'

'He organised the bike and the equipment for me. Picked me up at Calais and brought me down to Reims. It was just like having my very own Base Camp, a slightly more chaotic and overwhelming version than the one you're used to. But you can't fault the enthusiasm. He was tempted to come along for the ride too until I managed to talk him out of it.'

'Is he here now?'

'He decided in the end that having him around too would be more than we could handle. And Karina flat out told him to leave us alone. So he just dropped me and left.'

'I'm glad she's on our side. But why did they do all of this?'

Steve shrugged. 'I think they're trying to make amends. They were so single-minded in wooing Nick for their own ends, they didn't realise the effect it might have.'

She turned again and paced to the end of the grain hall. Steve waited until she turned, then he said, 'Decision time, Catherine Pringle. No more talking. No more delay. Just, yes or no?'

'Of course, it's a yes. A thousand times yes, one for every kilometre still to go. But there's just one thing. The way I see it, the end doesn't come when we reach a ferry port. If you come on this ride, we're signing ourselves up for a permanent arrangement. Is it a deal?'

He took her hand and replied, 'Yes, it's a deal.'

My Tandem Tour de France
By Catherine Pringle

Day 87, Monday 12 September
Roscoff

Other than an occasional – and, in my opinion, entirely reasonable – exaggeration for effect, this column has strayed only once into the journalistic dark side. I bitterly regret The Big Lie (see Day 66, Monday 22nd August) and hope that post-confession you have decided to give me the benefit of the doubt.

The Big Lie was my only real crime in four thousand kilometres of cycling. So it was something of a shock, just five kilometres from the finish line, to attract the attention of _les flics_ for the first time in sixty-seven riding days.

There were two of them, motor-cycle cops straight out of central casting – broad-shouldered, leather-clad, one with a wide, drooping moustache. They looked pretty serious and we gave them a weak, it-wasn't-us-officer smile when they drew level for a pretty intimidating once-over.

Officer Moustache, the one in front, let us sweat for a few seconds, then put his arm out and gestured to the side of the road. Somewhere, somehow, we must have committed a major transgression.

He stopped just ahead of us, leaving his partner to box us in from behind, and strutted back to ask for identification. I've never seen such an exaggerated scrutiny of our passports. I swear, he almost held them up to the light to inspect the watermarks.

Then he really shocked me. He saluted and said, _'Madame Pringle. Monsieur Munro.'_

It was hard not to laugh at this, especially when he elongated the first vowel in Preengell. Keeping a straight face, I asked, '*Il y a un problème, monsieur?*'

'*Nous allons ...*' The rest I didn't get. I shrugged and smiled helplessly at him, and he conceded that English was necessary. 'We are your escort for the final kilometres into Roscoff.'

'Escort?'

'We have our instructions from the office of the Mayor. You should follow us to the finish of your ride. When you are ready, of course.'

They didn't know, or wouldn't say, any more than that. We got under way with Moustache about ten metres ahead of us and the other the same distance behind.

Steve and I were quietly speculating about who might have been responsible for this when a cyclist swept up on us from behind. Like most French cyclists, he was on a road racing bike, still living the dream that he was the star of his favourite professional cycling team. He was middle-aged and had squeezed his ample belly into cycling shorts and a skin-tight team jersey. He smiled and *bonjour*ed.

He drew slightly ahead and was replaced by a second rider in the same livery. A third and fourth arrived. It was *Salut!* and *Ça va?* all round. I glanced over my shoulder and saw that they weren't alone; a peloton of twenty to thirty riders was about to swallow us up. They packed tight around us, riding wheel to wheel centimetres away on every side. It was thrilling and fun, but slightly worrying too – not quite the empty roads we were used to.

They were all in the same team colours: white cycling shirts with a small charcoal and pink logo. From a distance the design was subtle, but when they were close it resolved itself into the outline of two riders on a stylised tandem sitting on top of the words *Peloton of Two*. It was clear suddenly why Brendan had taken so much trouble last week to talk us into finishing the ride on the tandem. The whole thing was a Cruickshank and Spears marketing extravaganza.

The next surprise came on the crest of a small rise, the last before the outskirts of Roscoff. Standing at the side of the road next to a *Bienvenue à Roscoff* sign was a figure in a red-and-black caped costume. He wore a horned cap, and in his hands he held a trident which he shook over his head as we approached.

'El Diablo,' Steve said. 'The red devil. He always appears a few kilometres from the end of a real Tour de France stage. Looks like we're official now.'

This wasn't the real Tour de France devil, although we did find out later that he had borrowed the real costume from El Diablo himself. It was Werner. He was laughing so hard that he almost skewered Steve with the trident as we passed.

A reception committee, fronted by a small neat man in a suit, was waiting for us on Roscoff's waterfront along the Quai Charles de Gaulle. As we approached, he lifted a massive chequered flag and began to wave it elaborately.

This was it. The end of the ride. By now I could hardly stop laughing. It was almost uncontrollable, a reaction to the events of the last few kilometres that was soon mixed with tears.

Brendan was waiting for us in the car park at the end of the quai. He was grinning, but looking slightly anxious. 'Werner and I thought that something a little special was in order. It's not every day that someone you know completes their own Tour de France.'

'But how did you manage it?' I asked.

'Sponsorship money. Works every time. Aidan had second thoughts about blaming you for the break-up. He wants to make it up to you and thought this was a good start.'

Gesturing along the quai, he said, 'I'm afraid you have some duties to perform for the remainder of the evening. The gentleman with the chequered flag is the Deputy Mayor of Roscoff. And, of course, Aidan is here somewhere too. There will be speeches. And champagne.'

It was a bitter-sweet moment. In the two-and-a-half weeks since Fère-en-Tardenois, Steve and I had retreated into the same insulated bubble that had taken us across the South of France. We had deliberately avoided talking about what would happen when we got back to London. Now it was all I could think about.

As we followed Brendan across the cobbles towards the Deputy Mayor, we saw Aidan at his side. Behind him, ready for any eventuality, was Fi. I couldn't help gripping Steve's arm a little tighter.

He turned and smiled at me. We knew then that what we had in France was over. The circuit was complete, symbolically ending where it had begun thirteen weeks earlier. Everything from that moment was an incremental step towards a normal life again. There was, after all, a difference between the tandem ride and what came after it.

I smiled back in what I hoped was a conspiratorial way. We took each other's hand and started towards the reception committee, happy that we were at the beginning of a new journey together.

I hope it turns out the way I want it to. But either way, this journey will be very different. There will be no Big Lies, no exaggeration for effect. In fact no words about it at all. It's something that will remain strictly between the two of us. I won't write another public word about it.

Unless, that is, you really want to know what happens next ...

Catherine Pringle's Tour de France

www.ingramcontent.com/pod-product-compliance
Lightning Source LLC
Chambersburg PA
CBHW031030120726
47905CB00007B/2115